Grape Nuts or Corn Flakes

... and other decisions

by Jane Waters Bugg

Edited by Nancy Moyer Stock

DEDICATION

Dedicated to Scott, Alec, Christine and Claire.

CONTENTS

ACKNOWLEDGMENTS

This book goes out to the countless women who have encountered abuse, whether it was sexual, physical or emotional, and soldiered on with their lives.

I could not have written it without the help and support of my family and friends. I want to especially thank Nancy Moyer Stock for her guidance, editing prowess and discussions that made me think more than once about the book's trajectory. Terre Musselman provided much needed feedback and cheerleading. I'd also like to thank Sam Katz for my profile picture taken in 1976...it's still my favorite.

I've read the script and the costume fits,

so I'll play my part.

Wesley Schultz, Lumineers

Chapter One

Grape Nuts or Corn Flakes? It was a simple question. She looked at him, then quickly looked away. Grape Nuts lasted longer, their crunch unspoiled by the splash of skim milk, lying in the bowl like nuggets of rock defying the slushy snow that floated around them. Corn flakes soaked up the cold liquid, gathering it in and holding it, creating a mush that waited patiently for the spoon to make its impact.

She wondered which he would choose. He was reading the newspaper, carefully scanning the headlines, searching in vain for something that would help him answer her. Grape Nuts or Corn Flakes? Clinton or Sanders? Who could pick? He wasn't crazy about either one, yet in this ultra-democratic household, a decision had to be made. Still, Grape Nuts or Corn Flakes. Clinton, hoping to be the first female president, unashamedly deflecting the email and Benghazi criticisms like the Grape Nuts deflecting the milk. Or Sanders, the socialist wannabe, pulling in the ideals of the young wishing for a kinder, gentler world much like the Corn Flakes that deftly absorbed the watery avalanche.

"There's no right answer," he muttered, more to himself than her.

She glared at him. "I'm not looking for a right answer." *Just once,* she thought, *just once can he make a decision without turning it into some sort of apocryphal ordeal?* She reached into the cabinet and pulled out both boxes, plopped them on the counter. "I'm having Grape Nuts," she announced authoritatively.

That's just like her, he thought. *She's voting for Clinton.* She has to, what with all her post-60's feminism. Never mind the scandals. She was forthright in her conviction that Hillary was the victim of misogyny. None of the other candidates were attacked with the unrelenting force that was lobbied against Hillary. But she hung in there, just like the cereal that had no grapes and no nuts. Steadfast in the need to be the last one standing.

He watched her as she opened the box and filled her bowl, then carefully poured in just the right amount of milk. He marveled at the precision. Enough, but not too much. Can't have any left over when the cereal was gone. She hated those people who drank the crumb-sodden milk right from the bowl. Quietly, almost surreptitiously, she sprinkled sugar over the waiting nuggets, then quickly sat down at the kitchen table and started eating. Crunch, crunch, crunch. Spoon. Crunch, crunch, crunch. Until every last morsel and drop were gone. She dropped the spoon into the bowl with the smug satisfaction of a job well done.

She looked at him, wondering if he'd made a decision. He was still reading the paper, seemingly oblivious of the passing time. Oh, wait a minute. He's moving. He stood, tightened the belt around his robe, folded the paper and picked up his coffee mug. With a sigh he walked out of the kitchen. *Well,* she thought, *I guess his decision is no breakfast. Fine.*

With an air of resignation, she pushed her chair back and cleared the table, removing all evidence of breakfast. The dog watched her, noticeably disappointed that no food had made its way onto the floor.

It's morning in the Cromwell house. The same scene played over day after day. Sometimes he ate, sometimes not. Not that it mattered to either one of them. They had both come to realize that the day would unfold regardless of his full or empty stomach.

She spent the next hour straightening the house, making the bed, throwing in a load of wash, fighting the ever-present shadows that nudged at her memory fighting for recognition. As always, she pushed them aside, made a fresh cup of tea, and sat down in front of her computer. *I should check my email,* she thought, but instead opened up the Solitaire app. She used to love Solitaire on the computer. So many different games, no need to shuffle, easy to undo bad moves. But now it was almost a chore, just another thing she had to get done. There were 20 games she liked to play. And she played them all every day. She usually won at least five of them on the first attempt; most within the three tries she allotted herself. Winning at Solitaire was an accomplishment, something she prided herself on, especially when she won without any undo's. Solitaire was one of her guilty pleasures, an escape from chores she really ought to be doing. The problem was, the things she ought to be doing were boring, or futile. Like cleaning. Clean today and she would just have to do it again next week. Get the bathroom sparkling, the mirror streak free, the floors devoid of dust bunnies and the next thing she knew the faucets were dotted with heaven only knows what, the mirror cloudy and the floors littered with dog hair.

She used to have a job. Or as she would say, a job outside the house.

As much as she despised it, it gave her a purpose. Somewhere to go every weekday, projects to start and finish, people to talk to, an insight into how other lives were led. Now she understood what the Countess of Grantham meant when she asked, "What is a weekend?" One day bled into the other, no joy over hump day, no looking forward to Friday night or mourning Monday sunrise, no hurray-it's-a-snow-day. Just Solitaire and cleaning.

She heard him rustling around, getting showered, dressing, packing his electronic gadgets into his messenger bag. He walked into the room, clad in his winter parka, bag slung over his shoulder.

"Gotta run, Deb. Love you," as he bent over to kiss her goodbye.

She gave him a weak smile, "Love you too. Have a good one."

He turned toward the door thinking how lucky she was to have the entire day spread out before her to do anything she wanted. The house to herself. No one demanding or questioning or pushing. There were so many things he wanted to do if he only had the time. But no, he had to slog ahead. Go to work, check the data, write the report, answer the phone messages, email the clients. It never ended. It was like Whack-a-Mole. Just when you thought you were finished, up pops another fire that needs tending before it becomes a full-out inferno. He drew a sharp breath, "Damn the torpedoes, full speed ahead."

I'm so tired of this. Struggling to keep clients happy and on board, he thought as he walked to his meeting. *Like Sisyphus pushing that damn rock up the mountain. Never actually making it, teetering on the top until the rock tips to the other side and the big slide starts. Will this client call be my last? The one that'll cost me my job and throw me into an early, un-pensioned retirement? Who was it that said 'the struggle itself should be enough to fill you'? Yeah, right.*

His brain had a habit of throwing seemingly unrelated thoughts around and he was constantly afraid that they'd somehow come flying out of his mouth, Of course, they often did. Surprisingly, when it happened people tended to think him erudite, as if he were making connections that hadn't yet appeared to them. He found this terribly amusing yet somewhat unsettling. It was difficult to keep up what he felt was the pretense of intelligence. He just knew that one day he'd be uncovered as a fool, the well-masked village idiot.

He glanced up at just the right time and found himself in front of his destination. He checked his watch and happily realized he had time to hit the Starbucks on the corner. *Nothing wrong with showing up laden with muffins and caffeine*, he said to himself. He opened the door and got in line behind a scruffy-looking hipster. The kid ordered a decaf cappuccino.

You pussy. He smiled to himself as he remembered the line from some TV show or movie. *Which one was it? James Garner said it. No it wasn't James Garner as Rockford. Oh, that's right. It was that movie with Garner and Jack Lemmon about the presidents. What was it called?*

He ordered, picked up some creamers and sugar and made his way to the meeting, still trying to pull the movie name from the recesses of his memory.

Made it through another one. He almost smiled but the reality of 90 minutes of discussions on five minutes of take away was stifling. He fished his phone out of his bag and called her.

"Hi Joe," she answered. He wasn't sure he'd ever get used to the callee knowing who the caller was before any word was spoken.

"It's over," he said.

What the hell does that mean, she thought, but said, "Really? How'd it go?" Dreading but hopeful tone.

"Didn't get fired."

"That makes one of us," she said. Even though it had been almost a year -- a glorious, relatively stress-free year -- she still couldn't shake the resentment she felt at her dismissal.

"Uh, yeah." He never knew how to respond to those kinds of statements she occasionally threw at him. Sometimes he felt like he was walking through a minefield, artfully dodging the trip buttons. "Didn't really need to be there. Probably said more than I should have."

"I'm sure you did fine. You always do."

"Ok. Well, I just wanted to let you know."

"Thanks." *Should I hang up or does he want to keep talking?*

"Yeah. Well, see ya later." He clicked off.

"Ok," she said to dead air. She put the phone down, looking at it as if it could tell her something, anything. It was always this way. Clipped conversations volleying from one satellite to another. Both wanting to say more but having nothing more to say. After all these years, she guessed it had all been said.

She was pretty comfortable with the unsaid, knowing that usually it's just better. Better than the fights over petty things, the misunderstandings. Better than the crying, the door slamming, the moping. He was fond of saying "You're catching attitudes." She never really knew what that meant, but decided a long time ago to translate it as "Let it go."

Let it go, let it go. Breathe in, breathe out. Count to ten. Myriad ways to deflect those easy-to-misinterpret statements. A conscious decision was needed, let it bother you or let it go. She almost always let it go. She sat there staring at the computer screen, her mind going in twenty directions and yet nowhere at all. She was startled out of her reverie by the rude ringing of the phone. She moved to pick it up, see who was bothering her. Another robo caller? Oh good. It's her daughter.

"Hi, hon."

"Hi Mom. What's up?"

What's up, she thought? *You called me. I've got nothing up. Or down.* "Oh nothing. Just sitting here trying to decide what to do. I've got a hair appointment today with Tim. Need anything?"

"Yeah, get me that shampoo I like. Oh, and the hair spray."

"Ok." She made a mental note and wondered if she'd remember. "So what's new? How's Simon?" Simon, her daughter's significant other, would be fine. He was always fine, even when he wasn't.

"Good, good. We're thinking of coming over tonight. Can we have dinner with you guys?"

"Of course. We're not doing anything. Want me to make something special?" *Please, please, please give me an idea for dinner.*

"Simon really likes those enchiladas you make. Is that too much trouble?"

Yes, but she said, "No, that's fine. I have to go to the store anyway."

"Ok, good. We'll see you around 5 or so."

"Good. See you then." And she rang off. *Enchiladas huh? Well now, should I do them from scratch or cheat and buy the rotisserie chicken and salsa verde?*

She clicked on the Word icon and opened the chicken enchilada recipe. Cooking was one of those chores that she usually enjoyed. Except that you had to do it every day. Every day come up with a meal that at least one of you liked, wasn't too expensive or too much of a hassle to make and clean up. But at least now she had a direction. Knew what she was doing this afternoon. Knew too how happy her husband would be when he found out they were coming.

He always liked to see the kids. He became lighter, his face brighter. He'd figure out which cocktail to serve, Margaritas tonight for Zannah, Corona for Simon, no lime, he's a man's man after all. No fruit in his beer! He'd scurry around the kitchen getting everything together like Santa loading his sleigh, almost dancing with anticipation.

She made her grocery list, checked the liquor cabinet to make sure there was enough tequila and triple sec, checked her watch. *Gotta get moving.*

The salon wasn't busy yet. The shampoo girl was dutifully refilling the towel bin, loading the dryer, sweeping the floor. The receptionist was hunched over the computer checking the day's appointments. Tim and India, two of the stylists, were sitting on the couches playfully throwing barbs at one another and greeted her as she came in. She loved this place. You entered looking uneven and a bit unkempt and left dyed, cut, styled and clean. In

10

fact, she often felt like a whole new person.

She settled herself in the stylist's chair and studied her face in the mirror. A few too many lines. *Why is my one eyelid droopy like that?* she wondered. She vaguely remembered somebody telling her, or did she read it somewhere, it's from sleeping on that side, your face scrunched up against the unforgiving pillowcase. Whatever the reason, it was making her look old. And it seemed to be getting worse every day. Maybe Tim will give me long bangs on that side to cover it up. He was a wonder when it came to hair. Always chose the perfect color. So perfect that people would remark about how lovely and shiny it was. Silky, too. He instinctively knew how to style it so her jowl-y chin was minimized. Too bad he couldn't do anything about the lines that made her look like a ventriloquist's dummy. At least he'd get rid of that pesky mustache. They always joked about how much they both enjoyed the waxing process. He claimed he loved inflicting pain and she mused over the unpleasant pleasantness of the hot wax smeared under her nose waiting to grab and yank out those dark little hairs. Press, press, rrrrrrrip. Then the cooling balm as he gently wiped off the excess wax. Done. Sigh. Insert S & M joke here.

Watching Tim cut her hair was mesmerizing. He carefully gathered sections, clipped them out of the way, then snip, snip, snipped his way to just the right wave here, the perfect angle there, a few minutes with the blow dryer and voila! you were ready to face the world. She liked how he merged his utter professionalism with the ability to talk to clients like they were old friends. They discussed movies, recipes, politics, dogs, the latest scandal. Actual conversations. Sometimes he would tell her funny stories about what he called cranky hair, she liked those the best. Liked peeking into his world, snatching glimpses of his day-to-day, the frustrations inherent in dealing with the public. Then she would go merrily on her way, grateful that she didn't have to deal with those kinds of people.

Actually, she didn't have to deal with many people at all. At least not for more than the few seconds it took to check out at the grocery store. Slowly, over time, she had isolated herself, begun what she told her husband was merely a form of hibernation. Hibernation, right. In reality she was hiding. Hiding while she struggled with those shadows.

She knew, of course, that one day she'd rouse herself, wipe her one good eye and one droopy eye, force the darkness back in the closet and re-enter the world. One day. But not today.

Today she was content with Tim, grocery store and daughter for dinner.

Zannah was here. Announced by the slamming door and the rustling bags. She could hear her daughter greeting the dog who reacted like he hadn't seen her just a few days ago. With his tail wagging uncontrollably, he pounced on his squeaky toy and played keep-away with Zannah, racing through the house, up and down the stairs, almost taking out Simon on his way to the kitchen.

She suddenly remembered the day she and Zannah went to pick up the dog. Zannah was still getting over the death of Charlie, their crazy cat, and Deb was wondering if it was too soon to introduce another animal. It was unnervingly quiet in the car on the way to the breeder's, with clipped conversations and noncommittal replies from her daughter. But as soon as they walked into the kennel and Zannah saw the puppies yelping, clamoring and tussling with each other, the somber mask fell away, replaced by glowing eyes, a beaming smile and hoots of laughter. No, it was not too soon.

She was pulled back to reality by a gentle touch on her shoulder.

Long hug, quick kiss from both.

"Smells great!" Simon exclaimed. "I bought some flan for dessert." He unpacked the flan from the bag and after some extensive refrigerator rearranging, shoved it into the newly formed empty spot. He straightened, pushed aside that blond hank of hair that had a way of falling over his left eye and gave her a wide smile.

Zannah walked over to the stove and stirred the enchilada sauce bubbling away. "Yum," she said. "Can we help?"

"Absolutely!" Deb darted around her husband who had just come in, adeptly avoiding the father/daughter/boyfriend greetings that were happening in the middle of the room.

"You didn't tell me they were coming. What a nice surprise!" There it was, that brightening of the face, the twinkling in his eye. The memories of the workday momentarily erased. Happy to see him so pleased, she smiled at him and gave him a quick kiss.

Cocktail and dinner preparations began in earnest. Everyone had a job to do; Joe handled the drinks, Simon seared the tortillas, Zannah filled and rolled them, Deb grated and sprinkled the cheese and the dog greedily scooped up every morsel that dropped to the floor. With the enchiladas safely in the oven, they grabbed their drinks and went into the family room to munch on chips and salsa, effectively ruining their appetites, but what the hell.

When they were all settled, Zannah reached over to Simon and grabbed his hand. "We have some news."

"Oh?" She looked at her daughter questioningly, then at her husband, then at Simon, then back to Zannah, trying to get a read on what was coming. Zannah took a deep breath, but before she got started, the phone rang.

They all froze, waiting for the machine to tell them who was calling. Damn, it was her father's number. She had to answer.

Apologetically, she got up to grab the phone. "Sorry, this'll just take a minute."

"Hello?" Pause. "What? No, wait, wait, wait a minute. Say that again." Panic flooded through her. "We'll be right there."

Chapter Two

They sat in the hospital waiting room looking at the walls, the floor, their laps, looking at anything that wasn't a person. Waiting for someone to give them a glimmer of hope.

The glare of the fluorescent lights belied the darkness of the evening and their thoughts. Zannah sat erect, both feet squarely on the floor, moist eyes fixed on the Rob Ross-like landscape lopsidedly hanging in front of her, hands clasped together. Her face had the crumpled look it always took on when her heart was crushed. Simon, sitting next to her, had gotten out his phone and was busily texting, his fingers flying across the keyboard, sending some lengthy message to who knows who. Occasionally he reached out and rubbed Zannah's hand, letting her know he was there, that she wasn't alone, that he knew, understood somehow the fear and dread that washed over her.

Sweet, thought Deb. She looked at her husband, watched him write on the ever-present notepad he kept in his jacket pocket. She knew he was forming questions for the doctor, questions that she would be too numb to ask, questions that she didn't really want the answers to. This was how he coped. Removing himself from the emotion with the pragmatism of Henry Kissinger establishing relations with China.

Joe glanced up and gave her a wry smile, then went back to his self-appointed task. *Damn I'm hungry.* Guiltily he thought of the chicken enchiladas, languishing in the now cold oven. *Timing sucks.*

"Oh!" exclaimed Zannah. She quickly got up and ran to her brother who was slowly approaching them.

"Hi Sis," Miles said softly, gathering her in his arms. "You ok?" She nodded unconvincingly.

Deb remained where she was, pleased to see her children seeking solace with each other. Theirs was a strange relationship. Although close in age their bond never seemed very strong. But she could be wrong. She thought about when they were young, how they used to look forward to Friday nights when Joe would get them fast food takeout or pizza and they'd run upstairs to watch TGI Friday on ABC. She and Joe could hear them laughing at the antics of the Tanner family. And even now, they always asked her about the other one. Was it feigned interest or did they really care? She couldn't ask either one of them. They had a way of deflecting questions like that, making a joke of any serious topic she posed.

Like that time she told Miles they needed to have a talk about sex. He was headed up the stairs after telling her he was going away for the weekend with his girlfriend and her family. She said, "Wait a minute. You two seem to be getting serious so we need to talk about, you know, sex." "No we don't," he laughingly replied. "Yes, we do." "Uh, no we don't" and with that he was off. She remembered calling out, "This discussion will happen!"

To this day, she couldn't remember if it ever did. She figured it must have, the long forgotten girlfriend didn't get pregnant, no one got AIDS, all was well. Let it go.

Miles made his way over to her and gave her a long hug. His hugs always surprised her, how big he had gotten, this six pound seven ounce baby now a grown man. "Hey Mom. What's going on? How is he?"

"We don't know anything yet. We got a call from Mr. Rose, his neighbor. They were having dinner at his place and Gramps just kinda fell over. Mr. Rose called 911, then us. The nurse said someone would be out soon to give us an update. That was an hour ago."

She gave him one of her lopsided smiles.

The double doors to the emergency room slid open. A man, clad in blue disheveled doc duds, walked toward them, his face expressionless.

"Mr. and Mrs. Cromwell?"

She nodded at him. Joe came to stand next to her, latched his arm around her waist. She waited for what seemed an eternity. Too soon he said, "I'm sorry. We did everything we could, but his heart was too damaged."

"Oh." What was there to say? She stood there, inert. Her mind was blank. She was aware that she needed to say something, but what? She knew this was the probable outcome, thought she had properly prepared herself for it. Had prepared for years for the moment she was told she was an orphan. Can you be an orphan at 60? *Think, think, think. Say something.* She could hear Zannah crying, Simon murmuring, Miles breathing.

"Can we see him? I mean, if she wants to, can she see him?" Joe's deep voice jolted her.

Oh God, no! I don't want to see him now. I want to see him yesterday, this morning, this afternoon. Not now! But she didn't say anything. Just stood there in the endless moment that was speeding by too quickly.

"Hon, do you want to see him?"

She quickly shook her head as if to waken herself. "No, no, that's ok.

I'm fine. Maybe you should ask the kids."

She heard the doctor talking to Joe and Joe responding but she couldn't make out the words. Then Miles said, "No, I'm fine. He wouldn't want that."

Zannah sniffled, wiped her nose on her sleeve and looked wide-eyed at the doctor and shook her head.

The doctor said, "Suit yourself," turned and walked away, untying the facemask around his neck, disappearing behind the softly closing doors.

The funeral was, well, a funeral.

People came, not as many as would have had he died younger, but still people came. People she vaguely remembered from some time back, way back. Relatives she hadn't seen in ages. *When was the last time? Probably a family reunion or maybe when Aunt Flo died.* She glanced around, noting how everyone was dressed. *Funny how the rules for funeral dressing have changed over the years,* she mused. Time was when everyone had their special clothes just for funerals, stuck way back in the closet only to be retrieved when custom required attendance. The black suit for men and the drab, conservative black dress for women. Today the full gamut of attire was represented in all colors of the rainbow. Sure there were still a few in standard suits, a dress here or there, not much black, lots of pant suits and sweaters. She even saw one young girl in those ripped jeans that were all the rage now. *Now this girl really flies in the face of convention.* In addition to those jeans, she was wearing what appeared to be a red camisole and clogs! *Imagine. Well, good for her.*

Deb realized that some people actually were enjoying themselves, treating this funeral like an outing, a chance to see old friends or relations, catch up on the latest gossip and check out who was still with the living. Calling greetings to one another, moving across the aisle to shake hands. She could hear their quiet murmuring broken only by the unexpected laughter to someone's story. *Glad somebody's having a good time,* she thought as she stood in line greeting the mourners, nodding solemnly, accepting their condolences, trying to come up with something to say that wasn't trite. How many times can you say, "Yes, he had a good life" "Thanks for coming" "I appreciate you being here"?

Going through the motions, a hug here, a kiss on the cheek there. *Oh, here's my cousin.* "Sandy, thank you for coming. I can't believe you made that long trip."

"Well, I had to come, didn't I? After all, there aren't many of the old ones left. You know, we're next in line. For dying, ha-ha. You remember Ashley, my youngest?" Sandy reached back, grabbed her daughter's arm and pulled her toward Deb. Ashley was looking at her feet, embarrassed by this sudden attention.

"Yes, of course! Ashley, how are you? I can't believe how you've grown. The last time I saw you, you were just a child!" *My God, did I really just say that?*

"Hi Aunt Deb," she muttered, trying to raise her head to look at Deb.

"It was nice of you to come."

"Happy to be here!" she said with a crooked smile. As soon as the words left her mouth, Ashley looked stricken. Her face reddened, she started stammering, her eyes darted around desperately hoping nobody heard her.

"Oh no! Did you just tell your Aunt Deb that you were happy to be at her father's funeral? I can't believe you."

The poor child, thought Deb. She smiled at Ashley, and took her hand. "It's all right, sweetie. Not to worry" and winked at her.

Truth be told, Deb welcomed the change of pace, a little levity to break the monotony, something to laugh about later with Joe and the kids. She remembered when she had said almost the same thing at the first funeral she had gone to. Really, what is the right thing to say? Nothing. In Deb's mind, there was nothing anyone could say that would make her feel better at this moment. Except maybe "Happy to be here." Now that was funny. A bit of fun in this sea of solemnity.

Of course Sandy, with her feigned my-perfect-child, my-perfect-life persona, wouldn't see it that way and Deb felt truly sorry for the belittling that awaited Ashley. Dear, sweet Ashley. The last of Sandy's three children. The one that was always a disappointment to her parents, from the time she was accidentally conceived to her unmeritorious graduation and subsequent inability to enter a 'good' college. The child lurking behind her highly successful, intelligent, personable brothers, her shoulders hunched, head down desperately trying to shield herself from the ever-present comparisons that circled her, slowly seeping into her psyche.

They moved away, with Sandy tut, tutting at shrinking Ashley. On to the service.

During the eulogies, Deb found her mind wandering, stretching back to odd reminiscences. Her father whistling as he made his way to the house on Friday nights, frying up scrambled eggs for his bridge buddies at two in the morning, sitting in the dark with his glass of whiskey waiting for her to come home from a date. She remembered how, on her wedding day, he took her hands, looked her in the eye and said, "It's not too late. It's never too late." Well, it was too late for him. There would be no more funny stories, uncanny imitations, off-color jokes told in his nasally French accent. Now she'd have to rely on fading memories to bring him back to her. She couldn't shake the guilt she felt at not being by his side when he passed, knowing how he feared traveling to the other side, unsure what side he'd end up on. *If there is a heaven,* she thought, *he would surely end up there, if only because he'd keep them laughing.*

And with that thought, the music started and the mourners silently made their way out of the church.

The rest of the day inched forward as only funeral days can. The long, slow drive to the grave site always a little unnerving as the cars moved through red lights, the reception at the house that quickly became a loud raucous party in honor of her father. While she listened to her father's buddies telling intricate stories of times gone by, she busied herself refilling glasses and cleaning up the kitchen, knowing he would have been pleased with the usual exaggerations and sometimes complete falsehoods.

Finally the last mourner left and Deb closed the front door with a quiet finality that was only too fitting.

Chapter Three

Joe was jolted awake by the obnoxious blaring of the alarm clock. His hand groped the nightstand, searching for the button that would give him nine more minutes. *Just nine more minutes*, he pleaded but then his brain kicked in and reminded him that this was Saturday, golf day, the best day of the week.

He pushed back the covers and swung his legs to the floor. He sat on the edge of the bed, grabbed his glasses and tried to focus his thoughts. *What's my tee time? When do I have to leave? Is it raining? Who's driving? What time is it again?* The image of his wife came flying into his brain, jumping in front of everything else. *Damn. Deb. Just buried her father. Probably shouldn't play. Damn, damn, damn.* But then, a glimmer of hope. *Maybe, just maybe she won't mind. Want to be by herself. Yeah maybe. How can I find out without coming off like a jerk? Impossible. I am a jerk.*

He looked over at her side. She's up already. He felt the sheets. *Cold. She's been up a while. Ok. Could be a good sign. She's not languishing in bed. She's up and doing something.* He didn't hear her moving around downstairs. *Must be playing solitaire. Better go see. Coffee first. Definitely, coffee first.*

Entering the kitchen, he saw his mug waiting in front of the coffee pot. *Good. Coffee's made.* He filled the cup, and walked into the room that served as an office/computer room, expecting to see his wife sitting in front of the computer, glasses perched on the end of her nose, staring at the computer screen, busily clicking cards.

Hmm, not here. The dog, lying on the floor, stirred awake and lazily wagged his tail. *Not walking the dog. Where the hell is she?*

"Deb?" he called out. No answer. He opened the cellar door. "Deb?" Still nothing. No note on the kitchen table. He looked in the garage. Her car was gone. "Where the hell did she go?" he said to the dog. Thump, thump, went the tail.

If he had been more awake, had had more coffee, he might have been worried. But he wasn't and he hadn't, so he grabbed the newspaper from the kitchen table and went back upstairs to start his morning ritual, wondering if this meant that he could play.

They found her crumpled on the sidewalk between the Dollar Store and the shuttered All-Night Grocery. At first, the policeman thought she was a homeless woman sleeping it off. But when he prodded her with his baton and she pulled away, he realized he couldn't have been more mistaken. She was clutching the strap of a Louis Vitton purse, the telltale LV charm splayed against her body, the purse gone. His partner called for an ambulance while he bent down, trying to discover the extent of her injuries, all the while murmuring soft assurances.

She moved to sit up, shaking her head to wipe away the cobwebs that clouded her mind. Her head throbbed with the sudden movement. She tried to focus on the man bending over her.

"What? What are you doing? Who are you? Stop! Wait! Stop!" She pushed him away, her eyes darting back and forth, trying to figure out what was going on.

"Ma'am, settle down. I'm a policeman, Officer Shepherd and over there is Officer Lambo. We're here to help you."

She looked at him, taking in the kind face and worried eyes, and for the first time noticed she was sitting on the cold, unforgiving pavement. "What am I doing here?" she asked. She reached up and rubbed the side of her head. "Ow!"

"Ma'am, we've called an ambulance. Can you tell me your name?"

"Yes, yes. It's Deb. Deb Cromwell. What do you mean, you called an ambulance? What's wrong with me? How did I get here? What's going on?"

"Well, Ms. Cromwell, it looks like you've had some sort of accident. You've got a bad cut on your head and I don't know what else. Do you remember how it happened?"

"An accident? What kind of accident? Where am I?" She tried to concentrate, to pull together coherent thoughts, but it was useless. She struggled to her feet, her legs wobbling under her. She heard the ambulance siren closing in. Everything was fuzzy, her stomach flipping, her brain pulsing. She grabbed the policeman's arm searching in vain for an anchor. "I don't feel so good." she whispered and blacked out.

She felt a warm hand caressing her arm and slowly opened her eyes, blinking against the harsh glare of the fluorescent hospital lights. Joe was staring intently at her, his pupils the size of a pinpoint. "Joe," she smiled, "How ya doing?"

"I'm fine, hon," he said, "How are *you* doing?"

"I'm fine, sleepy. A bit groggy. It's so bright in here." *Hold on,* she thought, *where am I? This is a hospital room!* Images flashed through her mind, kind policeman, cold pavement, blaring sirens, flashing lights. Pain stabbed her brain and rolled down her neck.

"Joe, what happened?"

"Shhh. Quiet. I'll go get the doctor. Wait here, I'll be right back." He strode out of the room pausing at the doorway, deciding left or right. He choose left, then doubled back to the right, waving meekly as he passed her door.

She lay there, futilely trying to remember the events that brought her here. *Think, think.* No, thinking hurt. *I'll remember,* she hopefully reassured herself. *For now, I'll just close my eyes, maybe get some sleep.*

She had just begun to nod off when she caught the sound of approaching footsteps and Joe's nervous chattering. "Deb, you awake? The nurse is here."

The nurse smiled at Deb. "How are you feeling, Mrs. Cromwell? I'm just going to take your temperature and blood pressure and check on your dressing."

What dressing? wondered Deb. Furrowing her brow, she realized that there was something constricting up there and reached up to feel it.

"No, no. Don't touch that. I'll take care of it," the nurse said as she guided Deb's hand toward the side of the bed. She took out a thermometer, shook it and placed it between Deb's lips. Beep, beep, beep, ping. Removing the thermometer, she said, "Good. Ok. Now give me your arm" and clicked the instrument back in its sleeve.

She could feel the blood pressure cuff gradually filling, tightening around her arm like a boa constrictor around its prey and the nurse's fingers on her wrist registering her pulse. The nurse was humming some vaguely familiar tune; its notes strangely colliding with one another, making it difficult to discern exactly which song it was.

The nurse abruptly turned and walked away, still humming, only to return with a stainless steel cart laden with bandages, tape, scissors, ointments and other supplies necessary for successful wound care. In inimitable nursing style, she stridently set about tending to Deb's wound, carefully cutting away the bloodied gauze, gently dabbing the wound with a moistened cloth, cleaning it as tenderly as possible, then rewrapping fresh gauze around and around and around her head, securing it with tape. Instinctively, Deb knew Joe had retreated to the corner of the room, face averted, not wanting to witness the stomach-turning goings on at the hospital bed.

"There. All finished and just in time, too. Look, the doctor's here! Now remember, don't touch!"

In walked the doctor, a no-nonsense look on her face. Deb's first reaction was one of surprise. *Hmmm, a female doctor. Nice. And look how young. Why, she can't be much older than Zannah and Miles. That's probably good. Fresh out of medical school with the latest and greatest updates on medicine and patient care.*

"Mrs. Cromwell, I'm Dr. Hale. How are you feeling?"

"I'm ok. But my head really hurts."

"Well, there's a nasty cut there. We stitched it up but it's going to hurt for a while. We can give you something for that." She yanked a clipboard out of its holder on the bed-board and made some notes. "Tell me, Mrs. Cromwell, how'd that happen, that gash in your head?"

"I don't know," she responded feebly. "I've been trying to remember, but I can't. I don't know what happened." It hurt to think.

"Don't worry. That's common with head injuries. Looks like you've suffered a pretty bad concussion. I'm going to order some tests. You just rest and someone will be here soon to take you down." She made some more notes, slid the clipboard back in its holder and strode out of the room.

"I'll be back later," she called over her shoulder.

Joe emerged from his corner and sat on the bed. He smiled, "You ok?"

"Sure. Uh no. I don't know."

"Deb," he hesitated, "What were you doing there? Where were you going? I don't get it."

She tried to process the question. *Where was I doing where? What's he mean by that?* "I, I, I don't know. I can't remember. I can't remember anything, Joe." She felt frantic, her brain trying to process the situation, trying to remember something, anything. "The last thing I remember was, I don't know. I can't think. What happened? How did I end up here? What happened to my head?" She tried to sit up, but was forced back by a stabbing pain.

"Hon, if you don't know, I certainly don't. I got up this morning and you were gone. No note, no nothing. I figured you just ran over to Patsy's Pastries for some doughnuts." He tried to keep the annoyance from his voice, but damn, he was pissed. And scared. And worried.

She heard it, the bit-louder-than-usual tone, quavering words tumbling out accusingly. Her eyes welled up, tears started trickling down her face, following the contours of her cheeks through her chin and down her neck.

She tried to sniffle them back. "I don't know! I'm sorry, but I don't know!" she cried.

He looked at her, cursing himself for causing her more pain. *This is not what she needs right now, you ass,* he said to himself. To her, "It's ok. We'll figure it out" and he leaned over to wipe her tears away. "Here comes Uber. Time for your tests," he joked as the orderly and wheelchair came into the room.

"Ok," she nodded feebly. As they wheeled her out, she took him by the hand. "Don't forget to call Daddy. He'll be worried."

He stared at her, his mouth agape. "Hon, your father's dead."

The look on her face when he uttered those words. He had never seen so many emotions crammed together, fighting to reach the surface, to come out on top. Fear, panic, dismay, horror, dread, alarm, confusion, denial. Denial won, trampling all the others in their stampede to understanding.

"What? Don't be silly. Now is not the time for kidding around," she said with an uncertain giggle. "Just go call him."

When they brought her back from the MRI room, she was exhausted and seemed to have forgotten their earlier exchange. They helped her back into bed, asking if she needed anything. "No," she told them, "I just need to close my eyes. I'm really tired."

Joe dragged a chair to the side of her bed and sat down. He took her hand, told her to rest until the doctor came back. She nodded and quickly surrendered to her fatigue.

An hour later, Dr. Hale came in, studying her laptop as she walked. "Mr. Cromwell, how is she?"

They both looked over at Deb, sleeping peacefully. He shrugged.

"Please sit, Mr. Cromwell. I've got the results back from the MRI. It looks like your wife is indeed suffering from a traumatic brain injury; you know it better as a concussion. She'll need a lot of rest but she'll be just fine. I'd like to keep her here overnight, just to be safe." She delivered the news in the business-like atonal way that doctors tend to have. "Questions?" she asked, not expecting any.

"Well, um yes," Joe said as he pulled his notepad from his pocket. He flipped the pages until he found what he was looking for. "Um, I don't know if this means anything, but she doesn't seem to remember anything about what happened. You know, how she got this."

"Oh, that's common. People with concussions often can't recall how the injury occurred. It'll probably come back to her," the doctor seemed completely unconcerned and turned to leave.

Joe was not ready to let it go. He said, rather forcefully, rising to confront the doctor face-to-face, "But wait a minute Doctor. I'm not talking about just the injury. She told me to call her Dad, but he died a few days ago. I mean, she knows he died. We had the funeral. She knows it!"

The doctor stopped and turned to him, "Really? Well, that's something," she said. She plopped her laptop onto the bed table and started typing, her fingers moving rapidly across the keyboard. She paused, waiting as the page loaded, then started reading, scrolling as she went. "I'll have the neurologist come see her, maybe do some more testing." She typed a few words, slammed the lid down and left.

Nonplussed, Joe watched her leave, unable to verbalize the questions flooding his brain. He hated this, hated not knowing what happened to his wife, hated the almost flippant way the doctor dealt with his concerns, hated feeling useless, out of control. Hated damn hospitals.

He plopped down on the chair, defeated. He looked over at his wife, noticing the swelling on the side of her head, the circles under her eyes. He took a deep breath and slowly let it out, knowing he needed to calm down. He looked at his watch and realized he should call the kids. They'd be furious he didn't call earlier. With a deep sigh, he fished his cell phone from his jeans pocket and went out to make the calls.

As he entered the hallway, he saw a policeman talking to the nurse. She pointed at Joe. Oh God, what now? Joe thought. The policeman was approaching him.

"Mr. Cromwell? I'm Officer Shepherd. I'm the one who found your wife."

"Oh, yes. Hi. I appreciate your helping her," he managed to add.

"Mr. Cromwell, how's your wife? She wasn't doing so good when we found her."

"They say she'll be all right. She's got a concussion and she's sleeping right now."

"I was wondering if Mrs. Cromwell has told you anything about an accident. Looks like her car was rammed from behind, there were a few skid marks and broken glass like from the taillight. And there don't seem to be any witnesses." He held a notepad and pen and was looking at Joe expectantly.

Her car! Man, I didn't even think about her car! "Well, no. She hasn't said anything about an accident. She doesn't seem to remember anything."

"Well, we'd like to talk to her as soon as possible."

"I'm sorry, like I said, she's sleeping. Can I call you when she wakes up? Maybe by then she'll be able to tell you something."

"I hope so. We've had a rash of bump-and-run carjackings and we think this could be another one. Only for some reason, this time they didn't take the car. So you see why it's important we talk to her. Here's my card."

"Yeah, ok. Hey, and thanks for taking care of her."

"Just doing my job, sir. I'll wait to hear from you." And he was gone, leaving Joe to deal with this new information. *Damn,* he thought, *Deb in a carjacking.* He had read about these in the paper. Now he tried to envision the scenario, but found it difficult to imagine his wife in that kind of danger. He saw her getting out of the car with her purse, ready to hand over her insurance information. Saw some thug coming up to her. Then what happened? Would she have just stepped aside and let the guy take the car? *She wouldn't have been so stupid as to try to talk the guy out of it, would she? Hah, you never know with Deb.* The only thing he knew for sure was that she got banged in the head.

The neurologist was Dr. Chan. He was a slight man who wore black-rimmed glasses and slicked back glossy hair. He talked with Joe in the hospital room, making notes, nodding and smiling, asking questions with a surprising British accent.

He finally put his pen down and looked at Joe. "Mr. Cromwell, I'd like to do some tests on your wife when she wakes."

"What kind of tests? What do you think is wrong?"

"I'd like to do an AMI, that's an Autobiographical Memory Interview. I'll ask her names of relatives, personal information, job history, those type of questions. We try to get her to recall things from three broad time bands, childhood, early adult life and recent facts. This way we can determine the extent of the memory affected. I don't like to speculate, but I can see how worried you are. It's possible she has retrograde amnesia as a result of the traumatic brain injury." He said these words matter-of-factly, not waiting to see if Joe was understanding him.

Joe tried to take it in, find the area of his brain that would make sense of what this guy was saying.

"Retrograde amnesia?" he asked. "No, she doesn't have amnesia. She knows who I am." Flashes of old movies ran through him. Memento and the guy with his sticky notes, the Bourne Identity with Matt Damon running around trying to figure out who he really was, and of course Spellbound, that great Hitchcock film with Gregory Peck. *She doesn't have amnesia*, he reassured himself.

"Mr. Cromwell," the doctor replied, "there are two main kinds of amnesia -- retrograde and anterograde and of course, there are specific grades in each. I'm pretty sure, from what you tell me, that she doesn't have anterograde. Within retrograde, there's pure retrograde and temporally graded retrograde. Basically, retrograde amnesia is the inability to remember things that happened before a certain date, usually an operation or in her case, accident. You're thinking of the retrograde that extends back decades, the kind often seen in movies. In the majority of retrograde cases, the memory loss is only a few days or months. I'm pretty sure that's what we're dealing with here. I'll know more after I examine your wife."

Joe was furiously making notes on his pad, knowing the kids were going to pepper him with questions, questions he wanted to be able to answer. As he was writing, he was thinking that this didn't sound too bad. *She's lost a couple of days, that's all. I'd like to lose a few days,* he thought wryly.

Deb woke to find Joe talking with a well-dressed Asian man. She couldn't make out what they were saying and was still groggy from sleep, her head pounding worse than a New Year's Day hangover.

The man looked at her, smiled and introduced himself. *He has a good bedside manner,* thought Joe listening as the doctor explained to Deb why he was there. He asked if she felt well enough to talk with him.

Deb's head whirled but she nodded yes. She liked this man, with his quiet lovely accent and reassuring expression. *And he's not bad to look at,* she thought. The doctor gently asked Joe if he could leave so he could carry on his examination.

Joe looked questioningly at Deb who grinned at him. "At least he's not a head shrinker, " she laughed. "I'll be fine. Go ahead."

Dr. Chan settled himself in the chair Joe had just vacated. Smiling at Deb he said, "Well now, Mrs. Cromwell, your husband tells me you're having trouble remembering what brought you here." He purposely left out the part about her father's death. "This is relatively common with head injuries, so we're going to talk a bit. I'll just ask you some basic questions, get some more information, start to figure out how to get your memory back."

"Ok, you're the doctor. Although maybe I just don't want to remember," she said with a noncommittal smile.

"That may be. But it's always better to know, don't you think?" he asked without expecting an answer. "Let's just start and see where we go." He paused, then "Mrs. Cromwell, how are you feeling? Does your head hurt much?"

"Yeah, I've got a pretty bad headache. It hurts all over, not just where they say the cut is."

"That's too bad. I'm sure they'll give you something to help with that. Have you ever had a concussion before, any kind of fall maybe when you were a child?"

"No, not really. I was never really that active. I was one of those sit around reading kids, never played sports or anything like most girls today."

"Never in a car accident? Fall off your bike? Trip down the stairs?"

"Nope, not even a broken bone, although I did sprain my ankle once," she smiled apologetically.

"So you were pretty lucky then. Tell me, what's the earliest thing you can remember from your childhood?"

Oh no, she thought, *I didn't know there was going to be a test. And here I am, not at all prepared, didn't study, as usual.* "My childhood? Oh, I don't know. I remember stuff from elementary school, you know, my kindergarten teacher, Mrs. Frannie. I thought she was ancient but she probably was younger than I am now. Sometimes I think I remember things from younger, but I never know if I actually remember them or if I just concoct memories from pictures I've seen and stories I've been told."

"What about friends?"

"Friends? I played with the kids in the neighborhood. There was Carol, actually two Carols, and Barb and Sue. We lived in town so there were a lot of kids." Faces floated into her mind, she could hear giggling and calling, she saw summer evening kicker games and the street lamps signaling the end of fun, time to go home. Funny how it all tumbled back, invited by a simple phrase. One memory ran into another and before it was completed, replaced by another and on and on. How much did he want her to say? She looked at him quizzically.

"That's fine," he said. "Any relatives you were close to? Maybe cousins or aunts and uncles?"

"I had some aunts and uncles that I didn't see very often. One lived in Los Angeles, that was my Uncle Bob and his wife Sunny. They didn't have kids. There was an aunt in Cleveland with a bunch of kids, but I don't think she and my dad got along. My mom was an only child, so no cousins from her. Some of my parent's friends I'd call Aunt, like Aunt Cam and Auntie Olivia. They were my favorites."

Scribble, scribble, scribble. Head nodding as if in agreement. "So what about high school and college? Did you go to college?" he asked, still scribbling.

"Uh huh. I went for engineering, then switched to social work. My parents weren't happy about it. I wasn't a very good student, ended up withdrawing," she admitted ruefully. She hated to think about those years. All the time she wasted flitting from one thing to the next, never settling on anything that made a career. "I wish I had been more like my friends, dutifully attending classes, cramming for exams, staying up all night writing papers. Oh I stayed up all night all right, but only to go to concerts, drink and smoke weed, do the odd bit of mescaline. So useless, so trite, so 60's." She began to well up as the shadowy figure nudged her mind and she wiped at her eyes with the sleeve of the robe she wore over her hospital gown. She made an effort to turn her attention back to the doctor.

He was studying her now. Was that pity she saw in his eyes? *Damn, why did I say that?* The doctor cleared his throat, "Yes, We all have regrets," he said. "But tell me, after you left school, what did you do?"

She forced herself to sound normal. "I went to work, taking whatever job I could get. I was a sales girl in a camera shop for a while, then you know, my dad said I had to get something that paid me enough to move out of the house, so I ended up working for an insurance company. Took some classes and became an underwriter. Really boring, stuck in a rut type of work."

"Uh huh," scribble, scribble, scribble. "How did you meet your husband then?"

"I used to go into the city on the weekends, to the discos. One night after the club closed, a bunch of us went to this all-night diner, Little Pete's, and he was there eating corned beef hash. We just sort of struck up a conversation." Embarrassed by all she had already revealed to the doctor, she decided to go with the version of meeting Joc that she told pretty much everyone. Truth was, she was a bit drunk and on a dare, went and sat next to him and asked him why he stood her up. He was noticeably annoyed by this intrusion, did not see the humor in it and completely ignored her. A few weeks later, in an odd coincidence, they ended up sitting next to each other at a reading by John McPhee at the community college. He must have decided she wasn't a total idiot because he asked her to coffee afterwards.

The conversation continued with Dr. Chan probing for memories of specific dates, personal milestones, people past and present as well as current news and historic events.

"Ok," said the doctor at last. He paused in his writing and willed her to look at him. Staring intently, his eyes seemed to bore a hole in her pulsating brain. "Mrs. Cromwell, can you now tell me the last thing you remember before today?"

She stared at him. What was the last thing she remembered? She remembered a policeman, but before that? She wracked her brain. She saw herself in the kitchen making enchiladas for Zannah and Simon. "That's it!" she said brightly. "I was making enchiladas. I must have tripped over the dog, he always gets underfoot when I'm cooking. I must have fallen and bashed my head against the counter! That's it!" she almost yelled, pulling herself up to a sitting position, relief washing over her like a welcoming warm spring breeze. She plopped back onto the pillow, grinning with delight.

Dr. Chan stopped his writing and said, "So the last thing you can recall is being in your kitchen. Do you know what day that was?"

"What do you mean? It had to have been yesterday. Yes, my daughter and her boyfriend were coming for dinner and I was making enchiladas. I'm sure I just fell over something and knocked myself out. Then somebody probably came home, either Joe or Zannah, and they called the cops."

Wait a minute. That can't be right. It doesn't make sense. If Joe or Zannah found her, why would Joe be asking her all those questions about where she was and why. Think, think. She saw the policeman and remembered pavement, cold, unforgiving pavement. She looked questioningly at the doctor, "There was a sidewalk. It was cold. How did I get on the sidewalk?"

"Well, Mrs. Cromwell, that's what we're trying to figure out. I think we've done enough for today. You just try and relax. I'll come by later to see you. In the meantime, you get some rest. And try not to worry." He patted her on the arm reassuringly. "See you in a while," then left to find Joe.

Deb watched the doctor leave. She felt in a daze, worried, just shy of panic, unsure what any of this meant. A bolt of lightning slashed its way into her carrying Joe's words, "Your father's dead."

Chapter Four

Joe had just finished calling Zannah and Miles, explaining as best he could what he knew so far, which in their minds wasn't much. Zannah, predictably, was beyond worried and insisting that she come to the hospital to see her mother immediately. She was probably already out the door. Pragmatic Miles said he'd wait to hear more, didn't want to come off as flying off the handle. Joe knew that as soon as he ended the call, Miles would be researching amnesia on the web, trying to glean as much information as possible, figuring out what, if anything, he could do to help his mother.

Dr. Chan approached Joe and waited a bit impatiently while Joe clicked off the call. He looked expectantly at the doctor.

"Mr. Cromwell, let's sit for a moment," as he motioned toward the chairs in the empty waiting room.

Obligingly, Joe sat, hopeful for good news but fearful as well.

"Mr. Cromwell, I've just finished talking with your wife and, barring results from more extensive testing, I feel my original diagnosis was correct, that she is suffering from retrograde amnesia. She has retained her long-term memory, her childhood, teen years, your first meeting and so on. The last thing she remembers is making enchiladas for someone. She mentioned a Zannah and Simon? When was that?" Pen poised above his tablet.

"Really?" Joe tried to place the day, then it dawned on him. "Wow, that was last week, the day her father died, but before that. You know, before we found out he had had a heart attack. Zannah's our daughter and Simon is her boyfriend. They came to dinner and, that's right, they were about to tell us some news when the phone rang. Never did find out what our daughter's news was."

"I see. That makes sense. Often this temporary amnesia happens after a traumatic experience and it seems that your wife experienced not one, but two traumatic events in a short span of time."

"So what do we do? Will she get better, I mean will she ever be able to remember?" There was so much he wanted to ask, so much to know. He felt shaken, unsure what to do.

"There isn't much we can do right at this moment. From reading her chart, I expect she will be discharged later today or tomorrow, but I'll have to talk with her doctor to verify that. She'll need to rest. As her physical injury heals, I'm hopeful that will her memory will return. I'll prescribe some medication to keep her calm."

Joe was torn, not sure he was ready to deal with an amnesiac wife at home, yet wanting everything to go back to normal.

Dr. Chan said, "I'm sure you have a lot of questions but they can wait for now. I'd like you to call my office, here's my card, and schedule an appointment. I want to see her again in a few days."

"Doctor, how about if I just tell her what happened that last couple of days? I know she'll be asking me. Maybe if I just tell her, it'll spark something and she'll remember," he was almost pleading.

"Ah, what you're talking about is known as the Reminder Effect or Reminder Treatment. Unfortunately, simply telling someone about his or her personal experiences and identity is ineffectual. That type of treatment has no scientific bearing on recovering memory. Fortunately, however, memory can be and usually is, recovered by what we call Spontaneous

Recovery. I'll go into that in more depth at her appointment."

Joe nodded, trying to appear like he understood. He thanked the doctor, shaking his hand and assuring him he'd set up an appointment.

He watched the doctor walk away and thought that maybe it wouldn't be so bad. *Just get her home. Maybe being in the hospital is screwing her up and when she gets in familiar surroundings, she'll be her old self.*

Deb tried to yell for Dr. Chan to come back but her words caught in her throat, unwilling to voice themselves out loud. She frantically pushed the call button, hoping to summon a nurse to fetch Joe. She wanted answers and she wanted them now. She kept hearing Joe's words, "Your father's dead" but they had no meaning. *It can't be,* she thought. *It just can't be. I would remember that. I might not remember how I got here, but I would certainly remember if my father died.*

Maybe it was some sort of a joke, a way to lighten the situation. Joe could be strange sometimes, his sense of humor on the dark side. He loved dark comedies, delighted in exploring taboo subjects and putting a comic spin on them. It would be just like him.

But somehow she knew he wasn't kidding. That whatever caused her to be here in the hospital had knocked out more than the memory of her accident. How much had she forgotten? She felt like she was coming apart at the seams, she could almost feel the little threads pulling away from the sturdy fabric that held her life, her sanity, her self together. She needed to get out of here. Get away. Now.

She began to tear at the tube that was holding her tied to this place.

Damn that hurts, she cried as she yanked it out of her arm. She fought back the tears that sprung up and swung her legs to the side of the bed. She quickly stood up and just as quickly sat back down, her head whirling. Her breathing was fast, shallow. *Gotta go. Gotta get out. Where are my clothes? Where's Joe?* She took a deep breath to center herself, then reached for the side bar of the bed to steady her legs as she again tried to stand. *Better this time. Now slowly walk to the closet, take another deep breath. Good, here are my pants and shirt. Now put them on.*

As she was making her way to the chair, she saw Joe coming into the room.

"My God, hon, what are you doing?" he exclaimed incredulously.

"I, I, I gotta get out of here," she stammered. "C'mon, let's go home. I need to go home. Now."

"Ok, ok. Settle down. Just sit down for a minute. Talk to me. What's going on?"

"I don't know. I just have to leave. I can't stay here any longer. Help me," she begged unable to hold back the tears.

"Ok." He didn't know what to do, how to help her. He wanted more than anything to pick her up and carry her out of that damned hospital. But he knew he couldn't. Not yet. He tried to stay calm for her, tried to quell the anxiety that was streaming from her straight into him. He guided her to the chair and gently pushed her into it. He caressed her shoulder as he talked. "Let me get the nurse. I know Dr. Hale said she wanted to keep you overnight, but Dr. Chan said maybe they'd discharge you today, so let me find out. Will you just sit here for a minute while I find someone?"

She looked at him, deflated, and sank back into the chair nodding.

Joe went to the door and looked up and down the hallway. "Nurse! Nurse!" he yelled. The nurse who had re-bandaged Deb's head came walking briskly around the corner.

"Yes, what's the matter?"

Joe took her aside and talked with her in low tones. Deb sat in the chair watching them. She couldn't make out what they were saying, but heard the urgency in Joe's deep voice. She leaned forward, hoping to listen in. A minute later, the doctor came in and joined the conversation. After what seemed an eternity, Joe looked over at her and smiled reassuringly. "It's ok Deb. They're letting you go home."

There was a flurry of activity. Getting dressed, signing release forms, enduring a final bandage change, half listening to medication instructions. Deb hoped Joe was paying attention to those because she certainly wasn't. Finally, the wheelchair came and an orderly wheeled Deb to Joe's waiting car.

On the way home, Joe kept up a steady stream of light chatter, talking about work, the debacle of the latest Republican debate, the latest gastro pub opening in town and the antics of the neighbor's children. The pain pills the nurse gave her before they left were starting to kick in and although Deb did her best to contribute to the conversation she found her mind wandering back to what everyone was referring to as 'the accident.' It was unnerving not knowing what had happened to her. She kept turning what little she knew over and over in her mind, willing some sort of memory to rise to the surface but with no luck. They drove past the Simm's Funeral

Home. She stared out the window noticing the hearse with its rear door open, patiently waiting for the casket of some poor soul on its way to the grave. *I'll bet that's where Dad's funeral was,* she mused, surprised that this thought no longer startled her. *Good old Percocet.* She smiled in spite of herself.

"What's so funny?" Joe asked, breaking into her reverie.

"Oh nothing. I think the meds are working. Thank you big pharma," she giggled.

"Well that's good. You should probably eat something when we get home." He knew she hadn't eaten at the hospital "What are you hungry for?"

"Potato chips and onion dip," she announced with certainty.

Yup, he thought, *the meds are taking hold. Usually it's me craving crap food and Deb chomping on carrot sticks and hummus.* Against his better judgment, he went along with it. "Ok," he said laughing. "I'll stop and pick some up."

After a not so quick run into Wawa -- Joe decided he'd better pick up a couple of sandwiches too -- they made their way home. Pulling into their street, Deb saw Zannah's car parked in front of the house.

"Look Joe. Zannah's home." Even though the kids hadn't lived in that house for years, Deb still considered it their home. Their bedrooms were still their bedrooms: posters adorning the walls, sports trophies and high school memorabilia crammed onto bookshelves and closets with clothes no longer in style crammed against out-of-season coats.

"Yeah, the kids are pretty worried about you. Miles will be here later," Joe said.

"That's nice," Deb replied dreamily. "Always good to see them."

She opened the car door as Zannah came running out of the house.

"Mom, here. Let me help you." She took Deb's arm to help her get out and steadied her placing her free hand around Deb's waist.

Deb smiled at her, "Here to take care of your old mom, eh?"

"Yup. Took the day off. Let's get you inside," she said a little too brightly as she led her mother through the garage into the house. Joe ran ahead, trying to ward off the dog impatiently waiting to greet Deb.

Zannah settled Deb on the sofa. She had already brought down a bed pillow and Deb's favorite blanket. Now she was fussily plumping the pillow, arranging and rearranging the blanket, making sure it covered Deb's feet.

"There now. Comfy? How about a cup of tea?" she asked.

"Really hon, you don't have to fuss. I'm fine. My head was hurting but they gave me some wonder pills and I feel just fine now."

Zannah looked at her father hovering in the kitchen. "Really Dad, is she? What did the doctor say?"

"She has to go see Dr. Chan, the neurologist." He snapped his fingers, "Oh, that's right, I have to make an appointment." As Zannah walked into the kitchen, he whispered, "I'll tell you more when she's settled." She shot him a look that was both questioning and concerned.

"No, it's fine. It's better to wait until Miles gets here so I don't have to say it twice, ha-ha."

"Hey, where's my chips and dip?" Deb yelled from her perch on the sofa.

"Coming right up." Joe unpacked the bag and arranged the snack in a bowl while Zannah set about making tea.

"So Zannah," Deb said, "your father tells me that Gramps died. You know about this?"

Joe saw the panicked expression on his daughter's face and said, "Of course she does, Deb. Don't worry, everything's going to be fine."

Deb closed her eyes, mumbling as she fell asleep, "From your mouth to God's ears."

It was a restless night for Deb. Her dreams traveled haphazardly from the real to the surreal to pure fiction. Here she was in her high school chemistry class sitting next to Guy, my word he was handsome!, listening to the teacher explain that night's homework. But wait, the teacher was Miles. What was he doing here? She saw herself shuffling papers, leaving the room and running into 30th Street train station with her dog dutifully following her. Someone she didn't know took her hand. They ran together as one, dodging the travelers walking zombie-like toward them. A gigantic blob was oozing its way toward them, gaining ground quickly. They leapt into the air taking flight, flapping their arms to keep afloat. She could feel the slimy mass seeping onto her feet, ever so slowly rising up her legs.

She woke with a start. Her feet were rubbing her legs trying to shed the ooze from the dream's blob. She could feel the cut on her head pulsating, her arm was asleep, the pins and needles pushing into her skin. She flapped her hand back and forth to shake off the stinging pricks.

That was weird, she thought, *I should write that one down.* She reached over to open the drawer of her bedside table, groping for the pad and pen she kept there to record her dreams. She knew it was silly, really, keeping a record of her dreams, but it was something she had done since she was a child. She felt that her nighttime images would become reality if she didn't voice them somehow. After all, it had happened. She had dreamt about things that had come true. Joe told her it was just déjà vu, but she knew it wasn't. The reality would occur days after the dream. Little flashes of the future, insignificant little pieces that popped up during the day. Nothing earth shattering, mind you, just a flow of conversation or a person seen before only in the haze of her dream. She only jotted down those images if they bothered her. The good ones she kept to herself, willing them to come true. Like when she dreamt of three numbers. She was sure they were winning lottery numbers. But as she stood in line waiting to buy the ticket, she couldn't recall exactly what they were. 23, 46 and 99. Or was it 96? Or 94? Damn.

Even though she knew tonight's dream would never would come true, she carefully wrote down every last detail, aided by the glow of the night light, then placed the pad back into the drawer and let herself drift off to sleep, lulled by Joe's steady snoring next to her.

Joe was bustling around the kitchen making coffee, filling the teakettle, feeding the dog, doing all the things he figured Deb usually did before he woke up. He went outside to get the paper followed by the dog whose bladder was about ready to burst.

Sitting at the table, he quickly scanned the front page. The above-the-fold headline told him the Republican candidates were still at it, savagely slamming each other. *Wow*, he thought, *how in the world can anyone seriously think about voting for any of these guys?* He was completely disenchanted with all of the candidates and surprised that so many people actually planned to vote for one especially brutish man among them. Joe had been waffling between the Republicans and Democrats ever since college. Like many of his 60's cohorts, he began adult life as a left of left-winger, then as he became reliant on earning a living he skewed farther to the right. But events since 9/11 and the succession of wars and the rise of the neo-conservatives with their blatant intolerance of anyone who wasn't white, Christian and straight had him running back to the left. *When*, he wondered, *did the word conservative morph from fiscal constraint to moral inflexibility?* It was mind boggling.

Deb, on the other hand, was always a staunch Democrat who leaned toward socialism. She constantly threw herself and her money toward supporting organizations that promised to give a helping hand to those less fortunate, non-profits like the Southern Poverty Law Center, the NAACP, Habitat for Humanity, Jewish Defense League, any and all of those. He supposed he should admire her passion but often found it irritating. He'd been around too long to see it as anything more than a waste of time and dollars.

Noises from upstairs roused him from his thoughts. He put down the paper, realizing he had let her tea steep for almost a half hour, far too long for most people, but probably just right for Deb. He popped her mug into the microwave to reheat as she slowly made her way down the stairs.

"Hey, what are you doing up? I would have brought you your tea."

"I just couldn't stay in bed," she replied running her hand through her mussed hair, wincing as her fingers swiped the bandage. "I'm fine, really." She pulled her robe around her and sat down. "Hi puppy, how are you doing," as she reached down to stroke the dog. She clasped her hands around the tea mug, pleased by its warmth.

"It's so strange to see you up before me." She took a tentative sip, not wanting to burn her tongue but desperate for her morning fix. *Nice*, she thought, *nice and sweet.* She usually eschewed sugar in the morning, saving it for her afternoon pick-me-up, but at this very moment it tasted so good she wondered why she didn't sweeten it all the time. She glanced over at the paper and considered picking it up, but quickly decided not to. "Anything interesting in the news?"

"Just the usual political stupidity. That's as far as I got. Don't even know if the Sixers won the game last night," he laughed, 99% sure they didn't. "How'd you sleep?"

"Ok I guess. Had some really weird dreams. Probably those pain pills."

"You feeling ok? How's your head?"

"I know it's there. You know how you usually don't realize you've got a head or a stomach until you get a headache or a stomachache? I know my head is there."

"You should take another pill with breakfast."

"No, it's not that bad. It'll be fine. I want to take a shower. What did the nurse say, can I wash my hair?" She wanted desperately to wash yesterday off.

"I'll have to look at the discharge instructions. I'm not sure." He took a deep breath and trying to sound nonchalant, added, "Listen, the cops are coming by today. They want to talk to you."

"Talk to me?" she sounded surprised. "What do they want to talk to me about? Didn't you tell them I don't know anything?"

"Sure I did, but they want to talk to you anyway. They're hoping something will come back."

"They probably know more than I do," she said ruefully, but nodded compliantly. "Guess I better get ready."

Chapter Five

Officers Shepherd and Lambo sat on the edge of the surprisingly comfortable ultra-modern chairs in the family room facing Deb across the coffee table littered with coffee and tea mugs. Officer Lambo, notepad at the ready, was eyeing the room, taking in the paintings on the walls, artsy family photographs on the piano, stuffed dog toys strewn on the rug. *Not my taste,* he thought, *but pleasing in an odd sort of way.*

His partner cleared his throat. "Mrs. Cromwell, your husband thought it was better if we came to you instead of you coming down to the station. Hope that's okay with you."

"Yes, that's fine," she answered a bit edgily. She was always nervous around law enforcement wondering if they could retroactively give you a speeding ticket or cite you for underage drinking. She felt like she was on an episode of Law and Order, though these cops weren't as good looking as the ones on TV. Maybe it's just detectives that are attractive. Of course, the men on the shows were never as handsome as the women were beautiful. She wondered if female cops in real life were that pretty if there'd be less crime or more. Probably more. All the men would want to get patted down by the lovely cop. She realized the officer was talking to her.

Embarrassed, she said, "I'm sorry, I didn't hear you. What was that?"

"I was saying that you're looking much better than when we last saw you." Those kind eyes now accompanied by a slight grin.

"Oh, thanks," she self-consciously ran her fingers through her hair. "Joe said you wanted to talk to me but I don't know what I can tell you. I seem to have forgotten quite a few things," she tried to laugh but it caught in her throat.

Joe, sensing her unease, piped up, "Yes, she's lost a few days. Doesn't even know why she was in that part of town much less any kind of accident."

"Mrs. Cromwell, we found you on Broad Street right by the Dollar store. Your car was near the curb and the door was wide open. The taillight was broken. You can't remember maybe getting rear-ended or how you came to be on the sidewalk?" He was really hoping she'd recall something, he needed a break in these carjacking cases and felt she could be the key.

She looked over at Joe then back to the officer. She desperately wanted to give him the answers he was seeking but for the life of her, she couldn't figure out what she'd been doing over there. "Nooo," she said cautiously. "Joe said the doctor is hopeful that I'll start remembering things soon though. I'm sorry to waste your time but it sounds like just an ordinary hit and run to me. They seem to be happening more and more often if you can believe what you read in the paper. People afraid to take responsibility."

"Well, ma'am, like I was telling your husband, we've had quite a few carjackings lately and we're thinking this could be another one. But this time, it looks like something went wrong. This time they didn't take the car. And before there were no victims harmed." He knew he was saying more than he should but he wanted to jolt her, thinking that would bring back the incident.

Deb was staring at him, her mouth open. She didn't like what she was hearing, wanted to un-hear it and quickly decided that they were mistaken.

After all, she was smarter than that, wasn't she? She shook her head in denial. "I am not a victim," she said uneasily.

"Look Officer," Joe said somewhat testily, "the doctor said it wouldn't do any good to try to remind her of things like this. She'll remember when and if she remembers. If she does, I'll call you right away. But I don't want to upset her any more than she already is."

Officer Shepherd cleared his throat again. "I'm sorry Mr. Cromwell, Mrs. Cromwell. I don't mean to upset you, we just want to get to the bottom of this, get these guys behind bars." His partner, Officer Lambo, mumbled something and flipped his notepad shut.

"We'll be going, but please call me if she remembers anything." They stood and turned to leave. On their way to the door, Officer Lambo stopped and said, "By the way, I'd change your locks as soon as possible."

Joe hurried over to him. "Wait, what do you mean, change the locks? Why should we change the locks?"

He looked at Joe pointedly, "We know they have her car keys. Usually people keep their house keys with their car keys. And when we found her all she had was the strap of her purse, so it looks like they've got that too and her wallet with her driver's license. And your address."

"Oh God, yeah. That never dawned on me, what with everything going on with Deb," Joe said.

"Frankly, Mr. Cromwell, I'm surprised they didn't pay a visit to the house while you were busy at the hospital. Goodbye, now." And they walked out the door leaving Joe scratching his head and Deb slouched against the sofa cushions.

The rest of Joe's day was filled with handling the household duties that usually fell under Deb's purview. He cancelled credit cards, called the locksmith (happy to come and take care of that for you, Mr. Cromwell), and the neurologist's office (we'll see Mrs. Cromwell at 10:00 Tuesday). He made the bed, did some laundry, screened phone calls, and straightened the house. He kept thinking about the officer's visit, Deb's memory loss and wondering how it would all play out. Could he go back to work tomorrow? She seemed to be all right, but knew how she didn't like to worry him. Was she just putting on a good front? He tried to imagine how he would feel if it were happening to him. He liked to think he'd be fine with it, but knew it would be driving him crazy. He didn't like not knowing something.

Too bad you can't pick and choose what memories you lose, there's a couple of things I'd like to forget, he thought. Maybe she did. Maybe somewhere in her unconscious she decided to lose her dad's death and the carjacking. Perhaps that's all amnesia really is. A willful choice to forget.

Deb, meanwhile, laid on the sofa intermittently watching TV, flipping through magazines and dozing. She found it difficult to concentrate on any one thing. She'd come upon a recipe in a magazine and it would remind her of the enchiladas and she wondered if they ever ate them. Certain commercials reminded her of her father and a deep sadness would overtake her. She'd then try to imagine how he died, what the funeral was like, how it had all unfolded. She'd start to nod off but would rouse herself, afraid of the dreams she might have. She did her best to focus on the kids who always made her feel better. She'd put herself in their day, thinking about how they spent it and then wondered if she had forgotten anything important about them.

She heard Joe joking with the locksmith and for once was glad that he guarded his privacy like a sentry guards his post. She knew he wouldn't explain why they needed new locks, he'd just dance around the topic. After all, it was no one's business. That was Joe's mantra. Keep yourself to yourself.

In this case, he was right. It was nobody's business what had happened or what was happening to her now. She didn't want to answer questions, didn't want people trying to force memories or emotions out of her. She just wanted to be left alone. She found herself getting confused, frustrated, irritable.

And claustrophobic. The walls were closing in, the air felt hot and heavy, it was hard to breath. She flung the blanket off and stood up too fast. Her head felt light and she could see stars swimming in front of her eyes. She plopped back onto the sofa, telling herself to slow down, take a deep breath and start over.

This time she held onto the sofa arm as she stood, waited a few seconds, then cautiously walked to the back door. She opened the door. The cold winter air rushed at her. *Man that feels good.* She made her way to the patio steps and settled down, welcoming the icy stone seeping into her backside.

She gazed at the barren trees and abandoned bird's nests, the clouds scuttling across the sky, the flower pot with the dead tomato plant that she never got around to emptying. She saw a bird fly by and land in the yard. *Why, it's a robin!* She smiled. *How lovely.* Almost immediately her mood lifted, lightened by the harbinger of the coming spring. Gratefully she watched as the determined bird pecked at the ground, hoping he'd find that worm he was after. "Thank you," she whispered.

"You're welcome," said Joe laughing as he came up behind her. "What are you thanking me for?"

"Hah! I was thanking that robin over there. See, over there by the lilac tree? Spring is coming!"

"Yeah, well it might be coming, but it's not here yet. It's cold out here and you're not even wearing a coat. Let's get you back inside."

"No. It feels good to be out here. Just sit here for a minute with me."

Joe sat down and put his arm around her. After a few minutes, he said, "It's going to be all right, Deb. Even if you never remember, everything is going to be all right."

She looked at him, "It's just so frustrating. I keep trying to figure it all out. How can I not remember Dad dying? Or a car accident? I know it probably doesn't matter, but it makes me wonder what else I have forgotten."

"If it's any comfort to you, there wasn't anything else important. You know how uneventful our day-to-day is. Your dad and the accident, why would you want to remember? It's over. It's done. Just let it go."

She nodded. "I'll try."

Despite reassurances from Joe that Deb was much better, Miles and Zannah were not convinced. They weren't used to seeing their mother unwell. She was always the caregiver, making chicken soup, taking temperatures, readying cool towels for fevered brows. Miles couldn't even remember the last time she had so much as a cold.

But last night she looked pretty feeble, a ghost of herself, staring into space, disconnected from the conversation. Maybe their father was right, that it was the meds keeping her so out of it, but they were still concerned. So much so that they held a protracted Facetime conversation that morning debating whether or not she was getting the right care and what, if anything, they should be doing. Simon wisely kept his mouth shut and his opinions to himself, not wanting to get in the middle of what could rapidly become a sibling battle. Zannah felt Deb should see another doctor, maybe a shrink; Miles was of the wait and see view. The result of the meeting was a solid decision to do nothing but make dinner for their parents that night.

So they showed up after work, arms loaded with bags of groceries. Zannah announced she was cooking, Miles would be her sous chef; Simon, the errand runner and busboy. Joe was relieved. He was exhausted from the events of the last few days and hadn't even thought about dinner.

Joe trotted off to the family room, happy for the respite and the chance to catch up on the latest sports news. Deb sat at the kitchen table watching her children slice, dice and sauté, attempting to follow their rapid-fire banter. Jokes about the latest movies and shows, bands and concerts. Quoting lines of dialogue or song lyrics. Discussing the latest restaurant openings and closings. *How*, she wondered, *could they possibly keep up with all of it?* She and Joe rarely went out any more but still had trouble finding the time to watch their favorite series, unseen episodes piling up on the now 85% full DVR.

They sat at the table, Joe and Deb oohing and aahing over the presentation and aromas wafting toward them. Deb, against doctor's orders, had a glass of wine, wryly accepting the toasts to good health and swift recovery. Joe, to his credit, made no sarcastic comments about the quinoa and mushroom side dish, but helped himself to a large portion of the Chicken Milanese. They kept the conversation light, mostly discussing the upcoming NCAA March Madness frenzy.

Deb kept looking at Zannah and Simon. Something was nagging at her, pecking away at her subconscious. She couldn't put her finger on it. What was it? They seemed fine, almost better than fine. The feeling went away when she looked at Miles. She made a game of it. Look at Zannah, feeling there, look at Miles, feeling gone, look at Simon, feeling there. Back and forth between the three of them like a Pong game.

"It's weird," she said breaking into the who's-making-it-to-the-Final-Four debate. "I get this weird funny feeling every time I look at Zannah and Simon."

Talking stopped. All heads turned to look at her.

"What kind of feeling, Mom?" asked Zannah.

"I don't know. It's like I remember something, but not quite. Something that has to do with you two. It's just hovering there out of reach. I can't quite get it, but it's there."

Zannah flashed a knowing look at Simon.

"Hey, I saw that! That look you shot at Simon," Deb said to Zannah. "What was that about? C'mon, give!"

Zannah looked uncertainly at her father, who shrugged. "It's nothing really," she said. "When we came to dinner last week, Simon and I had some news for you but then we heard about Gramps so we just decided to put it off for a while."

"Good news or bad news?"

"A bit of both, I guess. I'm just not sure now is the time to tell you, what with everything going on, you know, your accident and such. We don't want to upset you."

"This sounds ominous." Deb picked up her fork and started toying with her food, certain she didn't want to hear any bad news but knowing that she must. It wouldn't do any good to put it off. It would just be something else hanging over her, something else fighting for the light.

She put down her fork, grabbed the napkin on her lap and looked right into her daughter's eyes and sighed, "Ok, talk."

Zannah took a sip of wine, her hand shaking. Simon wrapped his arm around her shoulder reassuringly. Joe and Miles froze in their seats, both wanting this moment, this meal, this day, to be over. They knew better than to get in the middle of a Deb/Zannah discussion.

"You know that Simon has been looking for a new job? Well, he got one." Then, as the words were sinking in, added in a rush, "Mom, it's a really good job, he'll be a systems software engineer handling platform architecture. It's exactly what he wants to do, what he's been trained for. It's perfect for him. Really."

"Wow, that's great! Congratulations, Simon!" Joe raised his glass in Simon's direction. "You've been hoping something better would come along and it has. Way to stick with it."

Miles piped up, "Nice!" and reached over to high five him.

"What good news! I'm so happy for you, Simon," Deb said attempting to sound happy yet dreading what was coming next, what the 'bit of both' meant. She smiled at them, and, trying not to sound too worried, "So what's the bad news?"

"Oh, well it's not really bad news, it's just that the job is in Santa Clara."

"As in California?"

"Yeah." While Zannah barreled on explaining why this was not really bad news, Deb only heard muffled noises. Her mind was racing, carrying on its own conversation. *Was Zannah going with him? Of course she was. But what about her job, her career? She'll just get a job out there. What would Deb do with Zannah so far away. Oh you'll be fine, there's Facetime and Skype, you won't even know she's gone.*

Deb did her best to comment in all the right places, be the supportive parent she knew she should be but felt herself getting angrier and angrier. Joe and Miles were peppering them with questions, making jokes about West Coast lala land and vegans and pot head surfers.

Abruptly, Deb stood up. "I have to go to the bathroom" and bolted out of the room. Her stomach was turning, her head spinning. She felt herself running up the stairs to her bathroom. Once there, she slammed the door shut and retched, just making it to the toilet. She knelt there with her head on her arms, panting. She seized a towel and wiped her mouth. She was sweating and felt faint. She laid on the floor, hoping the cold tiles would bring her the solace she craved.

She automatically entered her survival mode, closing her eyes, concentrating on her breathing, blocking out all the anxiety bearing down on her. *Calm down*, she told herself. *Just breath. In, out, in, out.* She could hear them talking downstairs, their words muffled by the distance. *Just a few more minutes. I'll go back down in just a few minutes. But right now, I need to be here.*

She stayed there on the floor, breathing. She focused on her surroundings, retreating to that familiar, safe place. The floor that hadn't been washed since who knows when, the tub that needed regrouting, the fly that had somehow gotten stuck in the ceiling light. *I've really got to spring clean this room,* she thought. It's disgusting. *Look, there're even cobwebs above the shower stall. And when was the last time I washed the baseboards?*

She heard a soft tapping at the door. "Mom, Mom? You okay in there?" It was Miles.

Of course it was Miles. Miles who brought home abandoned kittens. Who was the first to befriend the lonely boy standing by the wall at recess. Who fished that fiver out of his pocket so the homeless guy could have some food.

"Oh, yes, Miles. I'm fine." She got to her feet and sheepishly opened the door. "I'm sorry, I don't know what got into me. All of a sudden I felt sick, so I came up here. But I'm feeling better now. Silly, really." She paused. "How about Simon's new job? Pretty great, huh?"

"Yeah, good for him." he said. "But what about you? Are you going to be alright?"

"Of course," she said with a weak smile. She couldn't tell if he was asking about her health or her feelings about Simon and Zannah moving. "It is what it is."

Miles hated it when she said that, it was her 'go-to' phrase. What did it actually mean? Was it merely an acknowledgment that the present and future were in the hands of fate? Or a futile, grudging acceptance that she had no power to change anything. He felt it was the latter. She was one of those people who just let the world move her, wouldn't fight for what she wanted. She'd stand back and let everyone do as they wished, never voicing any dissent. It was so irritating, yet there were times when he was grateful she let him feel his own way.

He watched her splash water on her face and brush her teeth. She turned toward him, "Guess we should go back down. Wouldn't want them to think they upset me."

That night in bed, Deb had trouble sleeping. Her cut was itching and throbbing a bit, not enough to warrant a pain pill but making itself known. She kept thinking about Zannah and what this move would mean for her. Sad, really. Even in this day and age the women were still following their men. Putting off their aspirations for another day some time in the future that never seemed to come. Sure, she might find a job out there but then what about grad school? Was she going to put that off? She was about halfway to her PhD in Art Therapy and it hadn't been an easy road trying to sandwich her education with her current job responsibilities and a budding relationship.

Her mind drifted back to the decisions Deb herself had made in her twenties. Decisions that, unbeknownst to her at the time, would affect the rest of her life. The decision to leave school. That wasn't a decision, it was a necessity, the shadows chased her away. At the time, she didn't care about school, figured if it was important, she'd do it later. But later never came. She had gotten a job that paid well enough to get her out of the house and into her own apartment, but not well enough to finance that final year and a half of college. Then she met Joe and she was so happy that school was the farthest thing on her mind. They worked, traveled and had fun. She was recruited for what would have been her dream job but they decided to start a family and that it was best for her to be a stay-at-home mom. After all, she had told herself then, I'll get another chance when they're older. But the other chance didn't come. By then, the recession had hit and all the good jobs required a degree. Yup, that degree that she didn't think mattered. She considered going back to school, but with the kids getting older any extra money was earmarked for their college fund. So she found work where she was paid pittance but required to do the work and take on projects far above her pay grade. Then they fired her. They called it a layoff, a restructuring. But everyone knew it was because she had the gall to ask for more money. It didn't help either that the boss's son's girlfriend didn't like her. Not that she minded that much. She hated the job and had lost all respect for most of the people she worked with.

And when it was all said and done, she had a good life. Perhaps an unfulfilled life, a something missing existence, but a decent life. She was grateful for those wonderful years when the kids were growing up and thrilled with the adults they had become. Still, she wondered what if she had made different decisions? Would it have been so bad? It brought to mind the movie Sliding Doors, where a woman's love life and career hinge on whether or not she makes a train.

And now Zannah was faced with what could be the most important decision of her life. It appeared to Deb that she had already made it. Had already decided to go with Simon, to postpone her degree. Deb could see her daughter falling into the same trap that Deb herself had stumbled into.

Not for the first time, Deb thought about how nice it must be to be a man. Men appeared to pretty much do what they wanted. Of course they would disagree. They'd say they were saddled with the onus of earning a living, making sure their dependents were taken care of. Blah, blah, blah. Yes, Joe was a good man. But he was still a man. He'd help out around the house, but only when she asked. There was this unwritten rule that housekeeping, social ties, family emotional stability were her purview and he was doing her a favor by emptying the dishwasher or addressing the Christmas cards.

Bitch, bitch, bitch. Stop it, Deb, she told herself. *It's your own fault. You need to own your mistakes. It's your problem that you just let this stuff happen. Can't put it on anyone else. What's that you always told the kids? If you don't ask, you won't get. Or was it you cannot win if you do not play? Either one works. And you'll never get to sleep if you don't stop thinking about this stuff.* She knew from her many previous insomnia-filled nights that the only way to halt her brain was to sing songs in her head, try to remember lyrics of old 60's Motown tunes.

She started with My Girl, moved on to Ain't Too Proud to Beg and by the time she was halfway through What's Going On, she was fast asleep.

Chapter Six

Deb had convinced Joe that she was well enough for him to go back to work. He had used up enough of his personal days, she said, and he would have to take off tomorrow for the neurologist's appointment.

The lack of memory from last week still unsettled her but she tended to agree with Joe that it didn't matter if she ever remembered. She knew from past experience that some things were best left untouched.

"I'll be fine," she reassured him. "I'm just going to putz around the house, maybe do some wash and pay some bills. Watch a lot of TV."

"If you're sure you'll be all right," he said hesitantly. "I do have a lot to catch up on. I won't be late. Promise." And he went, a little too eagerly in her mind, to get ready.

She watched him go, not sure if she wanted to be left alone but anxious for life to get back to normal. She made a cup of tea without the sugar, after all it would be spring soon and she wanted to look good in summer clothes. It was too late to hope for a toned bathing suit body, but maybe she could manage a decent visage in shorts.

Her solitaire games were calling to her. She seated herself in the desk chair and opened up Double Klondike, the first in her 20 game rotation. Clicking on the cards was therapeutic, letting her concentrate on the next move and relieving her of extraneous thoughts. After about an hour, she checked her email. According to Google, it had been almost a week since she had visited this site. So much spam! Russian girls who wanted to meet her. Flash in the pan Viagra sales specials. Hard to imagine these messages were effective. *Did people seriously think they could lose 25 pounds in two days? Ugh.* She spent the next ten minutes scanning and deleting unimportant emails. She started to read the messages from the Democratic Committee telling her why she should vote for the Democrats in the upcoming primary, but gave that up pretty quickly. She knew who she'd vote for, no need to waste time reaffirming that decision.

She was glad she had missed the latest ever escalating vitriol of the Republican candidates. Grown men acting like kindergarteners insulting every faction of the American people. It made her sick. It might actually have been funny if so much wasn't at stake. Why won't they talk about the issues, the real problems facing the globe today? Seriously, a wall choking off Mexico? It worked so well in Berlin...aughh. And that guy running for Congress who hyped his desire to keep children safe with the sponsorship of a bill requiring background checks for school personnel, which they all do now anyway, and yet voting for open carrying of guns on campuses. It made her so mad she could spit.

Forget it, Deb, she told herself. *Think of something else. Food. Yes, I'm hungry.*

She went into the kitchen closely tailed by the dog and started rooting around, first the refrigerator then the pantry. Too early for lunch. Nothing to snack on. She considered making popcorn but she really only wanted that when she was watching a movie. Maybe later this afternoon. She gave up and walked over to the window. The wind was howling, branches were bending from the force and she spotted someone's plastic flower pot rolling across the grass. Wonder whose that is. She toyed with the idea of going out and getting it but instead watched it head toward the neighbor's yard and get caught in the patio bushes.

Just then the phone rang. She waited for the caller I.D. to tell her who it was. Zannah cell.

"Hi hon."

"Hey Mom, how are you feeling?"

"I'm ok. Didn't sleep too well, but then I never do. What are you up to?"

"Not much. I have a paper due so I'm working on that."

"That's good." *Hmm, she hasn't withdrawn from school yet.*

"Yeah it's a bear, but I'll get through it. Dad there?"

"No. I sent him off to work."

"Oh." She sounded unsure about this.

"No, it's fine, really. He would have just driven me crazy staying home another day. I feel all right, so there's no need for him to be here. If I have any problems, he'll come home."

"I guess so." Pause. "Listen, last night after we got back to the city, we went to Sheila's for a drink. Guess who I saw there?"

"No idea."

"Tyler, Tyler McCann. You remember him? He was in my class."

"Oh yes! He was so sweet in elementary school. I lost track of him in the later years. I did hear recently that he was sort of walking on the wild side, getting in trouble and whatnot. How is he?"

"Ok, I guess. It was strange seeing him. I hadn't seen him since high school and even then we hung out with different people. But the weird thing was, he asked me how you were. Isn't that odd?"

"Really? He asked about me? That's so nice. Odd, but nice."

"Yeah. It was like 'how is your mother?' not 'how's your mom doing?' And he seemed really interested. You know, it was like he knew about you getting hurt but I don't know how he would've. I mean, it wasn't in the paper or anything, was it?"

"Lord, I don't know. Maybe your dad does. Could be he knows somebody at the hospital, maybe somebody else you went to school with worked there and told him. Still, it was sweet of him to ask."

"Yeah. But we thought it was weird. He was all nervous and twitchy. Simon and Miles thought he was on something."

"Maybe he was. You never know."

"I just thought it was strange. It seemed like he knew more about you and the accident than we did. Not that he said anything about it, it was just the feeling I got. So strange."

"Zannah, everything seems strange to me right now. It's easy to misread people and their words. I'm sure he was probably nervous about seeing you after all this time," Deb said, although she wasn't convinced.

"Yeah, you're probably right." Zannah didn't sound convinced either. "Well, I've got to go. Just thought I'd check in. I'll come out later this week. Call me if you need anything."

"I will. Thanks." And they hung up.

Deb stood in the kitchen looking at the blank phone screen. Tyler McCann. She searched her memory bank and came up with an adorable little five year old with close cropped hair and silvery blue eyes. Tyler was a shy boy. She remembered when she was helping sort the children on the first day of school. Tyler getting off the bus, clutching his lunch box, weighed down by his backpack with his teacher's name plastered on the back, crisp new jeans, an ironed shirt and those sneakers that lit up when you walked. He looked so tentative, a little frightened yet resigned to face the strangeness that awaited him. He had attempted a small smile when she greeted him. She laughed when she remembered how he thanked her when she directed him to his teacher's line.

Fast forward to junior high school. She would see him in Homework Help, the class designated for kids who were struggling with their assignments. He had grown, of course. His hair was no longer short, a graphic tee had replaced the ironed shirt, and branded sneaks had taken the place of the light-up ones. She had felt saddened that those silvery eyes were not quite so shiny any more. But he had grinned when he saw her. "Mrs. C," he called. "How's it going?" He let her help him with the math assignment that he couldn't quite grasp. Again, he thanked her for helping him. "I don't feel so stupid now," he had remarked when they were finished. When class was over, the teacher told Deb that Tyler's father had passed away that year. He was having a hard time dealing with it, but seemed to be getting better.

The last time she had seen him was at graduation. She almost didn't recognize him. A tear tattoo circled his wrist, a huge chain clung to his neck, jeans were hanging at crack level held up by the patterned boxer shorts underneath, feet now clad in Timberlands. His hair, now stringy, brushed his shoulders marring the beauty of his still shockingly blue eyes.

That tear tattoo. Something about the tear tattoo made her feel disjointed. *It's probably just that I hate tattoos,* she told herself.

She tried to remember. Did she talk to him that day? Yes, yes she did. He had nodded at her, "Whasup, Mrs. C?" As she congratulated him and asked after his mother, he looked at the ground and shuffled his feet, embarrassed. "I dunno," he said, "I haven't seen her for a few months." Just then, Zannah and some friends came running up to them laughing. Zannah said hi to him, he said hey and mumbled something about having to go, gave Deb a sad smile and shuffled off.

She remembered then that the encounter haunted her over the next few months and that she had considered reaching out to him but had no clue how to find him and wasn't sure he'd welcome the intrusion. What would she have said? Are you okay? And he would say of course thanks for asking but I'm fine. Which would be a lie because how could any child be okay after losing his father and becoming abandoned by his mother? She'd mulled over different scenarios, one actually had her asking him to come live with them. *Imagine what Joe would have said!* It turned out she never saw him again and it gradually slipped from her mind as so many things do.

Deb shook her head at the sadness of it all. Thinking about Tyler made her uncannily uncomfortable and she didn't want to go over old ground again. She forced herself to focus on the wash, then laid on the sofa scanning the channels for something good to watch on TV.

Tuesday morning Joe woke to the alarm clock blaring. He turned it off, rolled over and was startled to find Deb, covers up to her chin, head nestled in her pillow staring at him.

"What are you doing still in bed?" he asked.

"I've decided I'm not going today," she replied.

"Huh?" Still groggy from sleep he had no idea what she was talking about.

"The doctor. You know, the neurologist. I don't want to go."

"Deb, it's not up for discussion and I'm not awake enough to argue with you. Just get up and get ready," he said rather huffily.

"No," she said and flopped over wrapping the quilt tighter around her.

"Damn it, Deb," Joe flung his blankets back and got out of bed. He went into the bathroom and slammed the door. *What the hell,* he thought. *I do not need this right now.*

A few minutes later he emerged, put on his bathrobe and walked out of the bedroom, kicking away the abandoned dog toy in his path. In the kitchen he made the coffee and put the kettle on to boil. The smell of the freshly brewing coffee helped calm him. He was grateful, not for the first time, that they had bought the machine that lets you pull out the pot before it was finished. While he was feeding the dog and making her tea he listened for sounds of movement from upstairs. But none came.

This wasn't like her. She was not one to miss appointments. If she said she would be somewhere, there she was, usually a tad early. *What's gotten into her? When we talked about it last night she voiced no objections. What had happened between then and now?*

He picked up her tea mug and his coffee and went back to the bedroom.

71

"Here, I made your tea." He put it on her bedside table and sat down next to her. "I'm sorry," he said, "but you have to go. Why don't you want to? It's no big deal."

"No big deal for you," she muttered.

"No, it's no big deal for you. What do you think he's going to do? It's not like he's a dentist," Joe took a stab at humor.

"I don't know. I just don't want to go. Ok, so I don't remember some stuff. Maybe I'll never remember. I've come to terms with that. Even you said that that would be okay. I don't want him poking and prodding me with all kinds of questions." She yanked the covers over her head, hiding like a child fearful of the test awaiting her at school.

Joe reached over and gently pulled the covers back. "Yes, it's true. It doesn't matter if you never get those memories back. But wouldn't it be better if you did? Doesn't it drive you a bit nuts that there are these little bits of your life that are empty?"

"Not really," she lied.

"C'mon now. I know you. After all these years, you can't fool me. So just get up and let's get going. It'll all be over in a few hours and you can crawl back into bed when we get home."

"All right, I'll get up. But I'm not putting makeup on," she said a bit defiantly.

He kissed her and stood. She looked so sad that he found himself wondering again if somewhere, deep inside, she unconsciously knew everything that had happened, but was unwilling to let it come back. The mind is a strange thing. Maybe the doctor will know. I should ask him.

Better write that down.

They went about the house getting ready, Deb delaying the inevitable by ironing a blouse -- *Seriously?* thought Joe but said nothing -- and hand washing the breakfast dishes. By 9:30, Joe was standing by the door, keys and wallet in hand, tapping his foot and calling to Deb.

"You almost ready? It's time we left."

"I'll be right there. Just putting on my mascara."

Although she had said no makeup, Joe knew she wouldn't leave the house without at least mascara. And he fully expected the whole 'daytime' works.

He was right. Deb was almost finished, carefully stroking the mascara onto her lashes, making sure she got every last one. She was mindful of how the aging process affected her skin and although she knew she wasn't pretty, she felt at least presentable with foundation, blush and mascara. After all, you never knew who you might run into.

Makeup routine completed, she wiped down the sink and counter, checked her face once more in the mirror, tried on a smile, sighed and went to meet Joe.

The waiting room was a pleasant change from the hospital waiting rooms. Dark green walls, plush chairs, wooden tables loaded with the latest issues of U.S. News & World Report, Times, Newsweek, even the New Yorker. The plants on the windowsill were well tended and the carpet was plush. The receptionist was dressed like she belonged in management for a Fortune 500 company.

Expensive, thought Deb. *Hope our insurance covers this guy.* She took out her phone and scrolled through the latest Instagram pictures but finding only photos of people's grandchildren and cats, she closed the app. She didn't know what she expected. Grandchildren and cats were pretty much all anyone posted. Oh, and food. For some reason, a lot of people (and she was guilty of the same) posted pictures of food. Food from the latest hot restaurant, food from newly remodeled kitchens, food grilled to perfection on the Weber grill or smoked in the Green Egg. No wonder she was always hungry, looking at pictures of food all the time. Like right now. *Right now I could go for a toasted everything bagel slathered with cream cheese. Think the doctor has any food in his office? Probably not.*

The receptionist called out her name and, holding the door open, said "Make yourselves comfortable. The doctor will be in in a minute."

So they did. At least they went in. Making themselves comfortable was another story, but they did their best. They took off their coats. Joe sat in the visitor's chair while Deb hopped onto an examination table. They didn't try to make small talk because neither one of them could think of anything to say.

Dr. Chan came into the room through a door on the other side of the room and stood opposite Deb.

He smiled at her. "Good morning, Mrs. Cromwell, how are you today?"

"I'm fine," she answered thinking she's been saying that a lot lately.

"Good, good. Today I'm just going to check a few things out, give you a basic neurological exam. I just want to make sure that there is nothing else going on. Okay?"

74

"Whatever you say."

"Mrs. Cromwell, may I call you Deborah?" he asked politely.

"Deb, please. Deb is fine."

"Ok. I'm going to list five things and I want you to try to remember them."

"Ok."

"Good. Pencil. Truck. Gardenia. Giraffe. Thumb drive."

"Pencil, truck, gardenia, giraffe, thumb drive. Got it."

"Good. Now, here's a paper with some simple math problems. I'd like you to try and solve them without a calculator." He handed her the paper and a pencil.

"Ah, pencil," Deb said as she took them, "That's one of the words I'm supposed to remember. Are you going to give me a truck too?" she giggled nervously.

"Ha-ha, funny."

She looked at the paper. Question 1. 30 x 5 = ?. 150 she wrote. Question 2. Reduce 24/32. 3/4 easy. The remaining ones were a little more difficult, but she quickly figured them out and handed the paper back to Dr. Chan.

He scanned her answers and handed her another paper. "See the cube on the paper? I'd like you to copy that image." he said.

She didn't hesitate and started carefully copying the cube, making sure she had the size and angles as much the same as she could without a ruler.

He had her do some more paper and pencil tasks, then asked her about her days since she came home from the hospital, watching her carefully and continually making notes.

During the next hour, he ran a battery of tests. He had her do all kinds of things with her eyes and face. Follow my finger, close one eye, can you see this, can you feel this, touching various places on her face, head and neck with a metal tool. He called this the cranial nerve exam and moved on to check her motor system, deep tendon reflexes, coordination, gait and sensory system. For the most part, Joe was right, it was painless. Except for the part in the sensory system test where he kept pricking her with a pin-like instrument. That was no fun.

After he had her walk around the room a few times, he asked if she could remember the five objects from earlier.

She proudly said, "Pencil, truck, gardenia, giraffe, thumb drive."

"Excellent," he smiled at her.

Joe was fascinated watching the doctor and Deb move through the examination. He wished he could have videotaped it just to be able to see it all again. He knew from the research he and Miles had done what most of the tests were for, but he had no idea if she was passing. And it was important to him that she passed them all.

The doctor told her to relax a while and then meet him in his office, indicating the room through the door he had entered earlier.

A few minutes later they were seated in front of a large mahogany desk across from Dr. Chan. They waited nervously while he looked over his notes.

The doctor put down his tablet and cleared his throat. "Well Deb, you seem to be fine. All the testing revealed no severe neurological damage. I see no signs of early onset Alzheimer's or dementia, no impairment of your thinking processes or your motor skills. You suffered a diffuse axonal injury that sheared some large nerve fibers and stretched some blood vessels. Most of this damage was done in the frontal and temporal lobes. It appears that this damage was minimal and resulted only in memory impairment. You might find yourself being a bit disorganized or having trouble concentrating, but on the whole, you are fine, except for the memory loss."

"Except for the memory loss," Deb echoed.

"So what do we do about that?" asked Joe.

"Nothing. Really, there is nothing we can do. Either it will come back spontaneously or it won't. I think it will eventually return. The only thing I can tell you is to try not to fixate on it."

Joe pulled out his notes from his pocket and said, "Doctor, I was wondering if maybe these memories were all stored somewhere in her subconscious and she's just too scared to bring them back. Is it possible that a psychiatrist or psychologist could help?"

Deb shot a horrified look at Joe.

"Well," replied the doctor, "I'm not sure a psychiatrist or psychologist could help."

Deb let out a huge sigh of relief.

"However," he continued, "there has been some exciting research relating to neurons. The thinking is, based on experiments suggesting that unlike common theory dictates, memory is not stored in synapses. They claim that if neurons are intact that the brain can synthesize the proteins needed to form new synaptic links. It's early research and I'm not sure it applies here. It seems they're focusing on Alzheimer's patients." He continued after a pause, "If you'd like to see a psychiatrist or psychologist, I can certainly recommend one to you."

"That won't be necessary," Deb said loudly. "I'll just take what comes."

"But Deb," interrupted Joe, "I think we ought to consider it."

"No," Deb shot back testily and added crisply, "Thank you Doctor. If there's nothing else, we'll go now."

"All right. Best of luck to you and please, if you have any questions or start experiencing any new symptoms, please come back and see me."

"Yes of course. Thank you. Good bye." And Deb stood up, gathered her purse and coat and walked out with Joe hurrying to catch up.

The ride home was quiet and a bit tense. Joe drove purposefully, listening to the local sports talk radio program. Deb looked out the window, staring at everything and nothing at all. She knew she had been rude at the end of the appointment but really, what was that shrink stuff all about? *What the hell was Joe thinking? That she was crazy? That she deliberately chose to forget what happened? What rubbish.* She was in no mood to deal with this. People telling her what she ought to do. *Why couldn't everyone just leave me alone?*

She sighed and said, "I don't appreciate you bringing up that whole psychiatrist thing. I'm not crazy."

"Nobody said anything about you being crazy."

"You might as well have."

Joe didn't respond. He couldn't understand why she was adamant and angry about this. Deb was usually pretty complacent, but she really had her back up about this. *I'm just going to let it drop for now. Maybe we can talk about it later when she's calmer.*

He pulled into the driveway and before he put the car in park, she had unbuckled her seat belt, grabbed her purse and opened the door. She walked into the house, absentmindedly petted the dog's head, murmured something, threw her coat onto a kitchen chair, went upstairs and threw herself on the bed.

Joe came in and said, "If it's alright with you, I'm going to work."

"Fine."

"You need anything before I go?"

"Yes. I need you to leave me alone."

"Fine," He huffed and left.

She laid on the bed looking at the ceiling. She could hear Joe's car starting and the garage door closing. Good, he's gone. She closed her eyes and saw only black. None of those little bright swirly things that so often danced around her shuttered lids. Just a dark void. She was tired, so very tired. Tired of trying to remember, of Joe's coaxing, of the children's concern, of convincing everyone she was fine. Tired of paying bills, cleaning, cooking, shopping, showering. Tired of never being good enough. Tired of being 'fine'. Tired of moving through life with no direction, no passion. Tired.

She thought about that Anne Tyler book, Ladder of Years, and how the main character just walked away from her family at the beach. Walked along the ocean, just kept walking until it was dark and she was in a different town. Walked to a new life. At least that's how she remembered it. She remembered being angry at the ending, didn't like how the author closed it, but that's the way things always turned out, wasn't it? There was always an ending, but it was rarely the ending she wanted.

She wished she could go back to the person she was at 21. Before the world crashed in on her and changed her completely. But she couldn't. There was no magic elixir to take that away. A psychiatrist didn't help then and wouldn't help now.

She thought about killing herself. She often thought about it. How good it would be to be finished. Over. Done. Through the years, she had fantasized about how she would do it. OD on pills? No, she had heard that you choke on your own vomit. Hanging? No, she was never able to tie a good knot. Put her head in the oven? No, the gas would kill the dog too. Slit her wrists? No, she hated pain. Sit in the garaged car with the engine running? That was the most attractive method to her. There were times when she almost did it, considered what to say in the note. But something always held her back. She'd think about Joe and the children and knew they'd feel guilty, that it was their fault when it wasn't. It had nothing to do with them. Nothing, yet everything. Wouldn't it be better for them not to have to deal with her? They could get on with their lives and not have her to worry about. She had done everything she could for them. Her job was finished. How could she ever make them understand how tired she was?

She wondered if everyone had these thoughts. *They must,* she reassured herself. *How can people go through these pointless days, weeks, months, years and not at least consider how nice it would be to be finished.*

"Enough," she said out loud. "You haven't got the guts, you chicken shit, so just get up and do something."

A tear slid down her face as she struggled from the bed and walked downstairs.

Chapter Seven

The days went by, sliding into weeks with no beginning and no end. Spring had finally taken hold. Flowers were popping up, trees were almost in full leaf, birds were chirping happily while they busily built their nests. The April rains had swollen the little creeks that ran through the town and their pleasant gurgling could be heard beneath the robin's chatter.

At the Cromwell's, spring cleaning was in full effect. Deb was inside washing windows, removing winter's grime from the sills while Joe was outside struggling with the debris that had gathered in the front flower bed during the long winter, trying to make the patch presentable with brightly colored pansies.

Deb had just sprayed the bedroom windows that faced the street when she saw Joe motioning to her, miming hunger. She opened the window and called down to him, "Ready for a break? I can make lunch."

"Why don't we just get a pizza?" he called back.

"Ok, as soon as I'm finished in the bedroom, I'll go get it." Joe was a pizza fanatic. A true pizza snob who believed you could only get good 'pie' on the East Coast, preferably New York or Philadelphia. Something to do with the water, he claimed. It was preposterous to get it from one of those chain restaurants when the local Italian guys lovingly created the dough and sauce fresh every day, forming a perfect thin crust, crunchy cheese pizza strewn with pepperoni or sausage. He had his favorite places, Nino's for a regular pie and Giovanni's for Sicilian. Always get the large. Commit to your pie.

She called and ordered. "Tenna fifteen minna," she was told. It was always 'tenna fifteen minna.' Except on Friday night when the wait was usually forty five minna. She loved these guys, they worked so hard every day pounding out pizzas and cheesesteaks and hoagies, always laughing, so happy to see their customers, seemingly immune to the heat blasting from the 550° ovens.

She finished up the windows in the bedroom and stood back to admire the clarity of the streak-free panes. Uh oh, there's a smudge in that corner. She considered cleaning it up but didn't want to and decided that the curtain would hide it anyway. She hurried away to avoid seeing any more spots that should be taken care of.

On the way to Nino's, Deb thought about the chores awaiting her that afternoon. She was happy with what she had accomplished that morning and was more than willing to stop and sit outside on the patio in the warming sun for the afternoon, catching up on the novel she had started last week. But no, the vegetable and herb garden had to be turned over, she needed to get those plants in tomorrow. She thought about calling Zannah to help her, but realized with dismay that Zannah was in California. Would she ever get used to Zannah not being around? As each day passed, Deb missed her more and more. Missed seeing that beautiful face, missed hearing about Simon's latest antics.

Stop it Deb, she told herself, *you're just making it worse thinking about it all the time. Maybe Miles will come out and help. He was usually busy but there was always the chance he was just hanging around today. I'll call him after lunch and see.*

She pulled into the parking lot. Nino's was unusually busy for that time of day, she supposed a lot of people had the same idea. She found a spot, efficiently parked the car and made her way to the pizzeria. As she approached the shop, the door swung open and Deb almost ran into someone coming out. She began to say Excuse Me as she looked up, but was taken aback by the blue eyes looking back at her. She felt an odd thud in her stomach. I know those eyes. I'd recognize them anywhere, she thought. A shade duller than before, but still startling in their own right. "Tyler, hi!" she blurted.

Tyler looked like a kid caught with his hand in the cookie jar. "Uh, Mrs. C-C-C-C," he stuttered. "Sorry" and pushed the door back and quickly shuffled away. *Strange*, she thought as she entered the shop and was greeted by the smell of sizzling onions and freshly baked pies. She glanced behind her and caught sight of Tyler as he ran across the parking lot.

"Yo, Deb!" sang out Vinnie from the dough table. "You know that guy?" Vinnie nodded at the door.

"Yeah, he went to school with our kids. Why?"

"I dunno, I hear he's trouble."

"Trouble? What kind of trouble?" The thud in her stomach had begun to flip.

"Ya know, running around with the wrong crowd, maybe drugs," he shrugged.

"That's sad. You hate to hear things like that," she said fighting the uneasiness creeping in.

"Yeah, you just never know. So anyway, whatcha got today? Pie or sandwiches?"

"Pepperoni. I might be early."

"Got it ready right here ready to come out of the oven." He pulled a perfectly browned pizza from the oven, expertly slid it into the box, cut eight slices, closed the 'you've tried the rest, now try the best' emblazoned lid and brought it to the counter.

"How's the family?" he asked as he rang up her order.

"Just fine, thanks. Yours?" handing over the money.

"Good, good."

"Good to hear." She picked up the box and started to leave, but then turned around and said, "Vinnie, does he come here often? Tyler. Does Tyler come in here a lot?"

"Yeah, why?"

"I don't know. Just asking, I guess. Ok, see you later," she waved goodbye and left.

Deb sat in her car, mulling over her strange encounter with Tyler and her conversation with Vinnie. She felt unsettled, her stomach had calmed down but her head was beginning to ache. There was a nagging sensation in the back of her mind vying for space with the ever-present shadow, but she couldn't put words to it. She felt sorry for Tyler and what he had gone through but there was a tinge of anger rising that confused her. She started the car hoping that the radio would help her shake off this feeling.

Driving back to the house, Deb focused her attention on the radio. She clicked through the stations searching for a song she liked, one she could sing along to. 'Ti-i-i-ime is on my side, yes it is' came wafting through the speakers. *Ahh, I love this song,* she thought. *Nothing like the Rolling Stones to put you in a good mood.* She turned the volume up loud and started whining along with Mick.

Joe looked up as she turned into the driveway and waved. The dog ran toward the car, instinctively knowing there was crust in his future. Both followed her into the kitchen like eager children tailing the Pied Piper. *If Joe had a tail, it'd be wagging,* she thought.

As she was getting out the plates, napkins and red pepper flakes, she told Joe about seeing Tyler and Vinnie's comments about him.

"Tyler McCann, do I know him?" he asked.

"Probably not. I only know him from the kids' elementary school. He was in Zannah's class, but he didn't really hang around with her."

"Well, from what you say, that's a good thing."

"I don't know. He was a nice kid. He's been through a lot; what with his father dying, his mother leaving. I heard somewhere that he was living with his grandmother. I always wondered if there wasn't something I could have done for him, you know, to make his life easier."

Joe grabbed a slice and sprinkled the pepper flakes on it. "Oh Deb, you bleeding heart. You'll never change, will you?" he said laughingly as he took his plate and the pizza box out to the patio.

"I hope not." she replied softly trailing after him.

While they ate lunch they discussed what was left to do in the yard and exchanged over-the-fence banter with their neighbors. After giving the dog her last piece of crust, Deb closed her eyes and lifted her face to the sun, reveling in its warmth, and propped her feet on the chair next to her. The dazzling sunlight made those funny little squiggles behind her lids a bright yellow, they were dancing around tiny dots of white. Slowly the squiggles darkened, turning into a blurry image. The blur resembled a black ski mask. The white dots transformed into a sky blue and traveled to the holes of the mask.

Startled, she flashed open her eyes and sat up.

Her abrupt movement gave Joe a start. "Oh," he said, "you all right?"

"Yeah," she said shaking her head to dislodge the vision she had seen. "I'm fine. That sun is really bright." She considered telling Joe what she had seen but quickly decided against it. It was just one of those weird things, most likely brought about by seeing Tyler. And the ski mask, she was sure she had seen them when she was checking out the post-winter sales online. *It's funny, the tricks your mind plays on you*, she thought and pushed the image away.

She stood up. "I'm going to see if Miles can come by and help me with the garden," she announced and left in search of her phone.

Joe watched her leave. Something about her demeanor since she came back from Nino's bothered him. She said all the right things, but her words had an unfamiliar edge to them. During lunch, she seemed distant, not quite concentrating on their conversation. Even Donna next door had remarked on it, but Deb had brushed it off saying she was just tired.

Was that all it was? he wondered. Ever since 'the accident' (that's how everyone but Deb referred to it, placing it in air quotes whenever it came up) she's been off. He'd find her sitting alone, curled into a ball, blanket folded around her like a cocoon, staring into space. Or in the middle of a show, she'd suddenly start talking about something completely unrelated, as if picking up a conversation from the day before. And just now, she had looked like she was dozing, then without any provocation, jumped like someone had shaken her. She appeared to be moving in a small world of her own and became agitated when asked about it.

And forget about discussing her memory. She'd either snap at him or ignore the question altogether.

He had talked with both her doctor and the neurologist about it. They said it was nothing to worry about. It takes time to get over a trauma like that. Dr. Chan would ask about her memory, if anything had come back. At this point, Joe didn't know if she'd tell him if it did.

It had been more than a month since the appointment with Dr. Chan and Joe weighed the idea of asking Deb again if she'd consider seeing a psychiatrist. *I could be lighting a powder keg with that one*, he mused and decided he'd need to think about it more.

As Joe was going over all this in his mind, Deb came out with Miles in tow.

"Hey Dad," Miles said.

"Hey Miles, how'd you get here so fast? Your mom just went in to call you."

Miles laughed. "I was up having lunch with some friends and thought I'd stop by. Didn't think I'd get roped into yard work though."

"She is a force to be reckoned with. Hey, did she tell you about seeing that kid, what's his name, Tyler?"

"No. Wait, she saw Tyler McCann? When?"

"Today when she was picking up the pizza."

"Nino's or Giovanni's?"

"Nino's. There's some left. Want me to heat some up for you?"

"Yeah, I'll take a slice or two. Can't turn down Nino's." He turned to Deb, "What's this about seeing Tyler?"

"Yeah, it was weird. He was coming out while I was going in. He mumbled something to me and rushed away. I didn't get a chance to talk to him but Vinnie said he's been running with a bad crowd." She didn't mention the drugs, it didn't seem right to put that on Tyler when she had no idea if it was true.

"Hmm. I don't know who he's hanging with. Last time I saw him I was with Zannah and Simon, it was a couple of weeks ago at Kellyanne's, that bar you like in the city. He was all fidgety and stuff. I thought maybe he was doing meth or something, Simon too."

"Yes, Zannah mentioned that, that you guys saw him."

"Did she tell you he was asking about you? Zannah thought that was pretty strange, but I don't know, everyone's always asking after you."

"Yeah, she did. I thought that was nice of him."

"Nice maybe, but it did seem odd, just the way he asked. Like he knew about you getting hurt. I mean, he didn't actually say that, but that's kinda how it came across. Zannah thought so too."

"Oh you kids. I'm sure you were just reading into it. After all, it was right after the accident. That was probably on your mind. You wouldn't have given a second thought any other time." She tried to sound convincing, but there was that thud and flip in her stomach again.

"I guess you're right." Miles said doubtfully. "Oh well, let's get started on that garden."

As soon as they finished turning the garden over, Miles rushed back to the city, off to an evening of fun and flirting, Deb assumed. The neighbors proposed an impromptu barbecue to celebrate the warm day. Although exhausted, Deb and Joe happily agreed and ran into the house to get ready.

Deb jumped in the shower, eager to wash off the day's dirt and hopefully any ticks that decided to hitch a ride. She knew Joe was selecting the wines for the evening and looked forward to the first sip of many.

Finally clean, she dried off and went into her closet to pick out her clothes. *Wonder if I can still fit into those jeans,* she thought, but decided it might be too irritating to try. Instead she chose a pair of tights and a long sleeved tunic top reasoning that the evening might get chilly.

She heard Joe come up and while he showered -- I'm not shaving, it's the weekend -- Deb threw together a fig and goat cheese salad. She was glad to have something different to do that night, tired of sitting in front of the TV scanning through the channels in search of an interesting show.

She really enjoyed the neighbors, Donna and Dennis. They were everything you'd want in a neighbor. Helpful but not intrusive, interested but not nosy, funny without being annoying. Like Joe and Deb, they enjoyed informal gatherings, good food, wine and testing new cocktail recipes.

Donna was an emergency room nurse and would regale them with stories about the people who ended up in the ER after some bizarre incident. Dennis, who worked in the city, repeatedly griped about his commute but grudgingly loved the hustle and bustle. They had moved in right after Joe and Deb and their children grew up together playing Capture the Flag and Midnight Murder on hot, lightening bug filled summer nights.

"I was thinking of trying to make those Little Dinghy drinks for cocktails. What do you think? I'm pretty sure we have everything we need," Joe said walking into the kitchen.

"Absolutely! Have we had them before?"

"I think we made them last summer once, at the shore."

"Oh right. Still know how? They were good."

"If I can't, Dennis and I'll figure it out." Deb smiled as she wrapped Saran over the salad bowl, knowing this was one of Joe and Dennis's favorite things to do at parties. They'd spend half the night at the bar concocting new drinks and then wonder the next morning why they were hung over.

"Better get over there. I can smell the grill heating up," Joe said putting various ingredients in the tote bag he kept for just these occasions.

He was right. Dennis was standing by the grill, loading it with shrimp skewers and chicken wings. He waved his tongs at them and opened the back door for Deb. Joe started unpacking his tote bag, answering Dennis' questions about the Little Dinghy.

Donna was applying a rub to the steaks and greeted Deb. "Hi, I'm so glad you got here first. I forgot to tell you I invited Annette and John over too. John called a few minutes ago and asked if we'd have dinner with them. I was kinda stuck, you know. So I asked them here. Hope that's okay." She flashed a rueful smile at Deb.

"Of course it is. Why would you even ask?"

"Well, you know. You haven't been out much since the 'accident' and I wasn't sure if you wanted to see other people yet. I promise to keep the conversation light and not bring it up when they're here."

"Oh, right. I guess I haven't seen them since it happened." Deb paused, then "No problem. It'll be fine." But she was nervous. Annette was the Mrs. Kravitz of the neighborhood, the gossipy one who always somehow knew everybody's business. While it could be fun to hear the latest dirt about the swinging couples around the corner, when you were the target, it was a different story.

"No, really. I'll have to face her some time."

"Face who sometime?" This from Annette who had just come in carrying a large casserole dish. "Oooh, who are we talking about? C'mon, give."

Donna rushed in to save her. "Nobody you know, Annette." She took the dish from Annette and said, "So glad you could make it. What's in here?"

"My famous scalloped potatoes. I had already made them thinking you were coming to our house for dinner, but... " she shot a look at Deb. "Anyway I thought they'd go great with the steaks."

"Umm, perfect."

Annette came up to Deb and gave her a loose hug, "Deborah, I haven't seen you in ages. How are you?" stress on the are.

"Fine, Annette, just fine, thanks. And you? Deb tried not to flinch from Annette's embrace. "It's been a long winter, hasn't it? About time we all came out of hibernation."

"Yes. I'm so sorry I didn't come see you after, you know. But you must tell me all about it."

"Not much to tell," Deb shrugged as she removed glasses from the cabinet. "I'll just take these out to the guys."

She could hear Annette quizzing Donna and Donna's noncommittal replies and was thankful that Donna ran interference so well. She joined the men on the patio and took over the grill duties while they made the drinks. They were acting like the bartenders from the movie Cocktail, flipping bottles and glasses and tossing ice cubes in the air.

She envied their ability to act like teenagers. That easy going machismo that seemed to take over when these two were together. Had they known each other in college, she knew they would have somehow gravitated to each other, the guys that disrupted classes with funny asides, the must-haves at every keg party breaking hearts at every turn.

She gratefully accepted the Little Dinghy Joe handed her.

Annette and Donna emerged from the house, cheese and crackers in hand. Donna grabbed a drink, Annette peppered Dennis about the ingredients. They gathered around the table to munch on the hors d'oeuvres, enjoying the first backyard dinner of the season.

"So, Annette, what's new in the neighborhood?" Donna inquired as she pulled shrimp off the skewer.

"Not much," Annette replied. "Any idea where the Campbells have been? I noticed his car is gone and there hasn't been any activity over there in days. Wonder where they've gotten to? Disney again? Weren't they just there in the fall?"

"No idea," said Donna. "They could just be at his parent's. They go there a lot."

"Mmmm, maybe. It seems they're always traveling. Here one week, gone the next. I heard he just got a promotion at work, some big muckety-muck job. Good thing the way they run through money."

Wow, thought Deb. *I'd forgotten how unrestrained that woman is.*

Annette continued, "And did you hear about the English's? Their daughter got a scholarship to play lacrosse for some school, can't remember which one. Was it Cal State or University of California?"

"Yes, isn't that great?" said Donna. "I'm pretty sure it's Cal State Fresno. I saw her dad posted it on Facebook."

"Well of course it's great. I'm just surprised, that's all. Who thought she was that good? She was always a gawky little girl."

"Children do grow up, Annette. Kids you thought weren't that bright are now getting into some of the best schools."

"Speaking of California," Annette turned her attention to Deb, "Isn't that where Zannah is now? I'll bet you miss her like crazy."

"Yup, Santa Clara. She and Simon moved out there a couple of weeks ago."

"She went with her boyfriend? My, my. I hope he put a ring on her finger before she tore up her roots and followed him."

Deb was not about to admit that she had some misgivings about Zannah's move, so she said, "It's a great opportunity for them. She's young, why not see life on the other side of the country. Anyway, she's able to continue her graduate studies while she's out there. You know, it's wonderful all the online courses."

To deflect any more Zannah probing, she quickly changed the subject to one that she knew would keep Annette chatting for quite a while. "So tell me, what's going on with your brood?"

"Jamie is doing great! Did I tell you she was pregnant? Yup, they've been trying for so long they thought they'd have to go the fertility route but finally things worked out."

Success! Now with Annette in full my-life-is-wonderful mode, Deb was able to zone out. Over the years, she had become expert at listening to Annette with only one ear, nodding and uh-huhing every few minutes, giving the impression she was paying attention.

The evening wore on. The steaks were delicious and even Deb had to admit that the scalloped potatoes Annette contributed were excellent. The weather had turned a bit chilly so after dinner, they moved into the house for dessert.

Deb had just gotten settled in the den when Annette came and sat next to her. "Deb, I swear I saw you with Tyler McCann today at Nino's.

Whatever were you doing with him? He's trouble, that boy."

"I wasn't with Tyler. It's true, I did see him today. He was coming out of Nino's when I was going in. We didn't really talk. And why would you say he's trouble?" There it was again, that thud in her stomach, followed by the flip, flip, flip. As much as she didn't like the tone of this conversation, she needed to hear what Annette knew.

"Everybody knows it. He's doing all kinds of drugs. I wouldn't be surprised one bit if he was running around breaking into people's houses to support his habit."

"Really?" Donna piped in. "Tyler was always such a nice kid. Where did you hear this?"

"Oh I don't know. I think one of my kids told me. Really, I mean, what do you expect. With a mother like that. It's in the genes."

Deb felt herself getting irritated and angry. "That's the stupidest thing I've heard in a long time, Annette," she blurted out.

Annette looked taken aback for a moment, but said, "Think what you want, Deb, but it's true."

Deb, usually one to avoid confrontation, started to retort, but was saved by Joe who said, "Time to go, Deb. The dog needs his walk."

She looked at him, both annoyed and happy and said, "Is it that late already?" She stood up and said to Donna ruefully, "Sorry. Sorry to rush out. I'll come by tomorrow and help you clean up."

To Annette, she just lied and said, "Goodbye, Annette, nice to see you. And congratulations on Jamie."

Chapter Eight

The dog was definitely ready for his walk. He met them at the door, plush toy in his mouth, tail wagging uncontrollably. Deb made a fuss over him as usual, while Joe grabbed the leash. Hearing the clink, clink of the leash, the dog bolted for the back door and waited impatiently to be hooked up.

After they left, Deb got herself a glass of water and went upstairs to get ready for bed. Once settled under the covers, she turned on the TV and searched for something that would help her fall asleep. This was one of her habits that she knew irritated Joe. He liked quiet and complete darkness when he slept, she preferred the comforting drone and glow emanating from the screen. As a compromise, she set the sleep timer for 60 minutes hoping she'd be sound asleep and the TV off by the time Joe came up.

She found a rerun of an old Law and Order episode with Jerry Orbach. A good one, as the comedian Jay Mohr says. She could always find some iteration of Law and Order, whether it was SVU, Criminal Intent or just the plain old original, some station on cable was usually running one of them. Lately though, NCIS was popping up with more frequency. Either way, there was a certain comfort to these shows. Something bad happens, the cops find the bad guys or gals responsible and the justice system does its job. Usually. She hoped that's the way it was in real life but she had her doubts.

The dog, fresh from his walk, nudged the bedroom door open and plodded to her side of the bed. She reached down and scratched his ears until he laid down, then turned her attention back to the TV. She had seen this one before, actually she had seen all of them before but somehow rarely remembered who the culprit was. No matter, she knew it was one where, after a questionable search and much legal haggling, the baddie was sent away to serve time for his misdeed.

She nestled farther under the covers, closed her eyes and concentrated on listening to the show, blocking out any stray thoughts and shadows that entered her brain and prevented sleep.

It must have been successful because when she opened her eyes, the room was dark and quiet except for the soft snoring from both Joe and the dog. She looked at the clock. 3:10. Gotta pee. She pushed back the covers, stepped carefully over the dog and made her way to the bathroom. Mission accomplished, she climbed back into bed and tried to lull herself to sleep with her tried and true method of singing old Motown tunes in her head. Didn't work. No matter which songs she chose, she found her mind wandering back to the past evening's conversations and Tyler McCann.

Why, she wondered, had his name popped up so much over the past few weeks? For years, she hadn't seen or heard anything about him but lately it seemed everyone was talking about him. First Zannah, then Vin, then Miles, and tonight, Annette. What really bothered her was her reaction every time it came up. A disconcerting physical reaction. Even now, her stomach was flipping. When she closed her eyes, she could see him staring at her, the sadness behind the silvery blue. She felt a wave of panic rising from her chest and flowing through her body. A shiver spread through her and she pulled the blankets closer around her body. Her head began to pound. Tears filled her eyes and ran down her face. She heard herself sobbing. Wretched sobs that had no beginning and no end. She curled into a fetal position, fists jammed into her brow, but the sobbing wouldn't stop. She wanted to get up, to leave, to run. But the sobbing paralyzed her. She was trapped. Trapped in the night with the darkness closing in, threatening to suffocate her.

"What the...?" and felt Joe's hand on her shoulder. Her body was shaking, she wailed, "No. No. No. Stop. No." She tried to pull away but the tangled covers held her in.

Joe grabbed her and brought her close to him, holding her tightly. "Wake up!" he almost shouted, then softer, "Deb, wake up. It's just a dream. A nightmare." He caressed her hair, trying to calm her down. Her body was shaking violently, he felt her tears wet his skin. Clutching her with one arm, he reached over and switched on the bedside lamp. Light flooded the room. He tightened his grasp on her, willing the shaking to stop, all the while murmuring, "it's ok, hon, it's ok."

Slowly, ever so slowly, the sobs dwindled, turning into quick short intakes of breath. The shaking subsided. She felt like a rag doll in his arms. She tucked her head against his chest and stuttered, "I, I, I remember."

She lay there like that, staring straight ahead, for what seemed to Joe an eternity. Thoughts and emotions were racing through him, rattling though him like a ping pong ball. He was happy (wasn't he?) that she remembered, he was worried about her reaction, should he get her some of that Xanax the doctor had prescribed?, he was scared about what she had remembered, he was exhausted, he wondered how long they would lay here like this, he was thirsty, he was unsure what to do next. He didn't know where to focus his attention.

Finally, he cleared his throat and gently took her shoulders and sat her up. She was unsteady but managed to remain as he placed her. He pulled some tissues from the box on the table and began to wipe her eyes and nose. He pushed her hair back, took her face in his hands and said, "It'll be ok now. Let's get you a cup of tea."

Like a child, she nodded and moved to the side of the bed. He got up and put on his pajama pants, glancing quickly at the alarm clock. Almost 4:30. What an ungodly hour. He resigned himself to the fact that his night's slumber was finished and retrieved her bathrobe from the closet. He helped her put it on and guided her downstairs, turning on every light as they made their way to the kitchen.

He sat her in the chair facing the stove, then busied himself filling the kettle and making coffee, grateful to have something to do. He heard the paper guy's car pass as the newspaper hit the driveway. *Funny*, he thought, *I didn't know he came this early.* When the kettle whistled, he filled her cup, added some sugar and placed it in front of her. She was sitting in the chair, her hands folded on her lap, heartache etched on her face.

He desperately wanted to know what she remembered. Was it everything? Or just pieces of information? Her father? The accident? Did it come bit by bit or was it a flood of memory like a dam bursting? His curiosity was getting the better of him and he fought it back. He was completely unprepared for this moment and had no idea how to help her. *Should I call someone? Too bad she wouldn't see a shrink,* he thought. *Then I would have someone to call. At 4:30 on a Sunday morning? Damn straight I would.*

He decided a Xanax might help more than the tea, so he went to the medicine cabinet and retrieved the bottle. He handed her a pill with a glass of water saying, "Take this. Maybe it'll help."

She looked at him with teary eyes, "Nothing will help," she said, but took the pill.

"Do you want to talk about it? Tell me what you remembered?" he asked timidly.

She shook her head no and answered quietly. "Not now, not yet."

"Ok. Well, look. Let's just go watch some TV. I'm sure I could find a Law and Order for you."

"No. No Law and Order."

"Ok. Um, how about we check out the Sixers? They played tonight. I DVR'd it." He knew she liked watching basketball, but when it was a team she cared about, she preferred to watch it in reruns, after their fate had already been decided.

She nodded as she watched him take the tea bag out of the mug. "C'mon," he said helping her stand. He took her to the couch and lay the blanket over her legs. "Just lie here and drink your tea." He opened the iPad and searched for the game results.

"Hey, they won!" he announced with inflated enthusiasm. "How about that? It'll be fun to watch."

She managed to conjure a smile and took a sip of tea.

They spent the next couple of hours watching the game and post-game show, zipping through all the commercials except for her favorite Jake from State Farm spot. As dawn began to peak through, they were both sound asleep.

The sharp ring of the phone wakened them. They instinctively looked at the television where the caller number and I.D. were automatically displayed.

Zannah. Joe, rubbing the sleep from his eyes, got up to answer it but was intercepted by Deb's weak voice, "No." Obediently, he went back to his lounge chair and waited for the message Zannah was sure to leave.

"Hi! Where are you guys? Sleeping in? Guess you had a rough night, ha-ha. Just checking in. Thought maybe later we'd do a Skype. About 5:00 your time? Text me. Bye."

Deb sighed. A conversation with Zannah was the last thing she wanted right now. Actually, she didn't want to talk to anyone. She was wrung out, depleted from the harrowing night. She needed time. Time to process. Time to regroup. If only she could find a hole and crawl into it, pull a lid over it and stay there, immersed in solitary confinement until she could figure out what to do.

But there was nowhere to hide. No escaping from the memory. Just like before. No matter how hard you tried to blot it out, relegate it to the recesses of your mind, it never went away. It stayed there, the ever present shadow, lurking like a termite gnawing away at the fiber of your soul.

You should tell. Answer probing questions, make them understand it wasn't your fault, you didn't ask for it, didn't go looking for it. Trouble was, even after you faced it, after you told people the truth, it changed nothing. If anything, it made it worse. You could see the doubt in their faces. Hear the faltering in their voices as they tried to console you, murmuring stock compassionate phrases.

No one would ever look at you the same way again. Sure, they'd say it wasn't your fault. But they wouldn't believe it. It was your fault. You knew it, they knew it. The unspoken questions lingering in the air creating a void, a vacuum so dense you could barely breathe. Why were you there in the first place? Don't you know any better? I thought you were smarter than that.

And she did too. She thought she was smarter than that, but apparently she was wrong. Because once again, she had been in the wrong place at the wrong time, saying the wrong things to the wrong people. Creating a mistake so devastating that it ripped her to her very core, changing the person she had been to one she no longer recognized. A person who lost all trust and faith and unbridled joy, lost the freedom to be herself.

There was no escaping these thoughts that played over and over in her mind, each one taking a bit more out of her, leaving her hopeless, defeated, resigned to the idea that she would never be the same. She knew she'd once again have to create a facade to face the world, to make everyone believe she was fine, that she was the same old Deb, they didn't need to worry about her. But to do that, she needed time. And she feared this was something she didn't have.

Joe sat in his chair pretending to watch the sports recap but keeping an eye on his wife. She looked smaller somehow, curled up under the blanket, staring at her feet. He wondered what she was thinking, what he should do. Should he try to talk to her or leave her alone? So he stayed where he was, hoping for a sign, some sort of signal from her to determine his next move.

He waited. Finally, getting nothing from her, he got up and went to the bathroom. He thought perhaps he should go about the standard Sunday morning routine. Only today, it would be him making the coffee and tea, walking the dog, fetching the paper.

I'll leave her alone for now, he thought. *Let her make the first move.*

He noticed the sky darkening and the wind beginning to howl, rattling tree branches against the house. Raindrops starting falling, at first softly then with increasing speed, beating on the windows. He and the dog ran outside to grab the paper, safely encased in its plastic bag. He stood in the garage, watching the dog wander about the yard sniffing grass, peeing here and there, completely undeterred by the rain. Joe was glad he could put off the walk until the rain let up.

He welcomed this reprieve, standing there, surveying the neighborhood, waving to the cars as they drove past on their way to church or the donut shop. His thoughts wandered to the golf course, and he took pleasure in replaying his last round in his mind. First hole, drive off the tee onto the fairway, dogleg left, ended up in the bunker, pretty easy shot from the bunker onto the green, but sadly, two putted into the hole. Second hole, lousy drive into the rough but thankfully rescued it and shot a great nine iron onto the green with a sweet putt making par.

His replay was interrupted by the dog running up to him shaking his drenched body fiercely, surprising Joe with the flung off raindrops. He grabbed a towel from a shelf and attempted to dry off the dog. He wasn't ready to go back inside yet, so he found a beach chair propped against the wall, opened it, sat down facing the street and unwrapped the paper. He dug out the sports section and read the articles on the Sixers game, then went through the golf update and the baseball news.

Finished with the sports section, Joe reluctantly folded the paper, put the chair away and went into the house. He picked up the tea kettle and was walking to the sink to fill it when he noticed Deb was no longer on the sofa. He strained to hear signs of her in the bathroom, but instead heard her coming down the stairs. He looked over and saw her, dressed in sweats, reaching the bottom of the steps. She bent over, picked up her sneaks she had left there, and put them on. She stood up and walked to the door, grabbing the dog's leash on the way.

"It's raining," Joe said.

"I know." And hooked up the dog and walked out.

Huh. He didn't know what to make of this. Usually in weather like this, she dawdled around until either the rain let up or he gave in and took the dog. *I guess nothing is usual any more,* he thought.

He decided to go ahead and make her tea and his coffee, figuring she'd need something to warm her up when she came in. Feeling hungry, he got the makings of breakfast from the refrigerator. He was glad to have something concrete to keep his mind occupied. He started the bacon and put English muffins in the toaster. A while back, a friend had told him how to do fried eggs in the microwave, but he couldn't recall exactly how to do it, so he readied a skillet for the eggs. When the bacon was done, he drained it on a paper bag and put it in the warmed oven to keep until Deb got back.

He looked at the clock. She had been gone for twenty minutes and the rain was still coming down hard. She'll be soaked.

She was. She came in, water dripping off her hair, clothes sodden and sticking to her body. Her sneaks sloshed as she plodded past him and slowly sat down at the table.

He took her tea mug over and set it down. "Here, this'll warm you up."

"Look," she said. "I know you want to talk about last night and we will. Just not now, not yet. I'm going to take a shower." Without waiting for a reply, she walked out of the room and up the stairs.

Deb went into the bathroom, took off her clothes and threw them into the bathtub, then started the shower. While she waited for the water to get hot, she studied herself in the mirror. I look like I feel. Like hell. She brushed and flossed her teeth, then stepped into the shower. She stood there letting the water wash over her, occasionally turning the faucet to the left, hotter and hotter, until the bathroom filled with steam and her skin reddened from the heat. She wanted to burn the images from her head and body, but no amount of heat would do the trick. By the time the hot water began to cool, she had made a decision. She turned off the water and stepped out to dry off.

Out of habit, she moisturized her body, sprayed deodorant under her arms and applied makeup to her face. As she finished each task, she put the products into her toiletries bag. Her routine was careful and complete.

She walked into her closet and pulled down her suitcase. She laid the case on the bed and filled it with underwear, socks, pants, t's, shirts and sweaters. She threw in a pair of pajamas and laid her toiletries bag on top. Finished, she zipped it closed and returned to the closet to get dressed.

She selected a pair of corduroys, an oversize fisherman's sweater and waterproof moccasins and put them on. Then she grabbed the suitcase and went downstairs.

Joe was setting the table for breakfast when she came into the kitchen. He started to say something to her but stopped mid thought when he saw the suitcase.

"I made some bacon and ..." pause, "What's going on? Where are you going?"

She looked at him, helplessly yet a bit defiantly. "I need to go away for a while. Please don't try to stop me," she pleaded.

"But, but why?" he asked.

"Because I need to. I need to get away. Away from here. By myself."

He was stunned. Surely she didn't mean it. She had had a breakthrough. He understood that it had been horrible, but it was a breakthrough. The end of a terrible ordeal. No need to go away. In his mind, last night was over. Now she could get on with her life. They could get on with their lives. What the hell was she thinking?

But he only said, "I made breakfast. You can eat something before you go, can't you?"

"No. I have to go. Now. I'll call you. I love you." She kissed him softly and walked out the door.

Chapter Nine

He watched her leave, heard the garage door open, the car start up and pull out into the street. The door closed and he was left alone with the dog. He sat down at the table unsure what to do. He was worried about her, about where she would go, what she would do. Out of the corner of his eye, he saw the message light on the phone blinking and was reminded of Zannah's call. *Shit. What do I tell her? Do I lie and just say she was out with friends and would call her later? No, that wouldn't do.* He had no idea when Deb would come back, much less when she'd want to talk to Zannah.

The more he thought about it, the angrier he got. It wasn't right that she left him with this. *Sure, it had been unsettling remembering whatever it was she remembered. But really, running off like that? Didn't she realize he was there for her? That he'd do anything she wanted? It's selfish, that's what it is. Leaving me to deal with Zannah. And what about Donna? She told Donna she'd be over this morning to help her clean up. What am I supposed to do about that? Shit. Shit. Shit.* He grabbed the paper from the table and flung it across the room, sending sections flying every which way.

The dog, startled from his napping, got up and slinked away to another room, trying to hide from the tension mounting in the kitchen.

Joe looked at him and immediately felt bad. "It's ok, buddy. I'm sorry. She'll be back soon, don't you worry." he said to the dog as he walked over to console him. He sat on the floor next to the dog and scratched his head reassuringly. "We've just got to carry on. We'll be fine."

And they would be. He made an effort to rationalize this morning's events. This was just another blip in their life. *We'll get through this,* he thought, *just like we've gotten through all the other random things that have happened in our lives. Bad things happen, you deal, and move on. They become as insignificant as that tiny spider carefully spinning its web in the corner of the ceiling. So much time and effort spent on that web, only to have it obliterated during one of Deb's cleaning forays.*

He shook his head, as if to clear his mind, gave the dog a final pat and walked back to the kitchen. The eggs were cold, so he threw them out and washed the skillet. He picked up the bacon, placed it on a plate and carried it to the table where he sat down to read the paper. Bacon is always good, he figured, even cold.

Joe spent a good hour with the paper, submerging himself in the articles and commentary on the upcoming presidential race, the Flyers, Sixers, golf and, of course, baseball. He began to realize that Deb had given him something he truly needed. A break from her.

With a shameful feeling of glee, he went to the stereo, picked out a favorite Grateful Dead cd and put it on, turning the volume as high as it would go without blowing out the speakers. He pulled a stool up to the music cabinet and started to go through the music DVD's he had collected over the years, pulling out ones he hadn't watched for a long time. There was the Simon and Garfunkel Central Park, the Eric Clapton Crossroads, a rare Rush one, so many he wanted to see. What a great way to spend a rainy Sunday!

Before he could really enjoy himself, he knew he had to figure out what to say to Donna and Zannah. Zannah he wouldn't have to deal with until 5:00, but Donna he should call now. Get it over with.

He got the phone and dialed their number.

"Yo Joe!" answered Dennis.

Good, thought Joe. A reprieve.

"Hey Dennis. I know Deb told Donna she'd be over this morning to help clean up, but she had to go off somewhere. Not sure where, but she felt bad about not helping." *A little fudging never hurt anyone,* he thought.

"No problem! It's already done. Donna was up early this morning scurrying about. She was finished before I even got up. She mentioned she saw Deb leave. Thought she looked kinda funny. Everything ok?"

I wish I knew, thought Joe, but said "Oh yeah, everything's fine. I'm sure she'll check in with Donna later. Well, gotta go. See ya."

"Good. Hey, you going to the game today?"

"Nah, got some things to do around here. You?"

"Uh uh. Same here. Donna's got her honey-do list out."

"Ok. Well, talk to you later. And thanks for last night. Good time."

"Yeah. Bye."

Joe clicked the phone off and let out a sigh of relief. That was easier than I expected. Zannah won't be so easy. He carefully replaced the phone on the dock and went upstairs to shower.

Deb felt a twinge of regret checking into the Rittenhouse 1715. She and Joe often stayed there when they spent time in the city and it felt weird not having him with her. But this was time for her, time she needed to rethink, regroup, redefine.

She accepted the room card from the desk clerk, musing about the demise of the standard key and wondering how much trouble she'd have making the card work. She'd have to put down her bag, fetch her glasses from her purse just to see which way the arrow pointed. Then sliding in the card and pulling it out quickly enough for it to register but not too quickly that it didn't have time to scan. Ugh.

She made her way to the elevator. It was one of those tiny elevators, reminiscent of the little London wood paneled ones crammed into a section of the one-time house-now-boutique hotel. Just big enough for three people or two with a suitcase. She really liked this hotel. Tucked away on a quiet street just off Rittenhouse Square, this place provided the warmth and seclusion she yearned for.

Surprisingly, the room card gave her no trouble. She went in and sat on the edge of the bed, taking in her surroundings. She marveled how every room in this hotel was different. Some were bright with a modern feel, some harked back to the Colonial period. This one was one of her favorites. A mahogany wall unit took up the entire wall facing the bed and was loaded with books and a few tasteful objet d'art and a fireplace. A beautifully carved armoire served as a closet. Yes, she could relax in here, get herself together.

She went to the window and looked out onto the street. The watchmaker was still in the building opposite, she could see him hunched over his worktable, peering through his loupe and carefully placing something in what looked like an antique clock. A couple of brunch-goers were making their way toward the square, seemingly indifferent to the rain pelting their umbrella. A man was walking his dog, one of those cute little white dogs so common in the city. The man wore a lime green poncho with the hood up and was trying to hurry the dog along. She could almost feel his irritation at the dog's insistence on stopping at every post and doorstep, sniffing, sniffing, sniffing, then moving on to the next, undeterred by the weather.

Deb pulled herself away from the window. She put her clothes in the armoire and checked out the bathroom. Nice. Clean. No sense that someone had been there before. She turned the water on for a bath, unpacked her toiletries bag while she waited for the water to get hot and opened the Pandora app. Tongue Tied was playing. *Appropriate*, she thought.

As she undressed, she carefully folded her clothes and threw her underwear in the dirty clothes bag provided. She artfully avoided looking in the mirror not wishing to see the mess that she knew she was and stepped into the hot bath.

She sank into the steaming water, feeling the heat work its way through her skin, deeper, deeper, until it seemed to reach her bones. She closed her eyes and wished she had the strength to just slide down as the water covered her mouth, nose, her entire face, and just stay there holding her breath until the moment when her body reacted and forced her mouth open for air but instead would fill with the warm, comforting sense of the end.

But she didn't. Didn't have the fortitude needed to stay down. Knew that the inexplicable innate will to live would jolt her up, gasping for the precious life sustaining air, delaying as long as possible the inevitable that would come some day in the future. It was just something else she was no good at.

She felt certain that one of the things holding her back was the uncertainty of what came next. Heaven? Ha ha ha. She laughed thinking about the stories told in churches of the pearly gates and St. Peter waiting with his list. Angels flying around playing sweet, wispy tunes on their golden harps. The relatives and lost friends hovering in the puffy clouds, waiting to embrace the newcomer. As a child, she would lie on her back staring at the clouds, hoping to spot her grandmother waving to her from behind the billowy hazes in the sky. Try as she might, she never saw her, or anyone for that matter. No, heaven was not in the realm of her possibility. And what about Hell? The flames lifting up from the ground, lapping at the feet of sinners wandering around doing terrible, unspeakable things to each other. She had a friend who, convinced she was going to Hell, was hoping for the upper bunk and bartender status. Now, for the Catholics, there was Purgatory. As she understood their definition of Purgatory, it was a place filled with the souls of sinners atoning for their misdeeds before going to heaven. She had heard that, in true Catholic fashion, loved ones could buy you out of Purgatory by frequently praying the Rosary and performing other actions (read making donations). Wow. Interesting that God is so into money.

Then there's reincarnation. The thought of beginning a new life in a new body was alluring. Unless the new body was a snake or a cockroach. She had thought dogs held the souls of good people until she became aware of all the abandoned and abused animals left to their own devices. It was a belief she had always meant to learn more about.

Then there was the belief that there is nothing. When it's over, it's over. That's the one Deb liked best. No moving on, no more goals to achieve, tasks to be done, people to disappoint, people disappointing her. How nice.

She shuddered. The water was getting cold. With a sense of dread, Deb lifted her body out of the water, determined to get her head together.

She put on clean clothes and noticed the rain was still coming down hard. She went down to the hotel cafe and got a large cup of tea, hoping it would fend off the chill she felt seeping back into her bones. She took her time going back to the room, sipping the tea as she went, pausing to look at the new art on the walls.

Finally, back in her room, she settled herself on a chair and opened her laptop. She considered checking her email, but decided against it. She had work to do and she might as well get started.

Okay, she said to herself. *Time to sort out those memories. Face them head on.*

First, her father's death. It was a bit fuzzy, but she remembered Zannah and Simon at the house, the phone call, waiting at the hospital, the doctor telling her that he had died. What did he say exactly? Something about doing everything they could. Really? She wondered if they worked as hard on an old man as they did on a young one. It didn't matter. Dead was dead. He had had a decent life. Actually, recalling her last few visits with him, he seemed ready, almost resigned to the end looming in the near future. He no longer made plans more than a few days in advance. He had made sure she knew where all his financial information was stashed. He even took her around the apartment, showing her the labels stuck on the backs of things indicating where or to whom they were to go. She smiled when she remembered that he bought potatoes one at a time, eschewing the five pound bag, perhaps knowing he wouldn't be able to use them all.

She spent some time thinking about him, their odd relationship, his disappointment that she wasn't a boy, that there was no one to carry on the family name. No one to play catch with or take on camping trips. In his mind, that was guy stuff, not for girls. Girls were supposed to play with dolls, wear dresses and have tea parties. And she obliged. She had spent her childhood living with him, yet always felt separate, distant, like a ghost rambling around the house avoiding the living. Until she married Joe. Then everything seemed to sort itself out. He finally got the son he craved. Someone to hang out with, share a ball game and a beer. He would spend hours with Joe, showing him how to fix things around the house. Every Saturday morning he would show up, tool box in hand, ready to tackle any task on the honey-do list. She became like a daughter-in-law to him. Strange, but at least he was happy to see them when they came to visit. As the years passed, his disappointment seemed to dissipate and he grew to accept her, wiping out all her past mistakes and some days, actually appeared to like her.

She regretted that she hadn't made more of an effort to fill the void. She could have tried to be interested in sports. Could have asked him to take her camping. Joined a softball team. But she didn't. And now it was too late.

Deb wondered how much of a difference it made that she and Joe also had a son. It kind of took the pressure off Zannah and let them develop a relationship completely different than the one Deb had with her father. Zannah and Joe were close, maybe because Joe always made the effort. He'd take her to dinner or out shopping, even to the ballet a few times. Zannah, bless her heart, made an effort too. She took up golf just to please him and would watch football or hockey, cheering on the hapless teams as though they had a chance.

But no matter how you looked at it, it was nothing like the bond between Joe and Miles. Joe seemed to understand Miles far better than Deb was ever able to. There were times when Deb wanted to press Miles about something and Joe would tell her to back off, leave the boy alone. She'd enviously watch their easy camaraderie and wish that she could relate to him like that. But for some reason, she was always afraid she'd say something wrong, probe too much. It wasn't always like that. As a child, Miles and she were very close. He'd tell her everything, no matter how silly. But as he grew older, he grew more distant, keeping his thoughts and feelings to himself. She was no longer privy to the innermost workings of his mind. She told herself that's how it's supposed to be. He's readying himself for adulthood, making way for another woman to be first in his life. And that's a good thing. She would have hated it if he had turned into a momma's boy. But still, it was a bit sad.

Luckily, Zannah hadn't drifted off like Miles. She still talked to her a few times a week. And while Deb didn't fool herself thinking that she knew everything about her, or that Zannah told her everything, she did feel that her daughter saw her as a safe port in the storm. Deb could only hope Miles felt that way too.

Wow, thought Deb shaking her head. *I've really gotten off track here. Concentrate, woman. Where was I? Oh, right, Dad. Yes, he had a heart attack and died.* She remembered the flurry of activity afterwards, making the funeral arrangements, cleaning, cooking, shopping for the wake-type reception at the house. Seeing all those people who never had time for him when he was alive, but somehow found the time for the funeral. She couldn't blame them really. She was the same way. There were so many people who flitted through her life. When she was with them, they were so very important. When she didn't see them for a while, they just sort of slipped out of her mind. Until they died. Then she'd go to their funeral and feel badly about not paying more attention and vow to keep in better touch with the friends and relatives who remained. Then life would get in the way and her good intentions never took hold.

Ok, so the funeral and after party went off well. People came, mourned, ate, told stories, laughed and left. She saw herself getting the house in order and going to bed.

She remembered having trouble sleeping that night, and finally, early in the morning, sleep still elusive, she decided she might as well go to her father's apartment and start cleaning out his closets.

She remembered quietly gathering her clothes and dressing in the bathroom, trying not to wake Joe. She considered leaving a note for him, but figured she'd be back before he was up.

It was still dark when she drove through the quiet morning, wending her way through the empty streets toward her father's place. She turned the radio on and listened to the early morning deejay with his voice hushed as if he didn't want to startle anyone who had just woken up.

She was absentmindedly singing along to some song, can't recall which one, when she noticed headlights approaching quickly in her rearview mirror. *Hmm, so I guess I'm not the only one out this early in the morning.* She slowed down as she approached the stop sign, expecting to cruise through when a jolt flew through her. *Damn. The stupid driver wasn't paying attention and rammed right into me. Probably drunk.* She pulled over, slammed the gear shift into park and turned off the ignition. Not a good way to start a morning.

The car behind her stopped, but kept the engine running. She saw a man get out of the passenger side and approach her car. Mumbling angrily to herself, she grabbed her purse and the insurance card, opened the door and got out.

Everything happened in a flash. There was the glint of something big and shiny, a rough hand clutching her arm, wrenching her body away from the car onto the pavement, a black ski mask with shimmering blue eyes staring at her. They were hard, cold, uncaring, then a flash of recognition rapidly replaced by dismay, then cold again. She looked straight into those eyes and said, "Tyler?"

She heard him say Fuck! then felt something hit her so forcefully she fell to the ground. Fade to black.

Chapter Ten

So, there it is. The accident that had everybody all concerned. Thinking about it in the light of day, she felt a little silly and embarrassed. Rationally, she knew that her reaction last night to the memory returning was far too dramatic and emotional than it needed to be. Why?

I guess that's why I'm here. Sitting in this hotel room. Alone. It's time to figure out why I get so absurdly upset every time I think about it.

What was it? That it was Tyler? No, the fact that it was Tyler was upsetting, but it certainly shouldn't have caused all this emotional upheaval. She thought about how her stomach would start flipping, how the nausea would set in and send her head spinning. She felt kind of nauseated now.

No, it wasn't the accident. It wasn't Tyler. Then it hit her like a ton of bricks. Her reaction to the memory was almost exactly like her reaction to the rape. Her helplessness, her loss of control, her inability to protect herself. The stark reminder that she and she alone was responsible for all the pain inflicted on her.

There was no getting away from it. She often put herself in the wrong place at the right time. Or was it the right place at the wrong time? Neither. It was the wrong place at the wrong time with her saying the wrong thing to the wrong people.

She thought she had learned. Spent the last thirty-odd years keeping her mouth shut, never saying what she really thought or felt. Sure, there was a price to pay, but it was small compared to the cost of her shooting her mouth off and getting herself into trouble. So what if she never moved to

France? Or lived in the suburbs? Or gave up that dream job? Or only watched the movies she wanted to see when she was alone? Those were trifles, easy enough to live with.

She thought about the times when Joe would get angry with her. How she would rush to get away, fearful that his anger would turn violent. It never did. He wasn't that type of man. But she couldn't help herself. She had trained herself to flee whenever she felt threatened. Better safe than sorry. Because you never know what someone is going to do. People you thought you knew, people you trusted, would all of a sudden turn on you, do unimaginable things to you, change you forever.

Deb felt her eyes well up and went over to the bed and got in. She laid there remembering the girl, stolen from her years ago, crying until she fell asleep.

It's 5:00 p.m.

Joe had spent much of the day waffling between putting Zannah off until he heard from Deb and just facing up to her, grabbing the bull by the horns, so to speak. He decided to leave it up to fate and texted Zannah, telling her that if she needed to talk to Deb, she was unavailable but he was around. He was a bit surprised that Zannah responded saying she'd Skype at 5 and would love to talk to him. She even added one of those annoying emojis with the smiley face and little hearts to the message.

He sat down at the computer and started up the Skype app. He wasn't fond of this computer face-to-face thing and usually had Deb get it going, but he had no choice today. It took him a while to figure it out, but eventually, there was Zannah's grinning face filling the computer screen.

"Hey Dad! How's it going?"

"Oh, there you are. Took me some time, but there you are. Ha-ha. I can't get used to this Skype thing."

"Ha-ha. I see you've got your baseball hat on. Bad hair day?"

"You could say that. So what's new?"

"Nothing much. Working on school stuff. Missing spring on the East Coast. You don't really get a spring out here."

"Yeah, well I'm sure you're not missing all the yard work I used to make you do," Joe laughed.

"Uh, nooo. Hey, so where's Mom? You were kinda cryptic in your text. What's this, she's unavailable stuff?"

"Oh," Joe shrugged. *Should I tell her? Guess there's no getting around it, Zannah will pick up that something's going on.* He took a deep breath and plunged right in. "Well, there's some news."

"Oh goody," Zannah exclaimed. Then seeing the expression on his face, said, "What's wrong? Is Mom ok? Tell me."

"Yeah, yeah, your Mom's fine. It's just that she woke up in the middle of the night last night and remembered everything she had forgotten. It kinda freaked her out."

"WHAT??? Really? Everything? That must be a relief for her." Zannah paused in her excitement. "But wait, what do you mean, freaked out? Is she ok? Where is she?"

"Yeah, I think so. Like I said, she was a little freaked out. She thought it would be good to be alone for a while. You know, to process everything. So she left. Not sure where but I'm sure she'll call soon and let me know. You know how she is. It's fine. She'll be fine."

"Wait. Wait. Wait. She left? Like did she pack a bag or just go for a drive? I don't understand."

"Calm down. She's fine," Joe kept saying that as much to reassure himself as Zannah. "Yes, she packed a bag, but it was a small one. I mean, she didn't take everything out of her closet. She just needed to get away for a few days. Really, think about it. Put yourself in her shoes. A lot happened in those days she had forgotten."

"Yeah, you're right I guess." Zannah sounded skeptical. "But I don't like it. Why didn't you call me? Does Miles know? What'd he say?"

"No, I haven't talked to Miles yet. And don't you either. Let me tell him." Actually, Joe wished that he wouldn't have to tell Miles, but he knew that it would be an easier conversation than this one. *Please, let it be over,* he pleaded to the air.

"Okay. But call him tonight. This is too much. What exactly did she say?"

"When?"

"What do you mean, when? When she left."

"Oh. She just said she needed to get away by herself. Really, Zannah, she is fine. I mean, she'll be fine. It's just the way she is. You know her, she's not like you. She likes to figure stuff out in her head before she even thinks about talking about it. Talking doesn't help her like it does some people. You wait, she'll be home in a day or two. No need to worry."

"If you say so. I'm just not convinced. I think maybe I should come home, you know, if she's that freaked out. Maybe I could help."

"Well, I don't think it's necessary. " Joe hesitated. "Don't get me wrong, we'd like to see you, but it's a big expense coming home. Why don't you wait until she gets back and you have a chance to talk to her?" Joe was getting nervous. He had no idea how Deb would react if she came home and Zannah was here. On one hand, she hated anyone making a fuss over her, but on the other hand, he knew how much Deb loved seeing Zannah. Maybe it would help. Maybe it wouldn't. He could imagine two scenarios. Deb walking in, seeing Zannah, breaking into a beaming smile and rushing to hug her daughter, giving a knowing, thankful glance to Joe. Or... Deb walking in, seeing Zannah, casting a dark look at Joe, turning around and walking out.

You just never knew.

Joe turned his attention back to the computer screen. He saw the back of Zannah's head. Apparently she was talking to Simon, filling him in on what she had just learned. Their words were muffled, but he could tell by Zannah's tone that she was explaining in a pleading sort of way to Simon why she needed to catch the next plane.

"Ahem," Joe interrupted. "Yo, Zannah. I'm still here."

"Sorry, Dad," Zannah turned back to face him. "Simon just came in. I was telling him what's going on."

"Yeah, I kinda got that. Hi Simon." He gave a slight wave as Simon's face popped into view. "How's it going?"

"Better here than there, I think," Simon replied with a little laugh.

"Listen, Simon, I was just telling Zannah that there's no reason for her to hurry home. Really. You two have a lot going on out there. It's silly to rush back."

"You're probably right, Joe. But you know Zannah." He patted her affectionately on the shoulder. "I'm surprised she's not packing a suitcase while she's talking to you."

"Hey," Zannah chimed in. "Enough of that! I don't think there's anything wrong with me wanting to come home."

"Of course there's nothing wrong with it, honey. It's completely understandable. But..."

Simon, sensing a standoff between father and daughter, quickly interceded. "Listen, how about a compromise? What if Zannah books a flight for, I don't know, like Friday or Saturday. Deb'll probably be back before then and that'll give you time to see if she'd want to see her. If she does, Zannah will fly out. If not, we can change the flight to another time."

Joe let out a sigh of relief. Thank heaven for level headed Simon. "That sounds perfect Zannah, how about that?"

"Yeah, I guess so." Zannah sounded a little deflated, but nodded her head in agreement. "But you call me as soon as she gets back."

"I will, I promise. And thank you, Simon."

"Sure, Joe. Keep us posted." He tapped Zannah on the shoulder and said, "Don't forget, hon, we've got dinner reservations."

"Oh, damn, yeah. I completely forgot." She looked at Joe, trying to keep the concern out of her face. "You okay, Dad? I know this must be tough on you."

"Me? Yeah, I'm fine. Uh oh, there's the doorbell. I gotta go," he lied, just wanting to end the call. "Now don't you worry about us. I'll talk to you soon. Love you." Before she could answer, he hit the disconnect button.

Chapter Eleven

Deb woke to the sound of birds chirping outside the window. She sensed the sunlight pouring into the room as it warmed the skin of her eyelids. It took a few seconds to remember where she was and why she was here. She pulled the covers closer around her body and over her head in a vain attempt to prevent the day from starting. It was useless. Slowly, she poked her head out and opened her eyes. She rolled over and looked at the clock on the bedside table. 7:33. Huh, she thought, p.m. or a.m.? Could I really have slept all night? Her bladder told her that yes, she had slept all night, but she picked up her phone and clicked it on to make certain. The screen verified it. Monday. Wow. She reached her arms over her head and stretched, yawning, then lay there as if waiting. For what, she didn't know.

Eventually, feeling she couldn't put it off any longer, she threw the covers off and hurried to the bathroom. Sitting on the toilet, she went over yesterday in her mind. At first it was all a blur, but then clarity came in fits and starts. She felt the familiar resignation setting in. It was a familiarity that was sort of comforting in the way that she knew how to handle herself. That was okay, she guessed. She could deal with that. It wasn't necessarily pleasant, but it was a known. Now all she had to do was figure out what to do next.

Tea.

Eat.

Call Joe.

In that order? No. Yes, tea first. Second? Hmm, I'm definitely hungry. Haven't eaten since dinner at Donna's. But no, I'd better call Joe first. He's got to be going crazy with worry. I'm such an thoughtless fool, running off like that.

Ok. So, tea, Joe, eat.

She called down to room service and was told they'd be up in about ten minutes. Enough time for a shower. The water heated quickly and she got in, shampooed her hair and scrubbed down. Turning the water off, she heard the door open and a voice call "room service."

"Thanks. Just put it on the desk. I'll be out in a minute," she answered wrapping the hotel-provided bathrobe around her.

She signed the tab and fished tip money from her purse while absentmindedly uh-huhing answers to the girl's chatter about the lovely day.

When the girl left, she poured herself a cup from the teapot and took a long sip, letting the hot liquid float around in her mouth for a few moments before swallowing. She sank into the chair with her cup cradled in her hands. The tea would help her gather the nerve to call Joe. What was she going to say? She had no idea, but putting it off wasn't going to help any. She picked up the phone and placed the call.

"Hello," Joe answered a bit gruffly. Even though the caller I.D. told him it was Deb, he didn't say her name.

Softly, she said, "Hi, Joe. It's me." She paused. "How ya doing?"

"Me? I'm ok. How are you doing?" Stress on the you.

"Better, I guess. Listen, I'm sorry, you know, for running out like that. You've been so good through all this and I'm afraid I'm not behaving well."

"It's okay," Joe replied grudgingly. "Glad you're feeling better. Not going to tell you I understand, 'cause I don't. But I guess you gotta do what you gotta do." His words were crisp, a little cold.

"Yeah." The ensuing silence was palpable. She was waiting for Joe to say something. Joe was waiting for her to say something.

Finally she said, "So what have you been doing? How's the dog?"

"He misses you." Pause. "Uh, Deb, I talked to Zannah last night, told her what's going on. She's pretty upset. Wants to come home."

Deb was taken aback. She had completely forgotten about Zannah and her proposed Skype session. The guilt she had felt before about Joe was now doubled.

"Oh, Joe, I'm so sorry." She didn't know what else to say. "I, I, I didn't think...I..."

"Yeah, you didn't think." He heard his voice, so cold, so harsh, but he couldn't stop it. His hurt and anger were getting the best of him and although he knew this wasn't the best way to handle his wife, he couldn't help himself.

"I, I, I'll call her. Don't worry, I'll make it all right." The words were tumbling out. "I just needed time. I'll make her understand. It'll be fine. No need for her to fly out. I'm so sorry. Really. Really, I'm so sorry. Please forgive me," she pleaded.

"Yeah, you had better call her." He felt himself softening, but wasn't ready yet to give it up. "This whole thing has been rough on everybody. Not just you, Deb."

"I know. I know. I'm sorry. I'll call her now. Bye." And, not waiting for him to answer, disconnected the call.

Deb sat there looking at the phone. She didn't know what she had expected, but it certainly wasn't this. He was mad. That much she was sure of. But why? Because she had left? Was her wanting to be alone to figure things out so horrible? It wasn't as if he never left. He did. Every week. Those trips to the golf course. He had even told her once that being alone on the long drive to and from the course helped him figure things out. Of course, he would say it wasn't the same thing. But it was, damn it. It was the same thing.

Well, he was just going to have to get over it. I'm always the one bending over backwards to make sure everybody feels better, always apologizing for things I'm not really sorry about. Being the understanding one, the regretful one. Swallowing my hurt and anger just to make peace. Well, not today.

She poured herself another cup of tea, knowing that in the end, it would be her, apologizing, smoothing everything out, stuffing her own hurt and anger deep inside. It's the price she'd learned to pay.

Joe looked disbelievingly at the phone. She hung up on me. He knew it was his fault, his inability to keep his anger in check. He knew it wasn't right, that he should have pretended that everything was fine, that he was handling it all well, but he couldn't help it. Sometimes she made him so mad.

Like when he would try to get through to her, find out what she was really thinking. He used to get angry and yell, thinking that would make her react, blurt out whatever it was that was eating at her. But she'd just close up and leave the room. Later she'd tell him it was to let him cool down. But he knew that wasn't it. It was simply her retreat back behind the wall.

That damned wall. The one that surrounded her, the dense cloud that formed when certain subjects were raised, her deft deflection of discussions about her time in school or those years before he met her.

After all this time, he should have known better. That letting her know how mad he was would do no good. He knew that, once again, he would apologize to her. Tell her he was sorry for getting angry. It was the only way to get back to their normal life. It was the price he'd learned to pay.

Chapter Twelve

Deb came home. There was no fanfare, no big scene. She just walked through the door, called out "Hi" to Joe, petted and scratched the dog while murmuring reassurances and plunked her purse, sunglasses and keys on the table.

Joe walked into the room and, after putting his coffee mug on the table, gave her an awkward smile. They hugged, each giving the other a kiss and said "I'm sorry" simultaneously. The embrace lasted longer than usual and was a bit more knowing than usual. Finally, she kissed him again, let out an embarrassed giggle and released him from her grip.

She was glad it was only Joe here at the house. She had been able to convince Zannah to hold off her visit. There were things she needed to say and do and having Zannah there would just make it weird. She hated having to explain herself and she knew that her decision was one that Joe, Zannah and Miles would disagree with, but she was determined to stick to it.

Joe would be the hardest to persuade, but she was sure she'd bring him around in the end. And once she had Joe on her side, Miles and Zannah would fall into place...hopefully.

"So..." she said to Joe as she walked over to the tea kettle, trying to keep her voice light. "Still mad?"

"No. Not really. A little confused maybe, but that's nothing new," he laughed.

"Yeah, me too."

He sat down at the table and rifled through the pile of papers lying there, not sure what to say. She put the kettle on to boil and busied herself emptying the dishwasher and loading it up again with the dishes soaking in the sink. It was easy to see what he had eaten while she was away. When the tea was made, she took her cup and sat across from Joe.

"Anything new here?" She felt like she had been gone weeks, not days.

"Nah. Just the usual neighborhood stuff. I'm pretty busy with work, but most of it I can do here." After a pause he said, "You ok?"

"Yup. You?"

"Yeah."

"Good."

They sat in silence, sipping their drinks, looking out the door to the patio. Maybe they were watching the birds build their nests, or checking out how the flowers were doing, but probably they were just trying to figure out what to say next.

Joe broke the silence first. "Yeah, well, I've got to get back to work. You mind?"

"No, no. It's fine. I've got plenty to do. We'll talk later, ok?"

"Yeah, good." He stood up, grabbed his coffee and squeezed her shoulder before he walked back into his office.

She watched him go. *That went pretty well,* she mused. She thought about what she should do while he was working. *Walk the dog? No, leaving again might not be such a good idea. Laundry? Ugh. Clean? Again ugh. Unpack. Yes, that's it. Unpack.*

She retrieved her bag from the car and headed upstairs, followed closely by the dog. As she unpacked, she decided it was time to switch her closet from winter to summer clothes, a chore she found both rewarding and distressing. She made four piles: keep 'cause I'll definitely wear it again; keep 'cause maybe I'll lose that weight; donate 'cause why in the hell did I ever buy that?, and toss 'cause it's too old, stained or ugly to keep or donate. She stood back and looked at the piles, every once in a while moving a piece from one to the other. The maybe I'll lose that weight pile got bigger every year and now contained three different sizes. She shrugged her shoulders in resignation, put the piles into their appropriate containers and lugged them downstairs.

This chore was easier when Zannah lived here. She never wavered about what to keep or what to toss. Unlike her mother, she wasn't one to hold onto things that may one day fit or come back in style. Miles was just like Joe, seeing absolutely no need to move his clothes around. They both liked having the option of pulling out a pair of shorts on the first warm day, even if it was February. Joe especially was overly optimistic about nothing ever getting too worn out to wear.

She supposed that was a good thing. The part of him that wouldn't throw out clothes or books or magazines bode well for their relationship. He might get sick and tired of her, but chances were good that he'd keep her around.

Finished with the clothes, she wandered aimlessly around the house. She could hear Joe, sounding very professional, on the phone with a client. She admired how good he was with clients and his ability to get right to the meat of a problem, the quick solution always at the ready. Sometimes she wondered if he was truly that sure of himself or if it was all just a really good act. Whatever it was, it seemed to work.

Deb, on the other hand, felt that she took forever to make a decision. Although once made, she was steadfast in her conviction. Unless, of course, someone exposed a crack in her logic. Even then, she often stoically remained unmoved, even to the point of ridiculousness. She was afraid that would be today's result.

She had spent a lot of time thinking about the interrupted carjacking and Tyler and what she was going to do. As sure as she was at the time about her planned actions, she feared Joe's reaction would make her doubt herself.

Stay steady, she kept telling herself as she settled in front of the computer with a fresh cup of tea. She turned it on and googled Tyler McCann.

"My word. Look at all of these!" she said to herself. "Well, I can rule out the black Tylers. And the guy in Alabama at the university. This one has a LinkedIn account, so I doubt it's him. Here's a guy who specializes in genetics and another who's a dentist. Nope, not either one of them." She decided to optimize her search and added Philadelphia. That narrowed it down a bit, but judging by the images that popped up, none of them were the Tyler McCann she wanted. After scrolling through pages of search results, she noted with some relief that there were no mentions of him cropping up in news articles, police reports or mug shots.

She decided to try Facebook. Apparently there are a lot of them in the South, but her Tyler was nowhere to be found. Flummoxed, she sat back and stared at the screen. Now what? The White Pages? Would he have a land line? Probably not, none of the kids these days seemed to have them, they all relied on their cell phones. But she decided it was worth a shot. Just as she clicked on the link, Joe came into the room.

"I'm going to make myself a drink. You want something?"

She looked at the clock and was surprised to see it was after 5:00. "Oh, it's that time? I didn't realize it was so late." She glanced back at the computer and switched off the monitor, not wanting Joe to see what she was up to. "Yeah, I think a vodka tonic is in order, thanks."

She stood up and followed him into the kitchen. While he made the drinks, she put together a cheese plate, knowing this might be all they'd eat tonight.

They went out to the patio, settled into their unacknowledged assigned chairs and sat in silence for a few minutes. Finally, Joe said, "So, you doing all right?"

"Yeah." Deb took a deep breath and exhaled. She stared at her drink when she said, "It was Tyler McCann. The guy who knocked me out that morning was Tyler McCann."

"What?" Joe said incredulously. "That kid you saw the other day at Nino's? That the kids know? Are you serious?"

"Yep," she nodded solemnly.

"Well, that's great! It'll make it much easier for the cops to pick him up. You know, since you've got a name and everything."

"No," she almost whispered, "I'm not going to tell them."

"What do you mean, you're not going to tell them? Of course you are. Don't be ridiculous."

"I am not telling them and I am not being ridiculous. I am not about to ruin someone's life because they made a stupid decision. I just won't do that. Especially to someone I know."

"Deb, this is crazy talk. You don't know him. Maybe you did once, but you don't know him now. And he didn't make a stupid decision, he committed a crime. He could have killed you!" Joe took a quick gulp of his drink. He was beside himself and needed a moment to think.

"But Joe," Deb said quietly, "I do know him. I know the boy he once was. The boy whose childhood was stolen from him. The boy he could have been. The boy he could be again."

"And exactly what does that mean? The boy he could be again? You think if you let him slide on this that he won't just do it again? To somebody else? Maybe with more serious consequences?" He stood up and started pacing around the patio. *What the hell was she thinking?* "This is sheer lunacy, Deb."

Deb watched Joe as he made his way from one end of the patio to the other. She was trembling on the inside but hoping it didn't show. She wanted to be firm, to appear resolute in her decision. She cut a piece of cheese and ate it.

"Joe, come here and sit down. Hear me out. Please."

Joe came back to his chair, plopped down and let out a big sigh. "Ok. I'm listening."

Now that the moment was here, Deb didn't know if she could do it, if she could make him understand how this really did make sense, how terribly important it was to her. She took a deep breath.

"Ok. Here goes. I've thought about this a lot over the past few days. I think the only reason he hit me was because he knew me. He was upset. Upset and afraid. I could tell how afraid he was. There was a split second where I saw it register in his eyes, you know, that he recognized me. I could tell it upset him."

"Of course it upset him, Deb. He knew you could I.D. him and they'd truck him off to jail."

"No. That's not it. Or not all of it. I don't know. I don't know how to explain it. It was as if he knew he was wrong but had no choice. He was at the point of no return. That if he could have just walked away, he would have, but for some reason he couldn't." She knew her words weren't quite making sense, that she wasn't getting through to her husband, but she pressed on. "Don't you see, Joe? Don't you see that I can help him walk away?"

"Help him walk away? Is that what you said?" Joe replied incredulously. "It's too late to just walk away."

"No, I don't think it is. Too late, I mean. He's still a kid, just twenty something. Like Miles and Zannah. Think of it, Joe. We've all done things, made mistakes, bad decisions. Especially when we were young. Decisions that change everything. And if you just had a chance to go back and you know, click undo, that you'd do it. Do it in a flash. I can do that for Tyler. I can erase that decision for him. Let him start over."

Joe reached over and took Deb's hand. "It isn't that easy, hon. You can't just wave a wand and make it all disappear." He paused. "I can't talk about this any more right now. But, Deb, think. Whatever made him go down that road, you had nothing to do with. It's on him and you can't fix it."

"Yes I can. And I will. With or without your help, I'm going to fix Tyler.

An uneasy silence took over the evening. Deb quietly moved around the house making dinner while Joe tried to immerse himself in a book, to no avail. His head was swimming, attempting to make sense of Deb's declaration.

Later, sitting at the table with their summer salads, Joe said, "Look Deb. I know this whole thing has been tough on you and I don't think you're really thinking it through." She started to interrupt, but he held up his hand to stop her. "No, now just wait a minute. Yes, you are right, we all have made bad decisions. But we've had to live with them, you know, pay the piper so to speak. Now it's time for Tyler to pay. It's not your responsibility to fix something that you had no hand in making."

Deb laid her fork down and looked at Joe. "I know it's not my responsibility in the clearest sense of the word. Maybe it doesn't make sense to you. But it is something I want to do, I need to do. Don't you understand?" She looked down at her salad, unable to meet his eyes. "That this is my way of finally making up for what happened in college?"

"God damn it Deb. Aren't you ever going to forgive yourself for that? It wasn't your fault. You can't keep blaming yourself for what those bastards did to you!"

Tears welled in her eyes and her voice shook as she blinked them back. She said, "Yes, Joe. It was my fault. I'm the one who shot my big mouth off to those guys. Calling them names, inciting them. I called them every name in the book. I remember it clear as day. Racist, chauvinistic white trash crackers. Shouting at them how real men stood up for the underdog. That their homophobia was just a mask for their unrealized homosexual fantasies. The words just kept spilling out, I couldn't stop them. Taunting them, goading them. Until they lashed out and showed me what real men they were." She said this last bit with a snort. "We were all so young, so stupid."

Joe couldn't look at her. She had never told him exactly what had happened that night. All she had said was that she had been raped. No names, no details, no back story. And he didn't pry. Once he had cornered her old roommate and asked her what happened. She'd only said that Deb came to the room, her face swollen, body bruised, clothes torn. Wouldn't say any more. Said it wasn't her place. If Deb wanted to tell him, she would. So, he figured that was that. And he pushed it out of his mind because he couldn't bear to think about it.

He had no words. There was nothing to say. He wanted to hold her but couldn't move. He just sat there, silently, barely breathing.

After a few minutes, she said, "That decision to lash out changed me forever. I don't want that for Tyler."

"Okay, Deb. Okay."

They sat at the table, pushing their food around, lost in their own thoughts. Deb seemed so far away. Still, he had never felt closer to her. His need to protect her was overwhelming. True, he couldn't protect her from her past, but he would do his best to shield her from the future. He might have to let her do whatever it was she felt she had to do, but he could watch over her, make sure it worked out. Somehow, he understood that if he got in her way, he'd lose her.

Deb wondered if she had said too much and was thankful she hadn't told him everything. She was sure that once someone knew the real circumstances, they would see her for what she really was. Unthinking. Stupid. Irresponsible. Harsh. Unworthy. Dangerous.

Now that Joe knew this much, would it be too much? What about when he learned the whole story? How could he live with the realization that she had brought this all on herself? Oh sure, he'd try to be understanding, put a good face on it, give it the old school boy try, but the ugly reality would not go away. Even now, sitting right next to her in the waning daylight, he seemed to already be moving away.

Joe cleared his throat. "What do you say, maybe after we finish dinner we'll walk the dog and figure out how to help Tyler."

Deb abruptly looked over at him. This man would never cease to amaze her. "Yeah, okay. That sounds good." She added after a pause, "Thanks."

The dog, hearing the word 'walk,' looked expectantly at Deb and Joe and thumped his tail against the deck floor. They saw the hope in his eyes and smiled. A little giggle erupted from Deb, and Joe, relieved to see some light from his wife, joined in, quietly at first, then the giggles burst into raucous laughter, an unexpected release from the hours, days, months of tension.

Deb didn't fool herself into thinking it was going to be easy. She had no idea how the scope of her revelations would play out in the days to come, but then again, Joe hadn't walked out then and there.

He even seemed open to the idea of helping poor Tyler. Who would have thought?

She quickly cleaned up their dinner plates, loaded the dishwasher and wiped down the counters. The dog followed her every move, stopping occasionally to catch sight of Joe as he watered the plants. It was a rare treat for him when they all walked together. It meant a nice long stroll, maybe even as far as the park, turning back only when the night air got too cool.

At last, Joe came in. "Almost ready, Deb?"

She dried her hands, "Yup, just got to pee."

Joe grabbed the leash from its peg and picked up a poop bag. The dog was having a hard time containing himself and shook with glee, making it difficult for Joe to hook him up. Deb pulled a sweater from the closet and followed her husband and dog out the door.

They headed toward the walking path, stopping occasionally to chat with the neighborhood children out playing basketball or making chalk drawings on driveways. When they reached the path, Joe took Deb's hand and said, "Ok Deb, you ready to talk about this?"

"Yeah, I think so."

"Well, dive right in. Tell me how you think we can help Tyler." Joe had decided earlier that he'd just let her talk, give her the time to lay it out for him, not rush to judgment.

"Well...." Now that the time was here, she wasn't quite sure where or how to start. "I guess ideally that I'd want him to move in with us. We could give him some stability. I think that's part of his problem. He hasn't had any kind of real family for quite some time." She paused and glanced over at him.

Joe fought the urge to blurt out how crazy this was and said slowly, "Oh kay.....go on."

"You see, if he came and stayed with us, he'd have, you know, a clean, dry roof over his head and food, real meals. He wouldn't need any money, so he wouldn't have to do those things, those bad things he's been doing."

"Uh huh...and then what?"

Deb had expected some push back by now. Bolstered by Joe's non-reactions, she rushed on. "Well, uh, then maybe he could get a part time job and go back to school. And no, I'm not proposing that we pay for his college or anything. He'd have to get student loans and stuff, but it would give him some direction. Just think of it, wouldn't it be great? To help this kid turn his life around? School and work instead of jail?"

"Mmmm. Maybe..." Joe said reluctantly. All kinds of questions and arguments were forming in his mind and he regretted his notepad wasn't tucked in his pocket, but he stayed true to his decision and just said, "I'm going to have to think about this. We'll have to weigh the pros and cons, not just jump into it without thinking it through."

She couldn't keep the excitement out of her voice. "Yes, yes. I know. I've pretty much done that. You know, tried to look at it from every angle. But I really do think it'll work."

"Maybe. But you've had the time to think about it. I haven't. You have to at least give me that."

"Sure! Sure! Take all the time you need." She added with a laugh, "as long as it's not three years." She smiled at him, "For now, let's just finish our walk."

Chapter Thirteen

Joe slept fitfully that night. Although he didn't really know any details, disturbing images streamed through his head. Deb, her eyes flashing, yelling hurtful words. Men, boys really, their faces fraught with anger and hatred. Hands grabbing, fumbling, ripping. Bodies pulsing. Running. Deb, clothes disheveled, lying on the ground, crying. Stumbling, dazed. Looking for safety when there wasn't any.

Feeling frustrated and discombobulated, he got out of bed and went downstairs. He poured himself a glass of scotch and sat down in the dark.

Was she right? he thought. *Was it her fault?* The rational side of him said, no of course not. But there was a nagging doubt that kept pecking away like a woodpecker searching for bugs in the oak tree.

He didn't want to go there, but his mind insisted on seeing the incident from the boys' side. What if he himself at that age had been confronted by a girl hurling insults about his manhood? How would he have reacted? It wasn't too hard to see the testosterone-fueled hurt and embarrassment of a teenage boy. How it could launch him, especially if aided by over imbibing, into monstrous acts.

Stop it, Joe. He felt guilty about even thinking considering the other side. There is no excuse for it. And there wasn't. However, he found himself beginning to understand what Deb meant when she claimed she was to blame. He hated to admit it, but to a certain degree, she was. That was a plain fact. She was right when she said if she had just kept her mouth shut, her thoughts to herself, none of it would have happened.

My God. She's been living with that all these years. It certainly took its toll. Explained her moodiness, her periods of darkness, the wall so solidly built. Until her run in with Tyler, when it just couldn't stand any more and began to crumble.

What now? Will her trying to fix Tyler fix her? He wished he could share her certainty, but he wasn't so sure. Selfishly, he wondered if he really wanted her fixed. He wondered if he would even like the woman she might become. What would that mean to their lives? He had to admit, up to now she never nagged or yelled at him like his friends' wives. She never argued, never really said anything that might anger him. Always let him decide what to watch, where to vacation, what to do in his spare time. His friends weren't so lucky. Did he really want that to end?

Wow. How narcissistic of me, he thought. *Worrying about how it will affect me.* Still, he couldn't stop. He sat there, sipping on his drink, thinking about what was to come and what he could do that would help her, but keep its impact on him as minimal as possible.

Deb woke to the warm, wet tongue of the dog licking her hand as it dangled from the side of the bed. She quickly jerked it back and wiped it on the bed sheet. She was surprised to find Joe's side of the bed empty. For the life of her, she couldn't remember what day it was. Maybe it was the weekend and he was out at the course already.

She dressed quickly and went downstairs only to find Joe sound asleep in his chair, empty glass by his side. She tiptoed to the kitchen and, as quietly as possible, set the kettle on to boil and made the coffee. Once her tea was made, she headed out to the patio.

Somewhere in the recesses of Joe's mind, he sensed rustlings in the kitchen. He knew he should get up, but attempted to ignore the call of the morning routine. When he heard the back door open and close, he knew it was fruitless. He had to get up. His neck was stiff from sleeping in the lounger and he swirled it back and forth to loosen the tightened muscles. He sat there for a minute, trying to wake up, then decided the only thing that would help would be his jolt of java.

As he walked to the kitchen he could see his wife sitting on the patio's stone wall. Not sure he wanted to see her yet, he poured his coffee and went to get the paper. Then he opened the patio door and said, "Morning" to Deb.

She turned and smiled at him. "Hey!" There was a lilt in her voice that he hadn't heard in a long time and he was distressed that, at the same time, a picture of her screaming flashed across his mind. He shook his head and closed the door. *This has got to stop,* he told himself as he settled at the kitchen table and opened the paper. He began to read the headlines, hoping for a distraction. More explosions in the Mideast. Soda tax dispute in the city. Some sort of sex scandal at a suburban high school. Nothing he felt like reading right then. He turned to the sports section and was immersed in an article about the Sixer's draft when Deb and the dog came in.

"How're you doing this morning?" she asked.

"Ok. Had trouble sleeping, so I came downstairs. Must have fallen asleep down here."

"Oh. You ok?" There was a hint of worry in her voice.

"Yeah. Fine. Just got a crick in my neck," he answered as he moved his head back and forth. He couldn't look at her.

"Want me to get you some Alleve?"

"No, it's fine. I'll take a shower. That'll loosen it up." He felt a sudden urge to get away from her, away from the images bombarding his brain. He stood, picked up his mug and paper and almost flew up the stairs.

Deb watched him leave. She noticed that he hadn't so much as glanced her way. She tried to remember. Was this usual? Or has something changed? She couldn't be sure. For once, she didn't care. She felt pretty good this morning and she wasn't going to let him change that.

Joe walked into the bedroom and plopped on the bed. He was jolted by the constant flow of pictures running through his brain like a tsunami building, building, building until it crashed on the shore. He went over to the bookcase where Deb kept all the family photos, and rifled through the various albums, hoping to replace the violent images with happy ones. The first one he picked out was supplied by Deb's mother one Christmas. It held memories of Deb's early years. On the beach in Ocean City pail and shovel in hand, Deb playing with her huge dog, Christmas by the tree, junior prom with her hair piled on her head, high school graduation, mortarboard tilted and eyes shining, surrounded by now absent friends.

The next album held their wedding photos, such as they were. He remembered how Deb refused to get a professional photographer, saying there was no need for the added expense. We'll just put those throw-away cameras on every table and get people to send us copies, she had told him. He smiled thinking back. We were so young, trying to be so frugal, he thought as he flipped through the pages.

He continued to go through the albums, filling his mind with the reminders of happier times. He stopped suddenly at a picture he hadn't seen before. Deb, leaning against a doorway alone. He studied the picture. She looked about 25 or so, attractive but certainly not stunning. Dressed in her Annie Hall outfit with the tie loosely knotted on the men's white shirt, sleeves rolled up, light brown leather vest unbuttoned, bowler hat perched on her head. She was looking right at the camera. Her face was pensive, her eyes held a wariness, almost sadness. Strange really, because she never posed for photos. Hated having her picture taken unlike the kids today who want to record every moment of their lives. He tried to remember when it was taken, who took it? His mind was blank.

He started when he heard Deb come into the room.

"What're you doing?" she asked as she walked over to him.

"Just looking through these old photo albums," he answered a little guiltily. He felt he had been caught doing something he shouldn't.

"Odd. Why?"

"Well," he stammered, "I just felt like it." He averted her gaze. He couldn't confess what he saw when he looked at her, how his mind was playing tricks on him and he was trying to outsmart it.

"Hmmm," she said glancing at the photo in his hand. "I loved that outfit. I so wanted to be Annie Hall. Of course, not with Woody Allen," she laughed.

"Yeah. I was trying to remember when that was taken. Do you?"

"Oh, Susie took that. You remember Susie, my roommate from school? She came up here to visit one Thanksgiving. I wonder what she's been up to," Deb replied her voice trailing off like it did whenever college came up. "She was always carrying around that damn camera snapping shots when you least expected. I think that time I had given up and hoped that if I let her take a picture, she'd leave me alone."

"Did it work?"

"Nah. Not where Susie and her camera were concerned. I think I tossed all the other ones. Don't know why I kept this one."

"Well I like it. It's one of the few where you're actually looking at the camera."

"I guess it's not too bad," she said more to appease him than to agree. She stood up quickly. She knew exactly why she threw out photos of herself. She never thought of herself as vain, but was truly dismayed how the camera caught her inner ugliness especially when she was looking right at it. It reminded her of Dorian Gray, the way the portrait reflected his misdeeds and innate evil.

Deb started to walk out of the room then stopped to say, "Don't forget. Zannah's flying in this afternoon."

"What? Oh right. What time are we picking her up?"

"We're not. She's getting Uber. She should be here around four. And Miles is coming out for dinner."

"Ok." With everything that had gone on the past day or so, Zannah's visit had completely slipped his mind. "You gonna tell them about your plans?"

"Guess I'll have to, huh?" she replied with some hesitation.

"Yup. It'll be good to hear what they have to say about it."

"They'll be fine," she said, trying to sound convincing as she continued down the hall.

Joe remained where he was going over last night's conversation with Deb in his head. What would the kids think of her decision to help Tyler? He was pretty sure he knew. Miles would be all for it. He had this strange rescue gene that seemed to permeate everything he did. He never realized before how alike Deb and Miles were but he could see them now, situated on one side of the argument, Miles steadfastly holding with his mother, facing ever doubtful Joe and Zannah. He knew, most certainly, that Deb would be able to convince Zannah. It might take some doing but in the end, she'd reluctantly edge over to Deb's point of view.

Out of the blue, an idea popped into his head. He knew then how he was going to handle tonight's discussion.

Pleased, he said to himself, "If nothing else, it'll be interesting.

They ate dinner on the patio. Joe grilled burgers and hot dogs, Deb made pasta salad and panzanella. Conversation was mostly light with Zannah telling funny stories about trying to assimilate into West Coast living. Miles, with his dry humor, kept making asides that had them all laughing. Donna and Dennis, hearing the uproar, poked their heads over the fence and offered to bring over dessert. Occasionally Joe would look over at Deb wondering if and when she would bring up Tyler.

She didn't have to. The kids did. It was innocuous enough. He and

Zannah were reminiscing about the 10th grade prank, something to do with moving the school 'established in 1952' rock, when Miles said. "Yeah, I think that's the first time Tyler McCann and his buddies got suspended from school."

Joe perked up his ears. "The first time? Tyler get into trouble a lot?" He lifted his eyebrows toward Deb.

"Well, I don't know if it was a lot. It was just kid stuff. A bunch of kids got suspended, right Zannah?"

"Yeah," said Zannah. "But speaking of Tyler. What's going on? Did you call the cops and tell them?" She looked expectantly at her mother.

"Noooooo."

"And why, might I ask?"

Donna chimed in. "I think this is our exit line. Come on, Dennis. As sure as I am that this is gonna be good, we should let them have the rest of the evening to themselves." The next few minutes were a flurry of goodbyes and so good to see you's as Deb helped Donna gather their dishes.

And then it was just the four Cromwells sitting around the table with their empty dessert plates and a fresh bottle of wine.

Miles and Zannah looked at each other, hoping for one of them to start the conversation again. Miles started, "Sooooo?"

Deb drew a deep breath. "Ok, here goes." So she told them. Told them about wanting to help Tyler, about how one mistake shouldn't ruin an entire life, about how she thought they could help him become the person she knew he could be. She didn't tell them that it could change her life too. That was too much information, some things your children shouldn't know.

Joe, meanwhile, sat back in his chair, arms folded, eyes moving like a tennis spectator from Zannah to Miles, gauging their reactions.

Miles kept his face pointed at the table top, occasionally squinting and rubbing his brow as if to push the information into his brain. Zannah leaned forward in an effort to hear, all the while keeping her focus on Deb's face, possibly evaluating the earnestness of her mother's softly spoken words.

Finished, Deb picked up her wine glass, took a large gulp, set it down, then looked at her children. "Well?" she said.

They sat there, Miles rubbing, Zannah staring, for what seemed to be a lifetime to Deb.

Zannah was the first to speak. "Uh, give me a minute here. This is a lot to take in."

"Ya think?" mumbled Miles.

"Of course it is," said Deb. "Let me clean up the dishes while you guys digest. I'll be back."

A bit trembly, she gathered the empty plates and utensils, placed them on a tray and carried them to the kitchen where she sat down, spent.

Hearing the kitchen door close behind him, Miles suddenly pushed back his chair and stood up with such force that his chair toppled over.

"What the fuck?" he screamed quietly, glaring at his father. "Are you in on this? You think this is a good move? Is she crazy? Are you?" He started pacing angrily around the patio. "This could be the stupidest thing I've ever heard and I listened to Trump's speech last night!"

Joe was taken aback. He had expected this incredulity from Zannah, but certainly not from Miles. Zannah patiently looked at him, waiting for his reply.

"Calm down, Miles. Sit." he said in an uncharacteristically stern tone. Miles obeyed but looked defiantly at him.

"Ok," started Joe, "Listen. No, I'm not crazy. Your mom? Jury's out. I do think it's an idea that is fraught with problems we can't even begin to fathom. But that being said, your mother has her mind made up. I don't think there's anything you, me or Zannah can say that will change it."

"Hey," Zannah piped up. "Leave me out of this. I think she could be right."

"Seriously?" Miles retorted.

"Yes. Yes. I'm completely serious." She looked at her brother. "What good is jail going to do for Tyler? You know as well as I do that jail doesn't cure anything. I doubt he'd come out any better and probably much worse. And really, he's not a bad kid. He was always nice to me."

"Not a bad kid? Right, 'cause good kids always knock out old ladies when they're stealing cars," Mile said sarcastically. "Plus, everyone says he's got a drug problem. He'll just end up stealing our electronics and selling them for his next fix."

"Oh don't be ridiculous. Like Mom said, he just needs a helping hand."

"I'll give him a helping hand," Miles sneered. "If I see him again I'll take him out, let him know what it feels like."

"You will not. You've never hit anyone."

"Just you wait and see."

"I don't understand you, Miles. You've always been the pushover in this house. I can't believe you don't want to help him."

"He fucking clocked our mother. Knocked her to the ground. Have you forgotten the hospital, the memory loss? He's gotta pay."

The argument continued with Joe the bystander sipping his wine, listening to the rapid fire exchange between brother and sister. He was waiting for an opening to tell them about his idea and hoped it would come before Deb came back out.

He got his wish. Suddenly there was quiet. They had reached an impasse, pausing to catch a breath or reload, he wasn't sure which.

He put down his wine glass and said, "I've got an idea that I think will either make her change her mind or at least make this whole 'fix Tyler' thing easier to handle."

Apparently, they had forgotten Joe was even there. They looked at him, Miles annoyed, Zannah curious.

"Ok, let's hear it," Zannah said.

"Maybe you don't remember or never knew, but Mom feels like she had done things a long time ago that ended up badly. Screwed up her life. I think she's using this to exorcise some of her own demons, sort of an atonement."

"What do you mean? What are you talking about?" Miles asked.

"Never mind the details. Suffice it to say that something happened, something bad and it's haunted her for a very long time. She thinks it was her fault and she's never forgiven herself."

The light dawned on both Zannah and Miles at the same time. It began to make sense. The days, sometimes weeks when their mother would be so distant, so sad, so closed off. They never knew why. Never asked about it. Were only relieved when it was over.

Joe continued, "I've tried to get her to see a shrink or therapist or something, but she's always resisted. But I think maybe now I can get her to agree. If we say she or we would need a professional to help guide us through this whatever it is, she just might go along. If she doesn't, then we say forget it. We won't support her, ah, let's call it her 'fix Tyler' proposal. It'll all hinge on how important this is to her."

Miles opened his mouth to say something but stopped abruptly when he noticed Zannah warning him off with a nod toward the back door. Deb was coming out.

As she walked to her chair, she gently touched each child on the shoulder. "Look," she said, "I know this is a lot to ask, but it's really important to me. So very, very important. You have no idea and yet, I really don't want to go into it. If I have to, I will. But I'm asking you to trust me. Please."

Joe nudged Miles under the table and looked questioningly at him. Miles gave him a resigned shrug. Then Joe took Deb's hand and said, "Deb.

The kids and I were talking and we've come to a decision of our own." And explained his proposal to his wife.

Chapter Fourteen

Deb perched precariously on the edge of the sofa in Dr. Nutley's office. She surveyed the surroundings. Exposed brick wall on one side with large windows looking out onto another office building. Subtle lighting, leather sofa with rust colored throw pillows, modern-ish armchair with two cushions, the obligatory coffee table, box of tissues at the ready.

Ugh.

In waddled Dr. Nutley. He made his way over to her, introduced himself and shook her hand. Then he sat in the chair facing her and smiled.

"How are you today, Deb? May I call you Deb?"

She looked at him warily. "Yes, that's fine." She didn't know what she expected, but it certainly wasn't this rumpled, overweight squirrely man eyeing her. *If he can't get himself in order, how does he expect to straighten anyone out?* she thought. Aloud, she said, "Am I supposed to lie down?"

"Only if you want to. Just make yourself comfortable," he answered as he fumbled through some papers on his lap.

"Does that mean I can leave?"

"Ha-ha." the doctor chuckled. "That's up to you, I guess. But first, why don't you tell me what brings you here?"

"I'm here because I made a deal with my family."

"A deal? What kind of deal?"

"It's a bit complicated."

"Life is complicated." He shoved his hand into the pocket of his pants, pulling out a handful of lint, papers and coins and dropping some onto the floor.

She bent over to retrieve the fallen coins and handing them to him, said, "Look, I don't know what my husband told you or what it says in that file you're holding. I don't want to bore you so why don't you tell me what you know and I'll fill you in. Let's just get this over with."

"Ha-ha." Again the chuckle. "I'm sure I won't be bored." He was examining one of the papers from his pocket. "It really doesn't matter what the file says or what Joe told me. I want to hear it from you. Why are you here?"

So we're going to play it like that, Deb thought. *Damn.* "Okay. A few months ago, I had sort of what the police called an aborted carjacking. Got hit on the head by a kid my children knew in school and now I want to have him come live at our house so I can help get him to live a productive life." She said all of this matter-of-factly. "My husband and son think it's a crazy idea and will only go along if you say it's okay. So just write a letter or something saying it's a great idea and I can go home."

"My, my, we're in quite a hurry, aren't we?" the doctor said, crumpling up the paper and tossing it toward a trash can.

"No sense in wasting time."

"We've got almost an hour so let's talk about this some more."

"You're the doctor," Deb said with a shrug.

"Why do you want to help this boy? It's a boy, right?"

"Not a boy exactly, he's in his late twenties. As I said, my kids knew him and I had known him a bit too when they were in school. He was a sweet boy who had some rough times. I see no sense sending him to jail."

"Uh huh. Well, he wouldn't go to jail if you didn't press charges. So why not just do that? Why have him live at your house?"

Frankly, she was tired of explaining herself, but knew she had to. As he fussily cleaned his glasses with his shirt front, she told him about Tyler's dad, mother, suspected drug use, how she felt that if he were exposed to a stable, normal household it might get him back on track.

"You see yourself as some kind of savior?" Dr Nutley asked, finally putting his glasses back on.

"Heavens no! Don't go reading into this more than it is. I just want to help him."

"Isn't that what a savior is? Someone who saves others?"

"I, I, I guess. In the strictest sense of the word. But I don't think I'm Jesus Christ or anything."

"Okay. We'll let that go for now. Why is it up to you? Why not let people who are trained to help help him?"

"I just think it would be better coming from someone he knows. Someone he trusts."

"And he trusts you." Fidgeting with the legal pad on his lap.

"I don't know. I hope he would."

"You mentioned a drug problem. Do you have any experience dealing with addicts?"

"I didn't say he had a drug problem. I said suspected drug use. You know how rumors swirl about people. Who knows if there's any truth to it."

"I suppose. Have you thought about the impact this would have on your family? A virtual stranger living under your roof? One who has done you harm?"

"Doctor," Deb said a bit defiantly, "I would think you of all people would be behind me in this. After all, you make your living helping people."

"Well, I try," he chuckled again. "It's not easy. Especially if someone doesn't want help." He looked pointedly at her over his now lopsided glasses.

"What's that supposed to mean?"

"Nothing. Just an observation. Listen, I can tell this is important to you, Deb. I just keep coming back to why. Why is it so important?"

"It just is."

"Nothing ever just is. There's always something more there, don't you agree?"

"No. No I don't. I think it's enough to just want to do it." She faltered. "And if there is something more to it, what does it matter?"

"It matters because I think there is more going on here than what we are talking about right now. I think we're on the surface and it would do you good to delve a little deeper. Figure out why you feel this need to help him. You have to admit, it's not the path most people would take."

"Maybe I'm not most people," she said quietly.

Silence. They sat there, Dr. Nutley scribbling furiously on his yellow legal pad, Deb looking at the floor lost in thought, tears beginning to well up. She blinked them back, sniffled, cleared her throat.

The doctor looked up at her and said, "I think that's it for today. We've made a good start, don't you think?"

"Okay." Deb picked up her purse, grabbed a tissue and headed out.

"Oh, Deb? Next time why don't you bring Joe in?" the doctor called as she closed the door behind her.

She slowly walked through the waiting area, nodding absentmindedly at the receptionist bidding her goodbye. She had agreed to meet Joe afterwards at the coffee shop on the ground floor and made her way there at a snail's pace, not really wanting to see anyone much less discuss the session.

She saw Joe seated at a corner table, huge coffee and tea cups steaming in front of him. He looked up as she approached and grinned.

"So how's the head shrinker?"

"Strange, strange little man," she answered as she settled into the chair across from him.

"Really? Strange how?"

"I don't know. He was all mussed up, you know, his hair, his clothes, always fussing with something. If it wasn't something in his pocket, it was his glasses. Almost like he wasn't really paying attention. Yet he kept asking me questions. I thought shrinks were just supposed sit there and listen."

"That's funny. So what did you talk about? Can you tell me?"

"You know what we talked about. Tyler, and him coming to live with us."

"Well, yeah, but did you talk about anything else?" He was fishing.

"Exactly what else do you mean?" She wasn't biting. "Look Joe, I know you think somehow this doctor is going to fix me, as if there is something wrong with me in the first place. But he's not 'cause there is nothing wrong with me. I'm perfectly fine. Whether you think so or not." She almost harrumphed.

"Now Deb, don't be like that. I never said there was anything wrong with you. I just think talking to somebody will help you with your ah, ya know, bouts of depression."

"They are not bouts of depression," she said emphatically. "I get sad sometimes. Everybody gets sad sometimes. I don't know why you have to make a big deal out of it."

"Okay, okay." Joe threw up his hands as if in defeat. "Let's just hope this guy can help us figure out what to do about this whole Tyler mess."

"Yeah, well you'll find out on Wednesday. He wants you to come in with me."

"Really? Why?"

"Didn't say. But I figure if I have to go through this, you should too," she replied trying to sound amused but coming across as accusing.

"Fine."

"Fine."

The two of them sat in the reception area waiting for their appointment. Joe had expected that the doctor would want to see both of them together at some time, but was surprised at the timing. After all, he had only seen Deb once and she was not very forthcoming to Joe about her session. He had no idea what to expect.

A phone rang, the woman behind the desk picked it up, looked over at Deb and Joe, said something, nodded and hung up. "Go on in, Mr. and Mrs. Cromwell."

They got up, glancing nervously at each other. Joe cocked his head toward the door and said, "After you."

Dr. Nutley, lounging on the sofa, was immersed in reading some notes. Hearing the door open, he quickly jumped up, sending his papers floating to the floor. He stooped over, gathering the fallen notes into his stubby hands. He raised his head toward them, "I'll get the rest of those later." To Joe, "Hi, I'm Dr. Nutley. Have a seat." To Deb, "Glad you showed up again" chuckle, chuckle.

They all sat down, Joe and Deb on the sofa, Dr. Nutley in his armchair.

"So Joe, tell me. What do you think of Deb's plan?"

Wow, thought Joe. *He gets right at it, doesn't he?* "Wellll," he stammered, "I'm not sure. I mean, I guess it could work. But I have my doubts."

"And you've told her about your doubts?" He looked curiously at Deb staring at the floor.

"Yes. I, I, we've talked about it."

"Really? You've told her exactly why you think this is a bad idea?" Glasses off, getting polished on his shirt tail.

"Hey, I didn't say it was a bad idea."

"But you think it is, right?"

What, is this guy trying to goad me? "I don't know. Isn't that why we're here? You tell us if it's a good idea or bad one."

"That's not my decision to make. You two are the ones who have to live with it, literally. I'm just here to help you figure out what will work best for you." He fished his phone out of his pocket and checked the screen. "So let's get it all out in the open. Why exactly do you, let's say, have your doubts?"

"Look," said Joe. "I don't know what she's told you. I'm trying to be supportive here. I don't want anyone getting mad at me." He was becoming defensive.

"Why would anyone get mad at you?" Glasses back on.

"Because this is something that's important to Deb and damn it, yes, I think it's a bad idea!"

Deb continued to stare at the floor.

164

The dam had broken, words spilling out in a rush. "I'm sorry Deb, but I do. Doctor, I don't know if you know it but this kid is dangerous. It's not like he's a ten year old who stole a candy bar from the grocery store. He's twenty some years old. He's doing drugs, carjacking. My god, Deb, he knocked you out. And you want to save him? You're going to fix him? I know we've been through this before. You think if you turn him in, it'll ruin his life. Well, so be it. Yeah, yeah, you say he just made a mistake. Face it, he made a ton of mistakes and bad decisions.

"You seem to feel that if you do this, it'll make up for that assault time back way back in college. But it won't. The only thing that'll make that better is if you just face the fact that it wasn't your fault. Not everything bad that happens is your fault, Deb. It just isn't. People make bad decisions all the time. But ultimately, the fault is on the doer. Just because you were at the wrong place, doing things that maybe you shouldn't have done, saying things you shouldn't have said, none of that makes it your fault. Those guys? They could have walked away. They should have walked away. But they didn't. It's on them."

Deb, still staring at the floor, hands clasped in front of her, was biting her trembling lower lip.

Dr. Nutley, scribbling away on his notepad, kept switching his gaze from Deb to Joe and back again.

Joe, spent and trembling with pent up frustration, flounced back on the sofa with a big sigh.

After a few minutes, he took Deb's arm and said softly, "I'm sorry, Deb."

She shook her head no and sniffled.

The doctor laid his pad down and said gently, "We're below the surface now, aren't we, Deb?"

To Joe, he said, "Joe, I'd like to talk with Deb for a few minutes. Would you mind waiting outside?"

Joe, heading out the door, was thinking how good that felt. To have it out right out there in front of a professional. Now Deb couldn't get away from it. With any luck, Dr. Nutley would make her see. He was glad though that he had stopped short of talking about the disturbing images that seemed to constantly confront him. That would have done more harm than good. A discussion perhaps for another day.

While the doctor waited for the door to close behind Joe, he studied Deb, mindful of her reaction. Her face, still pointed at the floor, had the look of a child caught unawares. Embarrassed. Frightened. Waiting for the punishment.

He cleared his throat. "Ah Deb. Something Joe said in his tirade was very telling."

No reply.

"He said," quick glance at his notepad, "and I quote, 'not everything bad that happens is your fault.' What did he mean by that?"

Nothing.

"Do you feel responsible for everything bad that happens? That it is, in fact, your fault?"

Head shaking no. Quietly, "Not everything."

"Okay. Give me an example of something that isn't your fault."

"The Mideast," she replied dryly.

"Right. Of course." Chuckle, chuckle. "Anything else not quite on that scale?"

Deb looked up, almost glaring at him. "Look Doctor. I don't think I'm the center of the universe or anything. That was just Joe exaggerating. Sure, I feel like some things are my fault. Because they are. I see nothing wrong with taking responsibility for them. Do you? Isn't that what we're supposed to do? Admit it and move on?"

"Maybe that's the key here. Admitting it and moving on. Have you admitted everything? Moved on? Are you able to let go? Forgive yourself?"

"I dunno."

"Perhaps that's where we need to start."

"I don't know why any of that matters. What does it have to do with helping Tyler?"

"Deb, let me put it this way. You won't be able to help Tyler if you refuse to help yourself."

"But, but..."

He held up his stubby hand to stop her. "That's enough for today. What I'd like you to do for our next session is think about the things that make you feel guilty. Try to separate them from the things that are truly your fault. Be honest with yourself. We'll see where that takes us." He motioned for her to leave, then went back to scribbling on his notepad.

Joe was waiting bashfully for her in the hallway. Seeing the door open, he hurried over saying, "Deb, I'm sorry. I really am. I don't know what came over me. That doctor's really something, isn't he? Knows exactly what buttons to push." As he talked, Joe searched her face for what? Forgiveness? Anger? Betrayal?

But what he saw was defeat.

"No, Joe," she said, "I'm sorry. I guess I was just being selfish." And walked out to the car.

He followed her, speechless.

They got in the car and he turned to her, "Deb, what did you mean by that?"

"Nothing. Forget it. Let's just go home."

At home, Deb went through the motions of a normal afternoon. Mechanically straightening the house, loading the dishwasher, starting dinner, anything to prevent her from thinking about her assigned task. She even took to answering the phone without checking the caller I.D., hoping for a diversion of some sort. It didn't work, of course. Dr. Nutley's words kept floating back into her head. Be honest with yourself.

At one point, she even laughed, albeit a tad derisively. Honesty with herself was not the problem. It was being honest with him. And Joe.

Chapter Fifteen

Back at the doctor's office. Deb waiting apprehensively for Dr. Nutley to finish cleaning his glasses and say something to her.

Finally satisfied, he placed his glasses back on his face and smiled at Deb. "So Deb, how was your week?"

"Fine."

"Good, good." Checking his notes. "Ok, let's start the morning off with you telling me about some of the things you'd feel guilty about when you were a child. You remember, when you left last time, I asked you to think about things you think were your fault and try to separate them from the reality."

Where do I begin? Deb asked herself. To the doctor, she said, "Ok, here's a for instance. My father and I were leaving church one Sunday and I noticed a cigarette smoldering in the butt can. I didn't do anything about it. All day long I worried that the church would burn down and it would be because of me not putting out the cigarette."

"And did the church burn down?"

"No."

"And why do you think you felt it would have been your fault if it had? Why not your father? Couldn't he or any of the other people leaving the church at the same time put the cigarette out? Or the person whose cigarette it was? Why you?"

"Because I'm the one who noticed. And I didn't tell anybody. You see, I worry about everything like that. Yes, I realize now, as an adult, that might not have been my fault or my responsibility. But that's how my mind works. Silly little things that happen every day consume me. If I called out to a friend riding her bike and startled her so much she fell off, it would be my fault. It would just escalate from there. I imagine the broken arm, the ambulance coming, the parents yelling at me 'she'll never be a concert pianist', and on and on."

"Uh huh. Concert pianist, ha-ha." Pause, look at notes. "Well now, let's move on to another topic. Tell me a bit about your family. No siblings, right? Just you, your mother and father?"

"Doctor, I really don't see what my family has to do with anything. I had a family. They raised me. End of story."

"Just humor me, okay?"

"Right. Not much to tell. Father worked. Mother stayed home doing the 50's housewife thing."

"Happy?"

"Who?"

"Anyone. Everyone. Would you say it was a happy childhood?"

"I guess so. Nobody beat me up or anything. The occasional spanking, but that was the norm back then."

"Your father, tell me about your father."

"Like I said, he worked you know, he was a white collar executive type. Came home every night, had a drink or two or three, ate dinner, watched TV, went to bed. Did the usual stuff, mowed the lawn, handyman fix-its around the house."

"That's what he did. What was he like?"

"Oh. Well, he was funny. Probably the best story teller I ever knew. Everybody loved him."

"You?"

"Of course," she replied curtly.

"Were you close?"

"Close? Not really. I mean, it seemed I always disappointed him. You see, he had wanted a boy. And I wasn't." She gestured toward her body. "He wanted his child to excel in school, maybe be a doctor or lawyer, you know, ultra successful. And I didn't or wasn't." She shrugged, "He was nice enough to me but sometimes he scared me. He could make me cry just by looking at me. We sort of kept our distance. But he wasn't a bad guy. Like I said, everybody loved him."

"Uh huh. And your mother?"

"Yeah, she loved him too."

"No, I meant tell me about your mother."

"Oh. She wasn't a happy woman, though she hid it well in front of other people. To them, she was the kind of person they liked. You know, kind. Pretty. Stylish. Smart too. She was as smart as my dad. I don't think a lot of people knew that about her."

"So you were close to her?"

"I wouldn't say that."

"Why do you think that was? That you weren't close to either parent?"

"I don't know. They were my parents. They acted like parents. Never were very interested in what I was doing or who my friends were. As long as I wasn't getting into trouble, they pretty much left me alone."

Scribble, scribble. Look at phone.

"And you were happy with that?"

"What do you mean?"

"Did you like being, as you say, left alone?"

"It's what I knew."

"Ever wish you had a sister or brother to keep you company? Someone to talk to?"

"Hah. That was never going to happen."

"Why?"

"Why? You really want to know? Because," she laughed, "they didn't even want one child. Much less two or three."

"Really? Why would you say that?"

"She told me."

"Who? Your mother?"

"Yeah."

"Was she angry when she said that? You know, people say things in anger they don't really mean."

"No, she wasn't angry."

"So tell me, how did this come about? Do you remember the scenario?"

Deb let out a snort. "Like it happened yesterday. We were watching Perry Mason on television, I was about 10 or so. I said something about wanting to be a lawyer. She said 'well, don't have any children. Having a child ruins your life, steals your dreams.' Just like that."

"Oh my. That must have been hard to hear."

"Yeah."

"Then what? What did you do. Or say?"

"Nothing. Finished watching the show and went to bed."

"How did you feel?"

"Feel? How did I feel? Oh Doctor, how do you think I felt? How does a 10 year old feel? Responsible? I don't know. There I was, the reason she always seemed so unhappy around me. I kinda felt that if I just disappeared, then she'd be happy, you know, have her dreams back."

After a minute, she said, "It's not easy knowing you ruined someone's life." Then added with resignation, "No wonder she was so pro choice."

Dr. Nutley sat quietly, no fussing or fidgeting, eyeing Deb with his head cocked to one side, waiting for her to go on.

But Deb was finished. She had nothing more to say. She had never told anyone about that day and wished she hadn't now.

Finally, she sighed and said sarcastically, "So Doctor, can you fix that?"

"No, Deb. I can't," he replied matter-of-factly. "I can't make that go away. But I do think I can help lift the burden from you. You've been carrying this guilt that your parents imposed on you for far too long. It has colored your perception of reality, made you assume the blame for things you are not responsible for."

He looked knowingly at her. "You need to fully realize and understand where the fault or guilt or responsibility actually lies."

"Right," sarcasm again.

"No, seriously Deb. I can't tell you how often I see this kind of thing. Maybe not yours exactly, but I have, and had, many patients who are laden with guilt. Some deservedly so. Most not. A lot of professionals look to our religions as a major factor. We've all heard of Catholic guilt, Jewish guilt. So much of it is carried by women. Why? Possibly because one of the first things we're told is the story of original sin. It was Eve's fault, they say. She gave Adam the apple. So women are taught from an early age that when bad things happen, they should look to themselves for the reason."

He continued, "But was it Eve's fault? Who put the apple there? Or, for that matter, the snake?"

Deb grunted.

"In the end," the doctor continued, "it's a moot point. What we have to focus on is your guilt and whether or not it is justified."

He paused. Looked at his watch. "I want you to think about this. Go back over your list, if indeed you did make one, and see where the blame truly lies. Again I will tell you to be completely honest with yourself."

"And how do I do that?"

"Try to take yourself out of the equation. Take the situation and replace you with someone else, say, your daughter or son. If it happened to them, would you blame them? Start there." He stuffed his hands in his pockets. "And now, our time is up."

He stood, once again papers fell to the floor. He looked at her and pointed to the papers, "That, my friend, was my fault."

Deb walked down to the little coffee shop, ordered a Chai tea latte and sat down. She wondered if the doctor was right. If women are ingrained with the guilt gene. Snippets of conversations she'd had with other women floated through her mind. The head of the PTA guilt-ridden because nobody showed up for meetings, the young girl blaming herself because her dog ran after a squirrel and got hit by a car, Donna worrying that the reason her son was gay was because she had let him play with dolls, not insisting on trucks.

Was it just women though? No, she knew Joe always worried that someone had misunderstood an offhand comment he made. But in Joe's mind, it wasn't his fault really, it was the fault of the other person who didn't get that Joe was kidding. It seemed to Deb that men were always able to shift the blame onto someone else in the end. Look at all those cheating husbands who fault their wives for their wandering eye. And the wives often took the blame with the old 'I let myself go, I'm not interesting or sexy or smart enough.' Ugh.

Deb's musings were interrupted by, "Mrs. Cromwell?"

She looked up and saw Tyler McCann, blue eyes pivoting from her face to her tea, back to her face.

"Tyler?" Now this was a surprise. "Wh, wh, what are you doing here?" She heard herself say, "How are you?" and was shocked how normal she sounded.

"Um, ah, can I sit down?"

"Yes, yes, of course. Please." Mind racing, what do I say? How do I handle this? She glanced around, noticing the coffee shop was almost empty.

Tyler pulled a chair out and sat down nervously. He put his coffee on the table, and clenched his hands around it as if clinging to a lifeline. "I, I, I need to tell you something," he mumbled.

"Oh." It was a statement, not a question.

"Well, um, ah, you know that thing that happened to you?"

"Yeeess," should I stop him or let him go on?

"Well, you see, um, it was me."

"Yes, I know," faintly.

"Huh?"

"Tyler, I know it was you," almost inaudibly.

"Oh." Silence. Studying his coffee. "I, I, I'm sorry. So sorry. I don't know what's wrong with me. Why I did it. I didn't want to hurt you. I like you. You've always been nice to me. I was scared."

"I know."

"Why were you even there? At that time of the morning? You shouldn't be out running around like that. Don't you know bad things happen?"

"I do." Slight smile. Somehow she was answering. A confidence she didn't feel was inexplicably coming through her voice.

"I guess you've got the cops looking for me."

"No. At least not yet."

His head popped up. "No? Why not?"

"It's a long story, Tyler. One I'm not ready to tell yet."

"Oh."

"Tyler, what's going on with you? she asked plaintively.

"Oh Mrs. C, I don't know. I just fuck things up."

"You certainly did that day." She couldn't believe how sure of herself she sounded.

"Yeah."

"Tyler, listen. I want to know what's been happening with you. Really.

I care about you and I worry about you. Talk to me."

For the next hour, Tyler talked to her. Told her everything. Haltingly at first, then it just spilled out of him. How his mother started drinking after his father died. How she left him with his grandmother who did her best but was old and broken. How ashamed he was at school because his clothes were ragged and dirty. How nobody ever treated him the way they used to. How the girls always looked at him with those pitying glances and the boys with their nasty asides. How he couldn't find a decent job. How he felt so angry and hurt. How easy it was to escape, first by smoking pot, then moving on to other stuff. How there was never enough money.

She sat there listening, tears trickling down her face as she watched him lay his life on the bare Formica table.

At last, silence.

Then, "You asked," he said almost defensively as he picked up his cold coffee and took a long drink.

"Yes I did. Thank you."

He eyed her guardedly. "Thank you? Am I supposed to say you're welcome?"

"No, no, no. I just meant thank you for trusting me enough to tell me that. I know it wasn't easy."

"Now I guess I'm off to jail."

"Maybe." For some reason she didn't understand, she wasn't ready to let him off the hook.

Her phone rang. She fished it out of her purse and seeing it was Joe calling, clicked it to answer.

"Joe, hi. Hold on a minute, ok?"

She said to Tyler, "It's my husband. I'll only be a minute."

"That's ok, Mrs. C. I gotta go." He picked up his coffee cup, threw it in the trash can and walked out with Deb calling after him.

"Tyler, Tyler. Wait," to no avail.

Deb turned back to her phone. "I'm back. You still there?"

Stop to listen.

"Just checking in. Finished with Dr. Nutley?"

"Yeah. Joe, listen. This is unbelievable. After I left the office, I came down to that little coffee shop, you know the one. Anyway, I was drinking my tea when, oh my god, you won't believe this, in walks Tyler McCann!"

"No! Really? Did you talk to him?"

"More like he talked to me," she said thoughtfully. "I don't want to go into it on the phone, but Joe, it's just too sad. We've really got to help this kid. If I wasn't sure before, I am now. I'll explain when I get home. Wait for me." She clicked off before Joe had a chance to answer, still bewildered by the person she was able to become, talking to Tyler.

In her idling car, Deb mulled the coffee shop encounter over and over in her head. How was she able to stay so calm? So collected? Before, whenever she considered what this meeting with Tyler would be like, she always saw herself stumbling, faltering, searching for the right words. But today? Today she came off as so controlled, so sure of herself. Why?

Thinking maybe Joe would help her understand, she shifted the car into drive and made her way home.

Joe was outside, feigning interest in the clematis' progress on the mailbox post. He wished he had gone with her to her appointment, had been there when Tyler approached her. What, he wondered, would have been his reaction? *Certainly not welcoming*, he though wryly. He imagined decking the guy, but realized, of course, that he wouldn't. He had never hit anyone, except maybe his sisters or cousins when they were young. Probably too afraid of getting hit back. Joe, like Deb, feared pain and avoided it at any cost.

Deb's car pulled onto the street as he bent over to yank a weed from the clematis bed. He straightened up, waved and went to open her car door.

"Eventful morning, eh?" he asked.

"You could say that," as she followed him into the house.

"Tea?"

"I'd rather a drink, but it's too early."

"Never too early for a Bloody Mary. Want one?"

"Actually, yes," she replied gratefully as she made a fuss over the excited dog. "That would be great." She gave the dog a biscuit and checked the answering machine. Nothing interesting, just a lot of hang-ups from robo-callers.

"I'm anxious to hear about seeing Tyler," Joe said as he cut the celery for the drinks, trying to sound nonchalant.

"It was strange."

"I imagine so."

Joe handed Deb her drink and they moved out to the patio.

Deb took a long sip and closed her eyes as the cooling liquid washed down her throat. "Ummm, I needed that." She fondled the glass, wiping moisture down the sides while she considered where to start. *At the beginning,* she decided.

She continued fussing with her glass as she told Joe the whole story. How Tyler approached her, their initial interaction, how she was surprised how cool, calm and collected she came off, how Tyler just opened up and unleashed his entire life story to her.

She ended with "Then the phone rang with you calling and Tyler took off. I didn't have a chance to get a number to reach him or anything. He just left. I called after him, but he never came back. I waited a few minutes, hoping he'd change his mind. No luck." Another long gulp.

Joe sat quietly listening. He too fiddled with his drink, stirring it with the celery, occasionally taking a sip or a bite. He was letting it all sink in. When she finished, he continued to stir, contemplating what to say.

"That's some story," he managed.

"I know, right?"

Pause. "So what do you think, Joe?"

"I think you're right. It is pretty strange." he answered slowly. "I'm not sure what more you want me to say."

"Hah, I'm not either. Are you as surprised as I am that I didn't freak out? I was so controlled, it was like I was somebody else."

"I don't think that's all that surprising. You were always very controlled and calm with the kids. Not just our kids, but the neighbor kids, the school kids. Although I have no idea why you weren't scared. You should have been scared."

"Actually, I was. On the inside. But something seemed to overtake me. It was really weird."

"Uh huh." He looked at his wife and wondered what more he could say. He knew she thought Tyler's story would completely turn him around, convince him that Tyler needed their help.

"Deb, how do you know he was telling you the truth? Addicts are manipulative, you know."

"I just know. He didn't ask me for anything. Didn't even ask me not to go to the cops. He was so sincere, so lost."

"I don't know. This is too much." He added after a minute, "If only you had just stayed in the house that day, none of this would have happened."

There it is, Deb thought, the guilt. It's my fault once again. She felt the anger and shame swirl inside her like the waters of a whirlpool pulling away from the safety and security of the river bank. She stood, picked up her drink. "Thanks," she said sarcastically, "I needed that." She strode into the house slamming the door behind her.

Tense days followed. Neither of them spoke of it again. They spent their time deftly maneuvering around each other, Deb handling normal day-to-day chores, Joe working in his office more than usual. When they did speak, Joe was overly nice, Deb was curt.

He was afraid of saying the wrong thing again. She knew he was right and hated him for it.

The morning of Deb's next appointment with Dr. Nutley found them in the kitchen. Joe, eyes focused on the newspaper said, "Want me to go with you today?"

"What for?"

"For you."

"Me? Why?"

"Well, you have a lot to tell him and I thought maybe it would be easier for you if I was there."

"Easier how?"

Joe was entering the mine field again, attempting to make the right moves but fearing his words would trip an explosion.

"Never mind, it was just a thought," he said.

"No, Joe. You've already done enough." She grabbed her tea cup and left the room.

Joe kept his gaze on the paper, afraid to look at her. *Damn*, he thought, *I should have just kept my mouth shut.*

A few minutes later, Deb came back into the kitchen dressed to leave. "I'm going now," gave him a perfunctory kiss on his forehead and walked out the door.

He was relieved to see her go. The air in the room, the whole house, cleared. He wasn't sure how much more of this he could take without blowing a gasket. He sat at the table mulling things over, then made a decision. He picked up his phone and called Sam, one of his golfing buddies.

"Sam," he said into the phone, "What's your schedule like the next few days?"

"Pretty empty. Summer ya know. Why?"

"Well, we've been talking about checking out some of the courses in Maryland and Virginia. I thought now's as good a time as any. We could see if Jeff and Dennis want to go too."

"Sounds great! I'll just have to clear some things out. When do you want to go?"

"Tomorrow?"

"Great. I'll call Jeff. You call Dennis."

They spent the next few minutes going over which courses and hotels they wanted to visit, then hung up, duties firmly placed. Joe sat back and smiled. He needed this. Needed it badly. At this point in time, he didn't even care what Deb would think about it. *She'll probably be happy I'm going,* he thought, as he went into his office to make his calls.

Chapter Sixteen

Deb stood on the porch, dog by her side, watching Joe's car drive down the street. She gave a final, weak smile and wave goodbye, turned and went back inside the house. It was eerily quiet, the echo of Joe's footsteps completely faded. She could feel the tension flowing out the door as his car traveled farther and farther away.

She roamed around the house picking up stray shoes, straightening magazines, tidying the kitchen, a tad surprised when she heard herself softly singing. Should she be upset that he decided, at this critical point, to take off on a buddy trip? Maybe. But she wasn't.

Really, who could blame him. There he was, caught in the middle of this made-for-Lifetime-TV movie scenario through no fault of his own.

She patted the dog on his head and said reassuringly, "He isn't running away from you. He's running away from me. Anyway, he'll be back. It's just a little getaway." She sighed, knowing she was right. Joe wasn't the kind of man who would go away like this and not come back. If he ever did leave, he'd do it when she wasn't around. She imagined herself coming home from the grocery store and finding a note on the kitchen table. All it would say would be "Sorry." Since the day they married, she had expected him to walk out on her, realize he never loved her, found someone new, and so on and so forth. She had played various leaving scenes so often in her head that when it finally did happen, she would be fully prepared. She'd be disappointed, upset, angry, hurt, and relieved that she wouldn't have to wait for the so-called other shoe to drop any longer.

Deb went to the china cabinet, got out her rarely used English teapot and filled it with hot water. Satisfied the pot was warm enough, she spooned loose tea leaves in and filled it with fresh boiling water. While it steeped, she ruffled through the mail throwing out everything but the bills, which she took into the office. Returning to the kitchen, she fished some shortbread cookies from the pantry and took her tea out to the patio. The phone rang. Zannah.

"Hi hon."

"Hey Mom, what's up?"

"Nothing much. Just sitting on the patio enjoying my afternoon tea. It's a beautiful day."

"Nice. Dad golfing?"

"Sort of." Short laugh. "Actually, he and some friends just left for a golf trip, down to Maryland and Virginia."

"Really? Now? Had this been planned?"

"No, not really. I mean, they've been talking about it for a while, but they finally decided to go now. I think he just needed to get away."

"And you're ok with that?" A hint of worry crossed her voice.

"Sure. It's no big deal. We could both use a break. Things have been a little tense around here since I saw Tyler."

"Wait, wait, wait. You saw Tyler?"

"Yeah, I guess I didn't get around to telling you and Miles about it. I ran into him after one of my sessions with Dr. Nutley."

"Seriously? That's so weird. What happened? What did you do?"

Deb gave Zannah a brief rundown of the conversation, hoping it was detailed enough to allay any further questions. She ended with, "That's about it. He took off when the phone rang before I could get any more information from him."

Zannah, listening intently, interjected a few oh my's and wow's. Now she said, "That's some story."

"Yeah, isn't it?"

"So what are you going to do now?" The news of her father's trip had evaporated from her mind.

"I dunno. What is there to do? Guess I'll just wait until I see him again."

"So you're going to go ahead with your plan? Dr. Nutley okayed it?"

"Not really. I mean, he didn't okay it but he also didn't veto it. Says it's not his place. It's up to your dad and me."

"Hmm. I guess that's where the tension came in, huh?"

"You could say that. I think your father was hoping I'd never be able to get a hold of Tyler and it would become a non-issue. You know, days, weeks, months and years would pass until it was just a bizarre memory."

"That could still happen," Zannah said thoughtfully. Then, "Wow. Wait until I tell Simon and Miles. I can tell them, can't I?"

"Of course. I should have told you both before but I just didn't get around to it. It would actually be easier for me if you did, ha-ha."

"Okay. Good." Short pause. "You all right?"

"Yes, I'm fine. But my tea is getting cold," she had had about enough of this conversation and was ready for it to be over.

"Okay, okay. I can take a hint," Zannah laughed. "I'll talk to you soon, ok?"

"Yes, fine. I love you."

"Love you too, Mom."

Deb put the phone down and chewed on a cookie. She could just picture Zannah frantically texting Miles, interrupting his workday with news of their crazy mother. "Big news! Mom saw Tyler. Call me!!!!!"

Miles would quickly check the message, shake his head and wait until he was home, bottle of beer at his side before he called.

Kids, she thought. She understood that she'd never know what they really thought about this whole mess. Their world view was different. Had to be. She cringed when she thought about her parents and how much she kept from them, realizing her children did the same with her and Joe.

"Oh well, nothing I can do about that, is there?" she asked the dog perched happily by her side waiting for his share of her cookie.

He gave a small yip and wagged his tail as if he understood.

Just then, she heard the doorbell ring. She snuck around the side of the house surreptitiously checking to see if it was someone selling something or one of those political action committee people hoping for a donation.

It wasn't. It was Officers Shepherd and Lambo.

She straightened herself, ran her fingers through her hair, emerged from her hiding place and walked toward them.

"Officers, surprised to see you. How are you?"

"Good, Mrs. Cromwell, good," replied Officer Shepherd. Lambo nodded his head in agreement. "You?"

"Fine, fine. What can I do for you?"

"Can we come in for a minute? We'd like to talk to you."

"Oh, of course! I'm sorry." She moved past them and opened the front door. "After you."

The officers went in, quickly scanned their surroundings and settled at the kitchen table. After accepting Deb's offer of iced tea, they got down to business.

"Mrs. Cromwell, how are you feeling? It's been a while and we were hoping that maybe you've remembered something about your accident," Officer Lambo said. He seemed to be the mouthpiece for them. "Anything would be helpful."

"Umm, yes actually."

"Really? That's great!"

"Yes, I suppose."

"Well? What do you remember?"

Deb was torn, unsure how much she should tell them. "I was on my way to my father's, going to start cleaning out his place, he had just died, you know."

"Yes."

"I had slowed down for the stop sign and my car was rammed from the back. I got out to, you know, get the driver's information and stuff, when this guy came and hit me on the head."

"Can you describe the guy?"

"Wellllll, he had on a ski mask so I didn't see his face."

"Uh huh. How tall? Weight? Anything more?"

"It all happened so fast. He was taller than me, but not real tall. Weight? I'd say average build." She was looking at the table, fearing the officer would know she was not being completely forthcoming.

Officer Lambo was busily jotting notes.

"Anything else? How about the car that hit you? Color? Make? Model?"

"Gosh, I don't know. It was dark. I really didn't have time to notice."

"But there was just the one perpetrator?"

"Noooo," she said slowly, as if just recalling it clearly. "The one who hit me got out of the passenger side, so I guess there was a driver too. I didn't see that person." *Oh my,* she thought, *who was the other person?*

"Good. Good. This is all good information, Mrs. Cromwell."

"Um, Officer?"

"Yes?"

"Have there been any more of those, what did you call it, bump and run incidents?"

"Now that's the odd thing. Before yours, there were a bunch. After yours, nothing."

"Huh," she said with a slight smile. "Interesting."

"But don't you worry. We're continuing to investigate. We want to catch this guy, or guys. We'll get 'em."

"Oh I'm not worried," she said almost carelessly.

The officer gave her a sharp look.

Deb noticed and added, "I mean, you guys do a great job."

"Oh, right. Yes. Thanks. We do our best."

"If there's nothing else, I really should get dinner started," she said as she stood up from the table.

"No, no. I guess that's it. Thanks for your time. And please, if you remember anything else, give us a call."

"Sure, will do," she answered with a smile.

She led them to the door. Before leaving, Officer Lambo stopped, turned and said to Deb, "Just one last thing. Why didn't you contact us when you got your memory back?"

Startled, Deb took a moment, then said apologetically, "I guess I just forgot."

Deb closed the door with a calm she didn't feel. Her mind was racing. Did they know she was keeping something from them? She had never been a good liar and was always intimidated by authority figures, especially the police. If they didn't believe her, they had let it go. For now, at least.

She leaned against the door replaying the conversation in her mind. Someone else was there. Who? Tyler never mentioned anyone else. She was willing, in fact eager, to help Tyler, but what about this other person? This accomplice? What would she do about him? Or her?

This is crazy, she told herself. *Get a grip. The chances of you finding Tyler again are slim, so what's there to worry about? Deal with it when and if it happens.*

Chapter Seventeen

Joe sliced his drive off the tee, too busy pondering Deb's text message. It was the last day of his trip, which until now had been blissfully free of any drama. Slam. Back to the real world.

'Tyler in outpatient rehab. Staying at the house. Last minute decision. Hope you don't mind. Love you.'

He smiled ruefully at his golf partners. "Sorry, my head's just not into it today, I guess."

Later, sitting at the bar in the 19th hole, he filled his friends in on the latest Deb news. "I just don't know what to do," he confessed.

"You only have two choices," Dennis replied taking a swig of his beer. "Either go home and make the best of it or don't."

"What do you mean, don't?"

"I mean, don't go home. Go stay at Jim's until this works itself out. He's got plenty of room. I'd say you could come to my house but that would be weird, right next door."

"Hey, what about me?" Jeff interjected laughing.

"You two would just get into trouble."

"I couldn't do that. I'm not going to leave her," Joe said. "That just wouldn't be right."

"Was it right for her to just go ahead and move this kid in without talking to you first?"

"Well, no, but that's just Deb. Actually, when I think about it, I'm not all that surprised. You know her. I'm lucky she texted me."

Jim piped up, "Sounds like a midlife crisis to me."

"Aren't we too old for mid-life crises?"

"Yeah. Maybe she's bored with the empty nest. What with Zannah out in Lalaland and Miles doing whatever Miles does in the city," Dennis said. "Donna says Deb seems awfully lonely."

"Lonely? I'm around all the time!"

"Sure, but how much taking care of do you need? Face it, she's spent most of her life taking care of somebody. Not anymore. You guys don't even have any grandchildren."

"True," Joe replied thoughtfully. This was a completely different track that he had never even considered. He wondered if Deb had. She had definitely been at her happiest when the kids were younger. Always busy juggling work, scheduling, cooking, transporting, lending a sympathetic ear or doling out advice. Now she wasn't even working. Who knows how she filled her days? Playing solitaire and cleaning? Sounded pretty empty, even to Joe.

"You know," Joe said to Dennis, "You might have something there."

"Of course I do! After all, I'm the smart one of the group."

That comment started off a barrage of banter, going from comparisons to Einstein to simple one-up-manship to idiotic politicians and sports figures to the latest Mr. Robot episode, giving Joe a much needed diversion.

They ordered dinner and discussed what time to leave in the morning, which brought about "So, you going home?"

Joe thought fleetingly about how it would be, to be on his own. No one to worry about but himself. Do the single guy thing again. Then Miles and Zannah popped into his head. And Deb. No. The old 'til death do us part' meant something to him. He looked from one friend to the other. "As tempting as it is to just walk away, I can't do it. It wouldn't be right. I couldn't live with myself if I did."

"That's my boy," Dennis said raising his glass to toast Joe. "Here's to sticking it out!"

"To sticking it out," they yelled in unison, clicking glasses and spilling beer.

Deb paced nervously around the family room, checking the clock every few minutes. She had expected that Joe would call when he got her text, but all she got was silence. She looked at her phone. Yes, the message had been delivered. No reply. Dr. Nutley had advised her to wait and come to an agreement with Joe. But things had happened so quickly. Why hadn't he called? Because he was mad? Would she ever hear from him again? *Don't be silly*, she told herself. *He'll come walking through that door any minute now.*

With that thought, she heard the garage door open and went to the kitchen, trying to look busy.

Joe came in, laid his keys and wallet on the island and faced her. "Hi."

Deb turned toward him, "Hi."

She searched his face for a clue. There was none. She began chattering nervously about anything but Tyler, to fill the void.

He only half listened, looking around for signs of the unspoken guest. There were none.

"Deb," he said, breaking into her endless stream, "I considered not coming home."

She stopped short. "Oh."

"I didn't. I mean, I did. Come home. You should know, though, there were better ways to do this. Texting was the sneaky way. The epitome of passive aggressive."

"I know," she replied. "But you weren't here. I had to act right away or I was afraid I'd lose him again."

"So you were afraid of losing Tyler but not me?"

"I, I , I didn't think..."

"That's right." he interrupted, "You didn't think. Once again, you just barreled on ahead, not caring what I would think. Am I that much of a pushover, that insignificant?"

"No, no, I..."

"You knew, right? Knew that I was against this. But you didn't care. Didn't think how it could affect our marriage. Our home. Damn it, Deb." He slammed his fist onto the island, "You put me in a horrible place. It's just not right." He stalked to the family room and threw himself into his chair.

She stayed where she was, frozen. Eventually, she made her way to a kitchen chair and lowered herself into it.

They remained in their respective positions for quite a while. No one speaking or moving. The dog, aware something intense was happening, retreated to the corner.

Finally, Deb gathered her courage and moved to the family room.

She sat down across from him and waited for him to look at her. Then she said, "Joe, I'm sorry."

"I'm sure you are," he replied harshly. "A little late for that, don't you think?"

"Yes."

Long silence as each considered what to say or do next.

Deb broke the silence with, "How badly did I screw up? Are you going to leave?"

"I'm here, aren't I?"

"For how long?"

"I don't know."

More dead air.

This time Joe spoke first. "I suppose I should hear how this all came about," he said.

"Ok. Yes," Deb's relief showed in her voice.

She started at the beginning, with the visit from Officers Shepherd and Lambo. Told him about the realization there was someone else involved in the attempted carjacking. About how she became uncertain that this was the right thing to do, considering the new information.

"But then, Joe, the next day Tyler showed up here. Here at the house. He knocked on the door. I can tell you, I was shocked. Couldn't believe it. I wouldn't let him in though. I made him stay on the porch. He told me he was sorry he ran off. Somehow, and Joe, I don't know how I did it, but somehow I convinced him to go to the police and turn himself and the other guy in."

Joe looked up sharply. "Really?"

"Yes. Yes, I did. I told him I wanted to help him, but he had to come clean. I said I wouldn't press charges, but I didn't know about the other people. He said that time with me was the first and only time for him."

"Sure," Joe interjected sarcastically.

"It's true. The other guy had done it before and Tyler owed him a lot of money, so he had to go along. He didn't want to but the guy said it was easy peasy and they could get a lot for the car. His debt would be paid."

"Uh huh."

"But of course it wasn't, 'cause they didn't end up with my car. Tyler's been kind of hiding out ever since, trying to keep away from that guy."

She paused to catch her breath.

"So we went down to the police station to see Officer Shepherd. They had to call him in from the road, but we waited until he got there. Tyler was so nervous, he didn't know what they were going to do to him. Officer Shepherd took him into another room and Tyler told him everything. They booked him. God, I felt like I was in the middle of some crime show. Mug shots, fingerprinting, the whole bit. Then the cops ran out. It took a while, but they picked up the other guy. His name is Sam something, I forget, but he's a real shady character. Had a list of priors and everything, they told me. Anyhow, apparently this is what this guy does. Lends kids money, then when they can't pay, forces them to do all this bad stuff. A real modern day Fagin.

"They were so nice about it. To Tyler, I mean. Real understanding. Of course, they pressed charges but the judge let him off on, what is it? on his own recognizance? I think if he testifies against this Sam somebody, he might get let off."

Joe felt like he was in a dream, listening to Deb. He found it hard to imagine her taking control like that, finding some inner grit that he hadn't seen before.

He said, "I can guess where it went from there. When you two left the station, you told him he could stay here."

"Well, yes. Where was he to go? I admit, I should have called you. But I know you turn your phone off when you're playing. Then things just got away from me. And too, I was kind of afraid to ask you. But I was sure once you heard the whole story, you'd agree. I just wanted to tell you in person."

"So you have."

"That's not all though. I didn't just let him stay here. There are rules. I told him he had to enter a rehab program and go to AA. No more drugs or alcohol. He has to help out around the house. Get a job, even if it's just part time. If he strays from those rules, he's out."

"So where is he now?"

"He's at rehab, a meeting. When he gets back, he has to weed the garden," she let a smile erupt.

"Ok." Resignation filled his voice. "I guess we'll see how it goes. I'm still not convinced, but I'll give it a try. I might come up with some rules of my own, you know. You owe me that at least."

"Yes. Yes. Definitely. Thanks, Joe, thanks."

Shortly after, when Joe was unpacking and Deb was loading the washer, Tyler came in. He found Deb in the laundry room.

"I see Mr. Cromwell is home," he said uncertainly. "He ok with this?"

"Sort of. He's upstairs. You should talk to him."

"I don't know, Mrs. C. What should I say?"

"That's up to you, Tyler. Just do it. Joe's a good guy. Go."

Tyler squared his shoulders and went to find Joe. He saw him from the hallway putting some clothes in the dresser. He walked to the bedroom and knocked.

"Um, Mr. Cromwell?"

Joe turned and saw the lanky figure, head down, standing like a lost waif in the doorway. In spite of himself, his heart melted.

"Yes, Tyler? Come in."

"Thanks. I, I just wanted to say thank you, you know, for letting me stay here. It's real nice of you and Mrs. C."

"Yes."

"I was pretty screwed up. You must hate me for what I did, you know, to Mrs. C."

"Hate's a strong word, Tyler. Although I'll admit I had visions of decking you."

"Yeah. I get that."

"Just to let you know, I'm not the pushover that Deb is. I know how manipulative users can be. She's convinced me to give you a chance. You've got it. One chance. You mess up and you're out the door. I'll give you the proverbial inch. Don't think you can take a mile. You will not disrupt the life we've built any more than you have so far."

"Yes, sir. I understand."

"Good," he said with finality.

He pulled his toiletries bag from his suitcase. When he came back from the bathroom, Tyler was still standing there.

Joe said, "Deb tells me you're going to weed this afternoon. Why don't you get started on the front bed?"

"Yes. Thank you," he let out a sigh of relief. "Yes. I'll go now."

"Good. There's a bucket in the garage you can use for the weeds. There's gloves and a spade there too. Careful you don't pull out any of the perennials."

"Ok. You got it. And thanks again. I won't let you down."

"Sure. Ok," Joe said.

Tyler almost raced down the stairs. Joe watched him go, doubt clouding his mind. He wished he was as optimistic as his wife. *"Guess I'll just try to make the best of this,"* he said to himself, and went into his office to prepare a list of chores.

When he finished, he went outside to where Tyler was weeding. Tyler looked up and said, "Mr. Cromwell, you want me to trim back those bushes on the side of the house?"

"Why yes, Tyler, they are looking a bit scraggly. You know how to do it?"

"Kind of. When I was little I used to watch my dad do it."

"Let me show you." Joe went into the garage for the hedge clippers and proceeded to instruct Tyler. "First you've got to remove the dead stuff, like this here, and any stems that are damaged. Keep your eye out for branches that are crossing, fix them like this. Then get rid of these little growing shoots. See? "

"Like these here?"

"Yup. Get rid of those." He was pleased that the boy was paying close attention. He really did seem eager to help. *Just hope it lasts,* he thought.

The two set about clipping and pruning the remaining bushes, occasionally wiping sweat from their brows and necks. After an hour, Joe stepped back to look at their work.

"Looks pretty good. Nice job, Tyler."

"Thanks."

"Deb will be happy. She's been after me for a while to get these hedges in shape. Let's go get something to drink. Lemonade or iced tea? Or you want a soda?" They headed toward the house.

"Lemonade thanks. Won't drink soda."

"Oh? Why not? On a health kick or something?"

"They told me in rehab that I shouldn't drink anything I used to mix with alcohol. Guess it's one of those triggers or something."

"Makes sense, I guess."

They entered the kitchen where Deb was already filling three big glasses with ice. "What's your pleasure?" she asked.

Joe desperately wanted a beer but decided against it and said, "Lemonade, please."

"Really? I thought you'd want a beer."

"Yeah well," Joe replied as he cocked his head toward Tyler.

Tyler laughed and said, "Mr. C, you can have a beer. It's all right. Just 'cause I can't drink doesn't mean you can't."

"I don't want to make it harder on you."

"Believe me, it's hard anyway. I just gotta get used to it."

"No, that's ok. Lemonade is fine."

"Up to you," Tyler said as he put the drinks on a tray. "Patio?" and carried it out followed by Deb and Joe.

That night at dinner, Joe quizzed Tyler about his progress. "So tell me, Tyler, how often do you have to go to meetings or rehab or whatever they call it?"

"So far every day. That's the deal I made with Mrs. C. But, you know, I don't really need it. I'm not an addict or anything."

"Really? You think that?"

"Yeah. I mean, I like doing stuff, but I don't have to."

"So when's the last time you did any drugs?"

"The day before I came here."

"Huh."

Deb chimed in, "He's been doing really well. Going every day like he said. Helping me around here. We're going to start looking for a job for him."

"Yeah," Tyler said, "it's not gonna be easy though. I don't have any experience."

Joe looked at him, "Everyone has to start somewhere. Of course, that tattoo won't make it easy. You seem pretty handy in the kitchen. Maybe a restaurant. Start as a dishwasher or busboy, keep your eyes open and learn how it works, possibly move up from there. Or you could be a barista or work in a deli. Anything that will keep you busy."

"Maybe," Tyler was hesitant.

"But I'd like to go back to the rehab discussion, Tyler. Do you seriously think you don't have a problem?"

"Nah. It's all under control."

"Deb told me you owed this Sam guy a lot of money. What's that about?"

"I wouldn't say a lot of money."

"How much?"

"Only a couple of thousand."

"You don't think that's a lot of money?" Joe was incredulous. "For somebody with no job? I gotta tell you Tyler, that's a lot of money for me and I have a job."

"Well, I was sorta working," Tyler was becoming evasive.

"Doing what?"

"Sort of a messenger."

"I can only imagine what that means. Were you running drugs or money for a bookie?"

"What's it matter? I'm done with all that."

"Joe..." Deb started. "He's right. He's done with all that. Going down a new road, right Tyler?"

"Right, Mrs. C."

"It matters because I think he has to be fully open about his past. After all, we've opened up our home to him. I think it's the least he can do."

"Ok, fine," Tyler said, a touch of animosity in his voice. "I was picking up the stuff and taking it to the kids who were selling."

"So you were running drugs."

"Yeah."

"What? Crack? Heroin? What?"

"Whatever they gave me to move."

"I see. So how'd it come about that you owe this guy money? Let me guess, you used the drugs instead of selling, right?"

"Um, yeah."

"And you think you don't have a problem?"

"No. Like I said, I'm done with all that. I'm making a clean start."

"I don't think it's as easy as you seem to think it is. I mean, what's it been? Two, three days?"

"Something like that."

"I think that's enough grilling for now," Deb said. "Let's get these dishes cleaned up. There's that show, The Tunnel on TV I want to watch tonight. You can watch with us if you want, Tyler."

"Thanks, Mrs. C, I think I'll go to a meeting tonight though."

After the kitchen was cleaned up and Tyler left, Deb said to Joe, "You were a little rough on him."

"Think so? I don't. Deb, he's not facing reality. You heard him. Anyone who was doing what he admits to doing is probably only owning up to maybe half of it. I hate to think what the whole truth is."

"Oh you have so little faith," Deb replied dismissively.

"You have too much. I really have no idea where this whole new rosy outlook you have is coming from. It's not like you."

"Maybe it's a new me."

"I'm just saying, we have to be alert and ready for when he fails."

"He's not going to fail. I'm sure of it."

"I'm sure he will. When he does, he's out."

"Yes, yes, okay." Then under her breath, "but it's not going to happen."

Chapter Eighteen

Days passed uneventfully. Tyler went to meetings, applied for jobs at pizza joints, grocery stores and landscapers, helped with cooking and cleaning. Joe worked, mostly from home and kept a wary eye on Tyler. Deb appeared to delight in her new role as optimist and cheerleader and kept her appointments with Dr. Nutley.

Which is where we are today. Deb sitting in her usual chair facing a mussed-up Dr. Nutley, currently polishing his glasses on his shirt tail.

"Deb, it's been a few weeks now. How's Tyler working out?"

"Good, doctor, good."

"No hiccups?"

"Nope. Everything is good."

"Joe happy?"

"I wouldn't say happy. Perhaps cautious is a better word, yes. Considerately cautious."

"How so?"

"He watches Tyler like a hawk. I'm sure Tyler senses it too. He bends over backward to be nice to Joe."

"How does Joe react when that happens?"

"He's pleased things are getting done around the house that he doesn't have to do. That's the upside for him."

"And you?"

"Me?"

"Yes. How are you feeling during all of this? Any less guilty?"

"Hmm, I don't know."

"Go on."

"Oh, sometimes I wish I never got involved in this. It's really tiring, walking around on eggshells all the time. Keeping Tyler motivated and out of Joe's way. Making sure Joe isn't inconvenienced. Even though I don't want to be that person, I keep looking for signs that Tyler is using again. So I feel guilty about that. Sometimes I think Joe was right. I should have just turned Tyler into the police and let them handle the whole thing."

"Have you told Joe this?"

"Heavens no."

"Why not?"

"I don't know. Probably because he'd be relieved. And right. I don't want him to be right again. I want to be right for a change."

"That's important to you?"

"I guess it is. If I'm not right, then it's just something else I'm to blame for."

"Aren't you to blame for, as you put it, walking on eggshells all the time?"

"Thanks, doc," Deb said, sarcasm dripping. "I feel much better now."

"No. No. What I mean is, why are you walking on eggshells. Why don't you just be you?"

"Because the real me always gets me in trouble."

Quiet. Dr. Nutley waiting for her to go on.

"It's like I told you before, the real me is the one that screws everything up. Bad things happen."

"You're still holding on to a lot of guilt, aren't you?"

"I dunno."

"Seems to me that you are, you hold onto it almost like a comforter. If you accept the blame for the rape, and pretty much anything that goes wrong in your personal life, you make the people you care about blameless. Sort of saving them from the life you feel you've had to lead."

Deb stared at him. "That's ridiculous!"

"Is it? Tell me, that attack in college, you knew them, didn't you?"

She glared at him. "Yes."

"Not only did you know them, but you thought you were close to one of them. Perhaps in love?"

"Where do you get that from?"

"Little things you've said over time. I'm right though, aren't I?"

"Yes," she said in defeat.

"He and his friends were making fun of the black kids, taunting them with racist comments, throwing things at them, right? You stood up to them. And lost. Big."

He continued, "Much like with your discussion with your mother about becoming a lawyer. You told her what you felt and found out something no one should ever know."

Deb was staring at the floor.

"So years later, you're married, two children, nice enough husband..."

"He's a good husband," Deb interrupted.

"Ok, good husband," the doctor said, "that you're scared to show the real you to, because if you do, he'll take off, hurting you like everyone else you cared about. Which brings us to the here and now. You made a decision, not an easy one, mind you, to help this troubled boy. Who's not a boy really, but that's how you perceive him. Somehow you found the courage to stand up once again for what you think is the right thing to do and you started to do it. Got everyone behind you, albeit passive aggressively, but you did. I keep coming back to why."

"I told you why."

"I know what you told me, but I want the whole story about the attack, the truth. The unvarnished truth. You are holding something back. You know it and I know it. So I think it's time you gathered your courage and let it out. You need to tell somebody. I am a safe somebody. Nothing you tell me leaves this room without your okay."

Deb stared at the floor listening to the doctor. "I don't know what you mean," she said.

"Yes you do. I think when you decide to be honest about it, we'll understand the real reason you want to help Tyler."

The phone on the desk rang. He picked it up, mumbled something and hung up. To Deb he said, "My next appointment is here. Think about what I said. I think you're strong enough to face it. And Deb," he added almost as an afterthought, "I think it has very little to do with your mother."

Deb, in a daze, gathered her purse and jacket and walked through the door.

The afternoon loomed long and hot in front of Deb. She fixed herself a tall glass of iced tea and sat in the cool of the family room, drapes drawn to keep out the beating sun. She tried to read, but the words bounced around on the pages not making any sense. She looked for something on TV to watch. It seemed as though the Kardashians and Housewives of almost every county in the United States had taken over the airwaves. She toyed with the idea of brushing the dog but decided to keep her distance from the heat of his matting hair.

Annoyed and frustrated, she laid down and closed her eyes. Her session with Dr. Nutley kept invading her thoughts. *He really was a pill, that guy. Why wasn't what she told him enough? Why all the gory details? Why wasn't it enough that she wanted to help Tyler? That helping Tyler would help her? Nothing wrong with leaving it at that, was there?*

"It's enough," she said out loud.

Joe came into the room just then. "What's enough?"

She glared at him, "Nothing."

"Then why the look?"

"Oh just some stuff Nutley said at the end."

"Like what?"

"He said he wants me to figure out why I'm really doing this. Seems like he thinks I've got some subliminal reason."

"I'd guess pretty much all shrinks think there's a subliminal reason for everything. If there wasn't, they'd be out of work," he laughed.

"You got that right." She hesitated. "Joe, do you think there's some other reason I'm doing this?"

"Gee Deb, I don't know. Maybe."

"Like what?"

"I haven't got a clue. This is all on you."

"Thanks," she replied sadly. She stood up, "Guess I should get dinner started."

They heard the door open and turned around to see Tyler walk in.

"Hey Tyler, I was just about to get dinner started. Feel like helping?"

"Uh no, not right now, maybe later." He flashed her a big smile. "I've got to get an application filled out for some job I found online. I was thinking maybe you'd have time to help me."

Deb threw a victorious glance at Joe. "I'd be happy to. What's it for?"

"Some entry level marketing job."

"That's great!"

Joe looked unsure. "Don't you need a degree for that?"

"Didn't say that in the job description."

"Well good then. I'll leave you two to get at it."

Sitting at the computer, Deb read over the job description. Tyler, sitting next to her, read through it too.

"Doesn't it sound great?" he asked almost beside himself with anticipation. "See? It's a new start-up company, They say they provide the training. And there's travel opportunities. And fast growth. They even give you a laptop!"

He continued excitedly, "See here? They only promote from within. I've just got to get in."

"Tyler," she said cautiously, "did you read this part, the bit about an Associate Degree and prior leadership experience?"

"Yeah. But we can fake it, can't we?"

"I don't know how wise that would be. It's so easy for them to check that kind of stuff out."

"Yeah, but everybody wants you to have a degree. Can't we fill it out like I have one and then if they catch me, I'll say I'm working on it?" he asked defensively.

"I don't think it's a good idea to start out with a lie."

"But Mrs. C, how am I supposed to get it then?"

"I'm sorry Tyler. Maybe this isn't the job for you right now. Let's look for something else."

"No!" he said vehemently. "Just forget it!" Tyler shouted and pushed up out of his chair. "I'll never find anything decent. I'll just end of spending my life working in some grocery store putting shit on shelves."

He stormed out of the room and went upstairs. Deb could hear him rummaging around in his room. She didn't know what to say to him. He was right. Unless he got a degree, his prospects were pretty grim. Tyler came running down the stairs, headed to the door, mumbled, "I'm going out." and slammed the door behind him.

Joe, hearing the commotion, came downstairs. "What's going on?"

"We started to fill out the application. They wanted a degree and experience, neither of which he has. He wanted to fake it, you know, put in false information. I told him I didn't think it was a good idea to lie. He got pretty mad and left."

"Oh."

"I feel bad. He was so happy, excited, you know?"

"Deb, would it have been that bad to just fill it out? I'm with Tyler on this. They probably don't check that stuff out. Not for some entry level job."

"I don't know," Deb replied. "I don't want him thinking that lying is the way to get what you want."

"I know. I understand what you're saying. You're probably right. Although I think people in HR look at every application and assume it's filled with lies. Those are the ones that get hired. Not the ones who tell the truth. Look at you."

"Yeah, look at me. More than 400 resumes and applications later, still no job offer. Guess you're right, that's what the truth gets you." She shut down the computer and went to the kitchen to start dinner. "We'll talk it over with him tonight."

As she got the pork chops from the refrigerator, she said, "I wonder where he went?"

The next day, Deb and Tyler filled out the application. Deb was uneasy about what Tyler was typing in but kept silent. He appeared to have spent a lot of time figuring out the right things to say. His cover letter, although it needed some grammatical correcting, did a nice job of fudging reality. *Maybe he would be good at this*, she thought but said, "Tyler, don't get your hopes up too high on this. I think we should keep looking."

"Yeah, yeah, of course. This would be great though, wouldn't it? A real job. I could start taking classes at the community college. I'm on my way," He grinned as he clicked the submit button.

Within minutes, he received an email from the company. 'Thank you for applying for the entry level marketing and sales opportunity. We regret that, due to the high volume of applicants, we are not able to interview every applicant. However, if your qualifications meet our needs, we will contact you.'

"Now what?" he asked Deb.

"Now we wait and see. We should keep looking for other possibilities too, in case this doesn't come through."

"Don't worry, Mrs. C. It'll come through. I can feel it."

"I hope you're right, Tyler."

"You gotta have faith. Things have really turned around for me now. Because of you and Mr. C. You taking me in, helping me with the cops. It's all good." He beamed his blue eyes at her.

Deb smiled back at him, fighting off the niggling question thumping in her head. "Yes, it'll work out, Tyler. I'm sure it will."

It was Saturday. Joe had decided to show Tyler how to replace the leaky valve in the toilet and, of course, a trip to the hardware store was inevitable. Deb took the dog for a long walk. When she returned, the guys were busily deconstructing and refitting. Mission accomplished, they came down to the kitchen, making jokes about Deb's over-usage of the facilities.

"Hey Deb," Joe said as they came in. "It's almost 2:30. How about some lunch for your two handymen?"

She set about making sandwiches, marveling at what appeared to be a building camaraderie between Joe and Tyler. They chatted easily while eating about last night's Phillies game, other chores on Deb's to do list and amusing if not so scary political news.

"Hey Tyler. Dennis can't use his Phillies tickets for today, asked if I wanted them. How about you and I go? It's a 7:10 game."

Tyler hesitated. "Don't you want to take Miles?"

"Nah. He's got something else going on."

"Really? You want me to go with you? That'd be awesome, Mr. C. I've never been to a game."

"It's settled then. We'll leave early enough to see batting practice. You don't mind, do you, Deb?"

"No, that's fine. Maybe I'll see if Donna wants to do something." She picked up her phoned and clicked on Donna's number. While on the phone, Joe was filling Tyler in on tonight's starting pitchers.

After a few minutes, Deb put her phone down. "No luck," she announced. "Donna's busy. Looks like I'll just settle in here and watch a movie or something."

"That's too bad," Joe said. "You sure you'll be okay?"

"Yeah. We can stay here. It's no big deal," said Tyler.

"Don't be silly. You guys go and have fun. I'll be fine," Deb insisted.

Joe said to Tyler. "Let's get moving. I don't know about you but I need a shower."

"Yeah me too," replied Tyler. "And I've got to test out our work," he added with a laugh.

After Joe and Tyler got ready and left, Deb looked over her list of chores. She had been meaning to clean out the closet and medicine cabinet in the guest bathroom, and get rid of fraying towels and Zannah's old cosmetics and lotions left behind when she moved out. *Guess this afternoon is as good a time as any,* she told herself.

She went into the basement, grabbed three empty boxes -- one for Purple Heart, one for garbage and one for miscellaneous stuff she could still use. She went through the linen closet first, sorting through the towels, filling the Purple Heart box with slightly worn ones, tossing hole-y ones, carefully refolding the good ones and arranging them neatly on the shelves. She then moved to the medicine cabinet. Old Bed, Bath and Beyond bottles, crusted around the top, were trashed. Cotton facial wipes were moved to the miscellaneous box. She began sorting through the medications, checking expiration dates on antihistamines and cough syrups. She pulled out a prescription bottle marked Darvon and vaguely remembered Miles getting it when they pulled his wisdom teeth years ago. *Funny, I was sure he had only needed to take a few of them. This feels almost empty,* she thought to herself as she shook the bottle. She opened it. Two left. Hmmm. Maybe Joe took some when he hurt his back. She took the remaining two pills, threw them into the toilet, put the bottle in the trash box and moved on to the almost empty tubes of toothpaste.

After dinner, nestled under a lightweight blanket, Deb's thoughts returned to the almost empty prescription bottle. Was it possible Tyler had taken them? She didn't want to think that he had. After all, he had been a model guest, doing everything asked of him, going to meetings, helping around the house, looking for work.

She considered searching his room, but fought off the urge. *You're being silly,* she told herself. *He has given me absolutely no reason to doubt him. Don't be so suspicious.*

She turned her attention back to making popcorn and finding a movie to watch. She settled on French Kiss. Although she had seen it before, it was innocuous yet fun enough to keep her thoughts at bay. The phone rang just as Meg Ryan's character showed Kevin Kline's Luc she was wearing the stolen diamond necklace.

Damn, right at the good part. She intended to ignore the phone until she saw it was Miles calling.

"Hi Hon! What a nice surprise."

"Hey Mom. What's up?"

"Nothing. Just watching a movie. I'm surprised to hear from you. I thought Dad said you had something going on tonight."

"I do, just later. Thought I'd check in, see how things are going. Haven't talked to you in a while."

"Things are good. Dad took Tyler to the Phillies game. Do you know he's never been to one? How do you get to be twenty whatever in this town and not see a game live?"

"Ha-ha, I don't know. It's good Dad took him."

"Yeah, he was real excited. Tyler, I mean."

"So everything is working out okay?"

"Yeah sure."

Miles noticed a slight pause before she'd answered. "You sure? You sound a bit, I don't know, hesitant maybe?"

"No, no, it's probably nothing."

"What's probably nothing?"

She debated whether to say any more, then dove in. "Remember when you had your wisdom teeth out?"

"Yeah," he answered slowly.

"And they gave you that pain medication. Darvon, I think it was. Did you take a lot of that?"

"Mom, you really expect me to remember that? Why?"

"I was cleaning out the cabinet today and noticed the bottle was almost empty. It got me to worrying maybe Tyler had taken them."

"Why? Has he been acting like he's on something?"

"Well no."

"Then why do you think he took them? And really, if he was going to steal the meds, wouldn't he just take the whole bottle? Why leave just a few?"

"Oh you're right. I'm just being silly. I guess it's all those things you read about nowadays. How addicts relapse."

"Yeah," Miles tried to keep the concern from his voice and forced a laugh. "You read too much. Tell me what else has been going on."

Deb brought Miles up to date on Tyler's progress and asked about the latest in Miles' life. As usual, he stuck to the basics: things were going well, friends were good, he started dating some girl, she seems nice, too early to tell, etc. etc. etc.

The conversation wound down. Neither had anything more to add and it was beginning to get awkward. Miles said, "Guess I'll let you go, finish your movie. I've got to get going myself."

"Ok. Thanks for calling. Oh, and Miles?" she said, "don't tell your father about the pills. I'm sure it's nothing and don't want him to start worrying."

"Ok, sure," Miles said. "I'll talk to you soon."

They hung up. Deb felt a little better. Miles was right. If Tyler was using again, he would have taken the whole bottle. "Just put it out of your mind," she said out loud and went back to her movie.

She must have dozed off because the next thing she knew, there was a loud infomercial blaring from the television. What time is it? she wondered. She looked at the clock, it was after midnight. They should have been home by now. She picked up her phone to see if Joe had texted her when she heard the garage door open and the car pull in.

She straightened herself up to a sitting position and tried not to look worried. They came bursting through the door, Tyler waving one of those foam fingers and Joe sporting a new Phillies baseball hat.

"Wow, that was some game!" Joe roared. "You should have seen it, Deb. Started out as a pitcher's duel and then went into extra innings. Even saw a grand slam home run, right Tyler?"

Tyler grinned at him. "It was awesome. So much fun. And the food. Man, I love that Schmidter, that's what it's called, right Mr. C?

"Yup, that's it. I'm surprised you're still up, Deb."

"I fell asleep watching a movie. I'm glad you guys had a good time."

"What'd you do all night?"

"Cleaned out the closets in the bathroom, then just watched TV."

As she spoke, Tyler's head whipped around. "Uh, Mrs. C, I would have done that for you."

"I know, but you wouldn't have known what to do with all that stuff. Some things I have to take care of myself, you know. I think I'll tackle the closet in your room next."

"Yeah, ok. Well, I think I'll go up now. I'm still pretty keyed up but should try to get some sleep. Thanks for taking me. It was great, Mr. C," and he trudged up the stairs.

Joe sat down in his chair with a plop. "Nice night. Glad I did that. You know Deb, I think maybe you were right. Seems like Tyler is a good kid, just needs some positive reinforcement and guidance."

"Hmmm, yeah. I'm tired too. Mind if I go to bed?"

"No, no. I'm going to stay up for a while, unwind. Still hate that drive home from the ballpark."

"Ok, g'night." She got herself a glass of water before making her way to their room.

Chapter Nineteen

The next morning, Deb woke early. Her appointment with Dr. Nutley was scheduled for 10:00 and she considered cancelling. She wasn't happy with the way the last session ended and feared he was going to press her on the issue. Maybe she could deflect him with the latest on Tyler and the missing prescription pills.

With an air of resolution she didn't feel, she got out of bed and started her morning routine. Boil water, make coffee, get the paper. She tried to concentrate on the news, but found her mind wandering to Dr. Nutley and what he expected.

Tyler came into the kitchen still beaming from last night's adventure. "Mrs. C, that was so much fun! It was really nice of Mr. C to take me. I want to do something for him to, ya know, show my appreciation. Got any ideas?"

She looked at him blankly, trying to figure out what he was talking about. "Oh, Tyler, hi. What?"

"You okay? You look kinda out of it."

"No, no, I'm fine. Guess I was thinking about something else. What'd you say?"

"I was saying how much fun I had last night and I want to do something for Mr. C to thank him. Any ideas?"

"Oh that's not necessary. I'm pretty sure he had as much fun as you did."

"Maybe, yeah, but I'd still like to do something. Where's that honey-do list?"

"Over on the fridge. I'm sure he'd appreciate any of those chores taken care of."

"Got it. Great. Thanks!" Tyler grabbed the list and sat down with his coffee.

Deb watched him as he read over the list, humming to himself. *He's a good kid,* she told herself, *it was silly of me to think he had taken those pills. That's a relief.* She exhaled audibly.

Tyler looked up at her, "What was that for?"

"Oh nothing. I was letting my imagination run wild."

"Huh?"

"It's just that yesterday I was cleaning out the cabinets in the bathroom and came across an old prescription bottle. I was afraid you had taken some of the pills." She laughed. "Silly of me, really."

Tyler looked stricken. "Aw, Mrs. C, really? I wouldn't do that. You guys have been so nice to me. Why would I screw that up?"

"I know Tyler, I know. I said it was silly. But in my defense, the other day when we were filling out the application, you got so upset. Then you stormed out that night, didn't say where you were going. I was worried that you had relapsed.

Tyler looked crestfallen. "Really, Mrs. C? You really thought that?"

"I did. I'm sorry. I was wrong. Let's just forget it, ok?"

"Forget what?" Joe asked as he walked into the room.

"Nothing."

"Yeah, nothing," said Tyler, then added sullenly, "It's just Mrs. C thought I had taken some pills."

"What? Why?"

"Can't we just forget it? I made a mistake. I was wrong. Let's just leave it. I'm sorry Tyler, really I am." She stood up and said, "I'm going to shower. Got an appointment with Nutley today." She walked over behind Tyler and rubbed his shoulder, "Forgive me?"

"Yeah, of course."

Deb paced around the doctor's office. Dr. Nutley sat patiently in his chair, polishing his glasses on his shirt tail. After a few minutes, he fixed them on his ears, cleared his throat and said, "Why don't you sit down, Deb." It was more an order than a question.

She moved to her usual seat and plopped down, Dr. Nutley peered at her over the top of his glasses. "You seem a bit nervous today."

"Do I?"

"Yes. Pacing isn't in your usual repertoire."

She fiddled with her fingers, clicking her nails against each other, biting her lower lip. "I've got something new to feel guilty about. I sort of accused Tyler of taking some Darvon from the medicine cabinet."

"Oh?"

"Of course he didn't. I mean, he said he didn't and there's no reason not to believe him. He was pretty upset."

"Why should you feel guilty about that? He does have a track record after all."

"I know, but still. It wasn't right. I made him feel bad and that's not right."

"The good thing is, you confronted him with your worries. He talked to you about it. Didn't run away, didn't hurt you. Maybe he was sad that you thought he would do that, but it was a natural reaction. How did you two leave it?"

"He said he forgave me, but I don't know."

"Deb, sometimes you have to take people at their word. Right?"

"I guess."

"Okay. Now let's move on to what we had started last session."

"What was that?" She asked knowing full well what it was.

"Let's not play these games, Deb. You know exactly what I'm talking about. So let's have it. Let the honesty begin." He smiled reassuringly at her. "Start with the attack. Go over it all, one more time, start to finish."

`She sighed, letting all the air out of her lungs. She looked at him and said, "I don't want to."

"I know. But you have to."

She started in, slowly at first, faltering, then picking up speed, trying to get it all out as quickly as possible. She described the night, cold, dark, there was a basketball game, the last one before Thanksgiving break, everyone went. Their team, made up of the only black boys in the school, lost. After the game, they were walking back to the dorms. The guys she was with saw some townies, young black kids, making their way home. Johnny, her date, drunk, started yelling at the kids, telling them to get out of here, go back to your little shack, we don't want you niggers here. Johnny's chants were joined by the three other guys walking with them, shouts of watermelon, chicken, Boy. Someone picked up a stone and threw it at the kids. The kids, trying to ignore them, just kept walking. Johnny and the others started chasing the boys, throwing rocks, hooting and hollering. Deb ran after them, grabbed Johnny's arm, yelling at him to stop, leave those kids alone, they didn't do anything to you. Johnny stopped and glared at her. What, you nigger lover, and struck her across the face. She stumbled back and fell to the ground, then lunged for his leg. She called him white trash and anything insulting she could think of. He bent down and pulled her up by her hair. Oh yeah, he shouted, Want to see what we do to nigger lovers in this town? He pushed her up against a tree, called his friends over, held her there while they ripped her coat off, yanked her blouse open, pushed her skirt up, tore her panties, pushed her down on her knees, made her take Johnny in her mouth, pulling her head up and down, up and down. Then they wheeled her around and one after the other, forced themselves into her, punching her as she struggled, until they were all finished. They gave her a final push to the ground, and each one spat on her as they walked away, laughing.

She laid on the ground shivering, watching them go, patting each other on the back, joking. She felt the rock under her head, slowly moved her hand until her fingers could grasp it, then pulled it out and with all the might she had left in her body flung it toward them.

It landed with a thud against Johnny's head. She saw his head jerk forward, then he crumpled to the ground. She laid back and passed out.

She didn't remember how she got back to her dorm room or what she did when she got there. The only thing she had any clarity on was her roommate, Susie, sitting by her on the bed. Was it the next day? She didn't know. Susie was telling her that Johnny was hurt, in the hospital, in a coma, possible brain damage. Some were saying that he must have gotten mugged by one of the town kids after he dropped Deb off at the dorm. Others said he was just drunk and fell down and hit his head. Either way, Susie said, you're in the clear. Just go along with the story. It's best that way. And Deb agreed.

Dr. Nutley, for once, was still. After a few minutes, he stood up, handed her the box of tissues, said, "I'll give you a minute," and left the room.

When the doctor came back into the room, he was carrying a cup of tea from the cafe downstairs. He handed it to her with a nod and said, "You ok?"

She nodded unconvincingly. "Yeah, sure."

He sat down across from her.

"Do you know what became of Johnny?"

"No. I followed Susie's advice, went along with the story. Went home for Thanksgiving, came back, went to classes, took finals, went home for Christmas break. Never went back."

"What did your parents say?"

"Nothing. I didn't tell them. I just said I hated it there and wasn't going back. My mother said okay, I think she sensed that something happened but didn't want to know. My father was really angry, didn't talk to me for weeks."

"That must have been hard."

"No. Not much was hard after that. You know, in comparison. Nothing."

"Right." The phone on the desk buzzed. Dr. Nutley said, "Our time is up, but I can postpone my next appointment if you want. I want to make sure you're okay."

"No. Thank you. I'm tired. I want to go."

"Yes, of course. Listen, I know this was hard on you, but it's good you got it out. You might not think it now, but you did good work here today. I'll see you next time."

Deb walked out of the office. Out of habit, she smiled and nodded goodbye to the receptionist. She felt weak, but propelled her body through the door, down the hallway and out to her car. She sat there for a long time, staring straight ahead, too numb to cry. Her mind whirling but unwilling to focus on any one thought.

Eventually, she put the car in gear and drove home, ignoring the radio and her ringing phone.

Arriving home, she saw Tyler and Joe standing on the porch. They waved as she pulled in and came over to open the car door for her.

"Hi hon. How's Dr. Nutley?"

"What? Oh, fine."

"You okay? You look kind of, I don't know, weird."

Deb got out of the car and said, "Rough session."

Tyler piped up, "I know what that's like. Let me make you some tea."

"Thanks, but no. I think I'll just go lie down for a while."

She went into the house, saying no more. Joe and Tyler watched her go, then looked at each other and shrugged.

The dog ran to Deb but sensing something amiss, just licked her hand and followed her to the bedroom. She kicked off her shoes, climbed into bed and closed her eyes. *If unloading all of that was supposed to make me feel better, it failed.*

All those shuttered memories were present in this moment, all the anger, fear, hatred, disgust, guilt. She tried to push them back where they belonged but they refused to budge.

What am I supposed to do now?

Retreat, she decided and started singing those old Motown songs in her head until she fell asleep.

Chapter Twenty

Deb felt something touch her. Fear overtook her and she instinctively jerked away until she realized Joe was sitting next to her, rubbing her arm, murmuring, "Deb?"

"Deb, it's just me. Sorry if I startled you."

"That's okay. I must have been sound asleep. What time is it?"

"A little after four. That was quite an afternoon nap. You were really conked out."

"Yeah, I guess so."

"Look, Dr. Nutley called. Asked me how you were doing."

"Really?"

"Yeah. Must have been some session."

"You could say that. But I'm fine, really. Well, maybe not fine, but I will be. It sometimes takes me a while after seeing him to settle in, you know?"

"I guess so. You look pretty sad."

"Yeah, well. I'll get over it." She sat up and rubbed her eyes. "Guess I better think about dinner, huh?"

"Why don't we just get takeout? You've had a rough day."

"No. I have to get moving. Get my mind on something, anything, else."

Joe looked at her. "Deb, do you want to tell me about it? You know you can tell me anything."

"No, I'm all talked out."

Joe nodded and stood up, more than a little relieved. He knew he shouldn't feel this way, but he wasn't sure he could take any more revelations from his wife.

"Okay. Well, then, I'll just go down and feed the dog. You coming?"

Deb followed Joe to the kitchen. She took some chicken breasts out of the fridge and, deciding to make Chicken Parmesan, sliced them in half. She got out her meat mallet and pounded the breasts, perhaps too much considering the force behind every swing of the mallet.

Joe busied himself feeding the dog and filling the water bowl, but kept a wary eye on Deb. "Tyler has some news," he said.

"Really? What?"

"I'll let him tell you." He called out, "Tyler! Get in here and tell Deb your news."

They heard Tyler's door open and his fast approaching footsteps. He bounded into the room, smiling from ear to ear. "Hey, Mrs. C."

"Joe says you've got some news." She tried to sound cheerful.

"I do! Guess what? Those people I sent my resume to? They called and want to interview me. Can you believe it?"

"That's great! I'm so happy for you." Deb gave him a hug. "That's such good news. When? When's the interview?"

"Day after tomorrow. I'm pretty excited."

"Of course you are. Do you have interview clothes?"

"Interview clothes? I never thought of that. Not really."

"Well, Joe's got lots of stuff, but I'm not sure they'd fit you. Why don't we go shopping tomorrow and get you an interview outfit."

"An outfit, Deb?" Joe interjected with a laugh.

"Ok, wrong word. Suit. We'll get him a suit."

Deb welcomed this diversion. It let her push the session back to the shadows where it belonged. She threw herself into the conversation, and joined Joe in peppering Tyler with questions about the kind of suit he'd like, the job, and his preparedness.

Tyler didn't know many more details about the job than those in the online posting. "They did tell me though that I'd have to go to some training facility for two weeks if they hired me."

"That's not uncommon," said Joe. "Did they tell you where it was?"

"No, the conversation never got that far."

Deb turned her attention back to the chicken. "Okay, enough yakking. Now you guys get out of my kitchen. I want to get this dinner in the oven."

Joe and Tyler went into the family room and turned on the TV, making jokes about the diva chef, leaving Deb alone to battle her resurrected demons.

Deb and Joe waited on the patio for Tyler to get back from his interview. Deb tried to concentrate on a crossword puzzle but in fact worried about what kind of impression Tyler would make on the interviewer. Joe played a game on his phone. They were both excited and apprehensive, each hoping that they had prepped Tyler enough for his foray into the working world. Yesterday, when Deb and Tyler returned from their shopping trip, they made Tyler go through a fake interview, Deb asking him probable questions, Joe coaching with the best answers. Although Tyler seemed to do well, they were concerned with his sometimes overly casual style.

"How do you think he's doing?" Deb asked Joe.

"I don't know. I tried to impress on him the importance of being respectful and confident. To say enough but not too much."

"I doubt he'll say too much. What if the question of college comes up? I can't remember, what did we tell him to say?"

Before Joe could answer, they heard Tyler come in the front door.

"Out here, Tyler," Joe yelled.

Tyler burst onto the patio. "I got it!" he yelled. "I know I did!"

"What? Really? Just like that?" Deb was incredulous.

"Well," Tyler hesitated, "they didn't actually say that, but I know it. You know how you can tell some things right off? They were so nice, especially the main guy that interviewed me last."

Deb looked at Tyler. He was beaming and seemed about to jump out of his new dark blue suit with the freshly ironed white shirt, striped tie and gleaming shoes.

Joe said, "That's great! But hold off on getting your hopes up too far. Deb'll tell you that those feelings don't always pan out."

"I know, I know. Can't help it though. Mr. Cunningham, that's the guy I was telling you about, said he'd be in touch. That's good, right?"

"Absolutely. Sit down and tell us all about it. We want to hear every word."

Excitedly, Tyler filled them in, from the initial talk with the recruiter from HR to the woman who explained the details of the job and finally to the talk with Mr. Cunningham. It turned out that Mr. Cunningham had worked with Tyler's father and had even talked to Tyler at his father's funeral all those years ago. He had heard the stories about Tyler's mother and wondered how the boy was doing, so when Tyler's resume showed up, he took a special interest.

Deb was afraid to ask but couldn't stop herself. She said, "Nobody said anything about your, uh, tattoo?"

"Actually, Mr. Cunningham did. He asked me about it and I told him I got it in memory of my dad. He was okay with it. Said the kind of company it was wanted young, hip kids in that position. How about that? He actually said young, hip kids." He roared with laughter.

Deb was surprised to admit it, but it did sound like everything was working in Tyler's favor.

Tyler was still explaining the job when the phone rang. Joe picked it up, listened, smiled and handed it to Tyler.

"Hello, this is Tyler McCann." Smile.

"Yes, Mr. Cunningham. Yes." Bigger smile.

"Next week? Atlanta? Yes, of course, I can be there. No problem. Thank you. Thank you so much. I won't let you down." Beaming.

"Yes, I'll come by the office tomorrow. See you then. Bye."

Tyler clicked off the phone and laid it on the table. He stared at it for a minute, then "Yahoo!" he cried. "I got it. I really did!" He jumped up and started dancing around the patio, grabbing Deb's arm and pulling her up. "Thank you so much! You guys did this. You've been great. This is the best."

There was much hugging and a few tears, mostly of joy. Finally spent but still excited, Tyler sat down.

"He said the training would be in Atlanta. Next week. They said they'd pay for my airfare and hotel. Isn't that great?"

"Yes, yes it is," said Deb, a tinge of jealousy seeping into her voice.

"Ever been to Atlanta?" asked Joe.

"Mr. C, if I had never been to a Phillies game, what makes you think I could have been to Atlanta?" Tyler asked with a laugh.

"Ha-ha. Right. Deb knows some people from Atlanta, don't you Deb?"

"Yes, yes, some guys I worked with were from down there."

"And isn't Susie? You old roommate, Susie?"

Deb looked up sharply but tried to sound nonchalant. "Yes, she was born there. Still lives there, I think, if you can believe what you see on Facebook."

"Maybe you should go down there with Tyler. See Susie. Catch up."

"I don't know about that," Deb said slowly.

"Yes, Mrs. C. Come down with me. I've never flown before, and to tell you the truth, I'm a bit nervous about it. It would sure make me feel better if you were along."

"Yes, Deb," Joe added. " I think you should. You and Susie have a lot to talk about, I'm sure. It'd be good for you to get away for a bit."

"Do it, Mrs. C. For me?"

Deb just shook her head and shrugged in feigned exasperation.

Chapter Twenty-One

Deb followed the valet to her hotel room, half-listening to his instructions about the ice machine location and the in-room mini bar. Tyler, settled in the room next to hers, told her he needed to read over the instructions for his upcoming training seminars and would see her at dinner. She was drained, had used all her energy staying upbeat for Tyler and just wanted to be home on the patio surrounded by flowers and birds.

With a fleeting look at the bed, Deb unlocked her suitcase and went through the motions of unpacking. She checked her phone for messages, remembered Joe's advice about setting up the WIFI, then plopped on the too-hard mattress. She lay there thinking about the whirlwind that encompassed the past few days. Finding flights, reserving hotel rooms, packing, buying suitable work clothes for Tyler, prepping meals for Joe to have during her absence. At times, she welcomed the flurry of activity; it kept her from thinking about her last meeting with Dr. Nutley. Just when she started to feel comfortable, something would pop up, like a reminder from Joe to contact Susie, and the whole affair would flood back, washing over her like a tsunami of grief.

In the end, she did contact Susie. A message via Facebook. As she typed, she wished fervently that Susie would be away that week, too busy, or simply not see the message. Her hopes were dashed when Susie messaged back right away. She would love to see Deb. It's been too long. She'd take time off of work. When will you get here? I'll meet you at the airport.

No need, Deb replied. I'll call you when I get in.

Augghhh. Don't misunderstand, Deb loved Susie, was forever in her debt, would do pretty much anything for her. It was just that now, especially now, Deb wanted to stay as far away from the old reminders as much as possible. She was sure, however, that Dr. Nutley would have a completely different view. He'd probably say, "Stop retreating, Deb. This is exactly the right time to see Susie. Lay the past to rest." She wished she had been able to talk with the doctor before she left, but time got away from her and before she knew it, she was on the plane buckling her seatbelt for a probable bumpy ride.

She wondered, could this be the right time to see Susie? She doubted it. After all, what could Susie say or do that would change anything? Did it matter?

The next morning found Tyler and Deb having their complimentary breakfast in the hotel restaurant, discussing the upcoming day. Tyler, excited and edgy, talked a blue streak. Deb did her best to calm him, nodding, uh-huhing, providing tips when asked. She dreaded the minute he got into the cab and fretted about the looming phone call to Susie.

The taxi was here. Deb hugged Tyler, wished him well and told him he'd do great. He flashed his gleaming blue eyes at her, smiling and waving as they drove away.

Left alone, Deb wandered around the hotel grounds, summoning her courage. She thought about calling Joe, but realized he might be sleeping in. *No*, she decided, *I've got to get it over with. It's just a phone call. Maybe lunch. Keep the conversation topical, in the present. I can do this.*

She went to sit by the pool, pulled her phone from her purse and clicked on Susie's number. A man answered the phone. *Husband, I guess.*

"Hi, this is Deb. Deb Cromwell, a friend of Susie's. Is she there?"

"Hi Deb! We've been waiting on you. You made it down okay?" said the man enthusiastically.

"Why, yes. Yes, got in yesterday. Thanks."

"Good. Good."

Deb could hear a muffled yell, "Suze, it's your old roomie. She's here. Pick up the phone." To Deb, he said, "She's comin'. She's so excited 'bout seeing you. Now just hold on a minute. Here she is."

The voice that came through the line was so familiar it caught Deb off guard. There was that musicality, the palpable tenderness, the rounded vowels that marked the authentic, homegrown Georgia girl. None of the exaggerated Southern belle accent so often heard in the movies.

"Hello? Deb? Deb, is that really you?"

"Hi Susie. Yep, it's really me."

"Ah am so glad you called. Ah can't wait to see you. What ah you doing right now? Right this very second?"

"Me? Oh I'm just sitting by the pool. Sorry it's so early."

"Early? Honey, I've been up since six this mawning. Thought maybe you would have called last night, but you wah probably tahed from the trip."

"Yeah, I was. So, how are you? Things good?"

"Things are great. Way-en can you get your body over heah? Want me to pick you up?"

Deb, surprising herself, slid right into the easy chatter she enjoyed with Susie. "Well, hon, I guess I can get my body over there this morning. No need to pick me up. I rented a car."

"But you don't know how to get heah."

"I've got Waze."

"What?"

"Waze," Deb laughed. "It's an app on my phone. Gives me directions. I'll just plug in your address and be there in no time."

"Ain't you the techie?" Giggle. "Well that's just fine then. I can't wait for you to meet Michael, my husband. The kids aren't heah, but I've got plenty of pictures for you."

"I'll bet. Still harassing everyone with your camera."

"You know it. And they-an some." She seemed to pause for a minute. "Now you hang up, get in that cah and get yaw a-ass ovah heah."

"Okay, okay. See you soon."

Deb clicked off with a mixture of gratitude and trepidation. Grateful because Susie sounded like she always had, trepidation because Susie held those remembrances of her past. *Buck up,* she told herself. *You're here, all you can do now is go forward.*

She went back to her room, eyeing the lounge bar longingly as she passed. *I could really use a drink right now.* She spent some time getting ready, collecting her bag and car keys as much as herself. Taking a final look in the mirror, she frowned at the image facing her, smoothed her eyebrows and tried to fix her droopy lid. With a feeble shrug, she headed out to the car.

Even with her Waze app directing her around the heaviest traffic, it took Deb more than a half hour to reach Susie's house. She parked on the street, and sat in the car taking in the perfectly manicured lawn and pristine exterior. Everything about the house fought Deb's picture of messy Susie. She had half-expected to see bikes and balls strewn across the lawn, but there was no real evidence that anyone actually lived a life here.

That is, until the front door opened and a woman came running out to the car, waving her arms excitedly. Susie? It must be. Even though she had seen recent photos on Facebook, she had a hard time connecting this person with the teenager she once knew. This was a woman, middle aged, carrying the weight of menopause like a well-earned trophy. The beautiful auburn hair had been cut to standard housewife length, white Capri pants and blousy floral top replaced the signature bell-bottoms and tie-dyed t-shirt so front and center in Deb's mind.

Susie reached the car, huffing and puffing, and yanked the door open. "My Lord," she screamed, "look at you! You're really heah! I can't believe it. Get yourself out of that cah and let me look at you."

The two old friends hugged, each holding on for dear life, as if transferring memories of their past youth. A happy, poignant embrace broken by Susie's husband.

"So this is the famous Deb," he said casually walking up to them. They let go of each other and looked at him.

"Michael, didn't I tell you? Isn't she just a sight for sore eyes?"

"Hi Deb. Glad you got here all right." He reached out to shake her hand. "Any trouble?"

"Hi." She accepted his hand with a smile, "No, no problem. Just a bit of traffic."

"Come on now, let's stop standing around heah and get in the house. I can just see Miss Lucy peeking out her window at us." Susie grabbed Deb's arm and walked her toward the house, through the door, past the foyer and into the kitchen.

"Heah we are. I've been keeping the water hot for your tea. See, didn't forget."

"Thanks. A cup of tea would be wonderful," said Deb as she surveyed the room. "So funny, I don't know what I expected, but it wasn't this."

"Oh, this old house? I guess it is kind of nice, huh? Michael has done quite well for himself. I get to reap the benefits. Now you just turn around and let me get a good look at you." She took Deb by the shoulder and spun her around.

"Same old Deb, although I spy a few extra pounds. Michael, doesn't she just look like an up Nawth city girl? All those stylish clothes. And look at the haih. Like something out of a magazine."

"She sure does. Maybe you can give Suze here some pointers." Michael winked at his wife.

Susie motioned Deb to the table set for two and put down a plate of pastries and biscuits, a jar of marmalade and the teapot.

"Isn't Michael joining us?"

"No ma'am. He's got to be getting to work. He'll be back later, I expect."

Taking his cue, Michael said his goodbyes, kissed his wife on the cheek, winked at Deb and said, "Now don't you girls get into too much trouble while I'm gone" and left.

"Good," Susie said as they heard his car pull out of the driveway. "Now we can really catch up."

They spent the next few hours sipping tea, munching on the goodies and bringing each other up to date on husbands and children, cautiously avoiding talk of school. Susie commiserated with Deb about missing children who lived far away. She had a son in the military who made it safely through two tours in the Mideast and was currently stationed in Germany. Deb talked about her unexpected retirement and the void it seemed to leave in her. She didn't talk much about Tyler or why he was living with them, just said it had to do with complicated circumstances. Susie just nodded, almost knowingly.

There were photos all over the house; taken by Susie, Deb assumed. Most were black and white pictures of people, close-ups of faces and hands, lovely portraits; some a little disturbing. She said, "I see you've kept up with your photography. These are really nice. You've developed into quite the artiste. Are you showing or selling anything?"

"Yes," said Susie glancing around. "Michael made me a dahkroom in the basement. I spend a lot of time down theah." She paused and looked guiltily at Deb. "Deb, there's something I've got to tell you. Now don't be mad."

Uh oh, thought Deb but said softly, "What is it?"

"Now promise you won't be mad."

"Can't promise anything Susie, but you've got a lot in the bank. Just tell me."

"Well, you see, I was asked to show some of my photos in this exhibit in Atlanta, some gallery, you know?"

"Uh huh."

"And the gallery owner came to the house and looked at all my stuff to, you know, pick the ones she wanted for the exhibit. Theah was one in pahticular that she just loved."

"Out with it, Suze."

"One of the ones she wanted was a picture I had taken of you. And I let her have it."

"Is that all? That's no big deal." Trying to sound calm, "I'll admit, I hate having my picture taken and I can't think which one you're talking about, but don't worry. It's ok. Where'd you take it?"

Susie took Deb's hand and looked her in the eye. "I took it in the room, when you got back that night."

"What?" Deb was sure she hadn't heard correctly. "What did you say?" Looking at Susie's face told her she had heard it right. She was shaken. "When? When would you have done that? Why?" Her voice rose higher with each question.

"I'm sorry," Susie said, pleading, "Don't hate me. It was just such a great picture. The expression on your face, it told a whole story."

"My story, Susie, my story. Not yours." She tried to regain her composure, bringing her tone down a notch. "I can't believe you did that. And when exactly did you take this? When I was crumpled on the bed. Or maybe when I was in the shower trying to wash everything off me?" Her eyes flashed in anger.

"You were looking out the window." Susie said softly. "It was like you were looking for someone who wasn't theah any more."

Silence. The two women sat in their chairs, one visibly seething, the other dejectedly staring at her hands.

Finally, Deb pushed her chair back and walked unsteadily to the bathroom. She closed the door and sat down on the floor. She tried to sort the thoughts tumbling around in her head. She had no recollection of Susie and her camera that night but that didn't surprise her. What did surprise her was that Susie had kept the photo. Not only did she keep it, she exhibited it. Feelings of exposure and violation welled up all over again. *Aren't you supposed to get permission to do that?* She hit her head against the door. Bang, bang, bang.

Crouched on the floor, she focused on home, on Joe, on Zannah and Miles. She could almost hear Joe saying, "Let it go, Deb. Just let it go." She thought about that, how she could let it go. *Was it really that bad? It had been so long ago; no one would know her or recognize her. As long as her name wasn't on the photo, it would be all right.* Grudgingly, she acknowledged that she owed Susie. Owed her for helping her, standing by her, making sure she got through. If the payback was to be this image of her at such a traumatic and horrific moment, so be it.

Deb stood up, straightened her clothes, washed her hands and unlocked the door. She drew a deep breath and went back to the table where Susie was still sitting, hands clasped in front of her.

She sat down and said, "I'm not happy about it. But ok. You did it. You showed the picture, and now it's safely back here, right? Somewhere in this house, that picture is silently filed away." She looked questioningly at Susie.

A look of relief mixed with worry crossed Susie's face. "Yes. Yes. It's heah. Down in the dahkroom. Want me to get it? So you can see it? "

"Seriously? No. I don't want to see it."

"Okay. Sure. We ok?"

"Yes. Like I said, you had a lot in the bank." After a minute, she added, "and now the account is closed. No more. Nobody ever sees that picture again. If it were up to me, you'd burn it and the negative. Got it?"

"Got it." The conversation continued, albeit haltingly.

Susie looked sideways at Deb. Finally she said, "I really didn't think I'd see you again."

"That shouldn't have mattered."

"I'm not talking about the picture. I'm talking about actually seeing you again."

"Oh. Right. Me too."

"But you're all right, right? Things turned out well for you, didn't they?"

"I suppose."

"Do you evah regret it? Leaving like that? Not doing anything about it?"

"I don't know. Yes. No. What was there to do?"

"You know, it would be different now. Georgia, hell the South in general, is different now."

"If you say so."

"I do. I do say so. Now they'd put them in jail."

"Hah. Me too."

"No. No. It was self-defense. You know it was self defense."

"It was anger. Pure and simple."

"He didn't die."

"Oh." A moment. "That's good." Pause. "I guess."

"Yes," Susie said. "He never came back to school, you know."

"No, I didn't know that." She wasn't sure how much she wanted to know. Would she want to know if he married, had kids, life was great? Or that he was forever damaged, living in total dependence on a family member? Did it matter? If the former, she'd be distraught. If the latter, the guilt would consume her.

"No. Why would you," Susie murmured, her words more a statement than a question.

Deb took a lingering look around the room as if an answer was hiding somewhere beneath the frames and appliances. Finding none, she didn't respond.

Susie started to say something more, then stopped. She seemed to be arguing with herself. She opened her mouth again, blurting out, "He's heah. In Atlanta. He's living in Atlanta."

"Oh kay...," Deb said slowly. "So what?" She said this with a nonchalance she didn't feel.

"I thought I should tell you. In case you run into him. Not that that's likely, but I wanted you to know."

"You're right. I'm not going to run into him. When I leave here, I'm going straight back to the hotel." In her mind, she kept repeating *Let it go, let it go.*

"Right. But just in case, you know, stay away from Maggie's Bar."

"Why? He hang out there looking for college girls?"

"No, well, probably. He manages it. Leastways that's what I heard."

"That's almost funny." She imagined Johnny, now in his 60's, kowtowing to a bunch of teenagers, sucking up to them to push the profits, a middle-aged beer belly, dull skull peeking through a noticeable comb-over. The picture she painted made her laugh with derision.

Neither of them said anything more for a while, each lost in their own thoughts. It was Susie who broke the silence with the announcement that a drink was in order. Deb agreed. As she was fixing Bloody Mary's, Susie asked quietly. "You think about it a lot?"

Deb accepted the glass from Susie, took a drink and said, "Think about what? Those beasts and what they did to me? Or what I did to Johnny?"

"Fahget about what you did to Johnny. He desahved whatevah he got and then some. I mean the attack."

"Hah! How can I not? You think out of sight out of mind? Sorry, it doesn't work that way. I've tried to forget. Honestly I have, but it's always there, hiding behind the every day. It's the shadowy gnat that flies around my head, flitting into my consciousness when it's most unwanted. Like when someone comes up behind me in my own house. I know they're there, but it startles me anyway. And making love? Forget it. I don't understand it. How people can associate love with that act."

"You mean you never have sex?"

"I didn't say that," Deb said with a dismissive laugh. "Of course we have sex. I just don't see that as love. Johnny and his pals made sure of that."

"Oh. Yeah. Still," she said trying to lighten the mood, "Just plain sex can be pretty good, huh?"

Deb heard the change in tone and appreciated Susie's effort. She took another long drink and remembered how much Susie liked sex. Barely a night went by that she wasn't off somewhere with somebody, rarely the same person, always coming back with stories about this guy's foreplay or that guy's penis size. She attacked the sex act with a gusto Deb had never witnessed before or since.

She said to Susie, "There were times when I'd pretend I was you."

"Really? Now that's funny. Kind of flattering."

"Yeah. I can't tell you how many nights you got me through. Even though he didn't know it, I think Joe really appreciated it. Thanks for that."

"Any time. Feel free to be me any time."

From there, the talk loosened into joking about Susie's old 'beaus' and where they might be now. It was quickly decided that most of them were busy begging their wives to do what Susie had done to them.

Although she was still unsettled from the day, she agreed to have dinner with Susie and Michael that evening. Susie insisted that Tyler come along. Deb reluctantly promised to ask him, uneasy about the two disparate worlds meeting.

When Deb returned to her hotel and Tyler came back from his training session, they sat in his room talking about the many things he had learned. He went into great detail, flush with excitement. Deb was pleased that Tyler appeared ready to jump through the up-the-ladder hurdles and join Corporate America, and envied his youth and exuberance, struggling to recall when she had felt that gung ho about anything.

"Of course," he said, "I'd love to go to dinner with you and your friends. Get a chance to hear about your old days." He winked slyly.

"Don't expect too much," Deb replied. "I'm happier when I'm living in the present." She went to her room to get ready, leaving Tyler poring over the stack of manuals he brought back from his training.

Tyler watched her go. She seemed different somehow, subdued. Sure, she listened to him talking, but in a detached sort of way. Eyes staring blankly into the air while her head nodded and her mouth said, "Really? Interesting," and "Uh huh."

It seemed to him that she didn't want to go to dinner with her friend and wondered why. He had realized a while back that she deflected talk of when she was at school and he had even asked Joe about it. All Joe would say was, "It was a difficult time, just let it be." So he did. After all, he was grateful for everything that Deb had done for him and wasn't about to jeopardize that, no matter how curious he was.

Chapter Twenty-Two

Susie and Michael were already seated when Deb and Tyler arrived at the restaurant. It was one of those high-end chain steak houses found in every city in America. Deb was comforted by the familiarity of the setting but a bit disappointed that there would be no collard greens on the menu.

The introductions took place. Tyler was his charming self, beaming his blue eyes at Susie who drank them in like a kitten lapping milk.

"Oh my, isn't he just adahable?"

"Ah, thanks," said Tyler. Deb could almost hear 'aw shucks' in his voice.

Michael started asking Tyler about his new job while Deb and Susie looked over the menu and discussed cocktails.

"Just a Coke or Pepsi for me," Tyler said.

"Oh come on, live a little," Michael chided.

"No, no thanks. I'm staying away from alcohol."

"Now why on earth would a young pup like yourself be staying away from the good stuff?"

"I guess Mrs. C didn't tell you." He glanced over at her questioningly.

Deb said, "Tyler prefers not to drink."

"It's all right, Mrs. C. I don't mind." To Susie and Michael he said, "I got myself into trouble. Had problems with drinking and drugs and a whole slew of other things. Mrs. C here sort of rescued me. That's how we got to be here."

"Really? This sounds like quite the story. Do tell."

Deb concentrated on her vodka tonic, at times checking Susie and Michael's faces for reactions. They were immersed in Tyler's story, which he began with the details about his father, mother, and grandmother; continued with the drinking, the drugs, the debt, Sam, and the carjacking, and ended with Deb, who, as he put it, picked up the pieces, realigned them and made him whole again. You would have thought he was in a group therapy session.

Finally, and in an effort to release Tyler from the hot seat, Michael let out a short laugh, adding, "Well these girls right here know all about getting into trouble, don't you?"

"That's enough, Michael," Susie said sharply. To Tyler, she said, "That's quite a story. I'm so sorry it had to happen to you. It seems like it's all working out though, right hon?"

Michael interrupted, "It's true, Suze. You and Deb got into all sorts of things. Nothing wrong with Tyler knowing that. Might make him feel better."

Tyler, fully unburdened, perked his ears up. "This sounds good," he said with a laugh. "C'mon, tell me about your misspent youth. I told you mine."

Deb was frozen, incapable of stopping this train wreck. She stood up quickly, murmured something apologetically, and took off in the direction of the ladies room.

While she was gone, Michael joshingly ignored pleas from Susie and started telling Tyler some of Susie and Deb's college escapades. There were stories about lowering a glass tied with thread out the window to retrieve pot, mescaline fueled Jethro Tull concerts, Purple Jesus parties. Wisely, he avoided mentioning the attack and its aftermath.

But Deb didn't know that.

When she walked back to the table and sat down, she looked at Tyler and said, "Okay. So now you know. I was sexually assaulted by four of my college classmates and I almost killed the guy who initiated it. Welcome to my hell." She looked at Michael but said to Tyler. "Feel better now?"

He and Michael stared at her. Tyler stammered, "Oh, no, Mrs. C. Something bad like that happening to you would never make me feel better."

Susie grabbed Deb. "No Deb no. Michael didn't say anything about that."

Deb looked at Susie's hand clutching at her arm, then looked at her face. "Oh. My. God."

Time stood still. Eventually, Michael picked up his menu and started blabbering about how good the New York Strip was and how large the baked potato. Tyler followed suit, eyeing his menu, casting furtive glances toward Deb. Susie called the waiter over and ordered another round of drinks. Deb, still in shock, filled with shame, subserviently took her cue from the others and pulled her glasses from her purse.

They ordered. Susie and Michael filled the awkward silence with talk about Atlanta, baseball, politics, global warming, funny neighbors, anything but the elephant in the room.

When the food arrived, Deb picked up her knife and fork, then laid them down again. She said, looking at her plate, "I'm sorry. Tyler, you didn't need to hear that. I'm not myself these days. Michael, I shouldn't have assumed. I'm sorry."

Everyone spoke at once, "Nothing to be sorry for." "No, I'm sorry." "It's okay, Mrs. C."

"No, it's not okay. But it's out there now. Let's eat."

They dutifully plunged into their food, remarking how good it was although no one in the party was actually tasting any of it.

Deb moved robotically through the meal, making a decent show of interest although her mind was far away. She thought about the past few months, everything that had happened to lead her to this time, this place. Why? Was this fate? Proving you could run away but never hide? Showing her life was meant to be led in the open, not buried beneath the guise of normalcy?

She reached down, down deep, gathering the strength she didn't know she had. She pushed away her plate, dropped her napkin on it and said, "Susie, I have a question for you."

Susie stopped mid-bite and returned the look. "Okay. Shoot."

"Where is Maggie's Bar?"

Michael, unaware of the power of this question, said, "Maggie's? It's right down the street. Why?"

"I think I need a drink."

"I'm not sure you do, Deb," said Susie.

"I am. It's time. Will you go with me?"

Michael said to Susie, "I don't get it. Why would she want to go to Maggie's when she can get another drink here?"

Deb said, "I've got some unfinished business."

"You're not going alone. We'll go with you."

To the uninformed Michael and Tyler, Susie half whispered, "That's where the guy works, the guy who attacked her."

"Ooooh." Light dawned on the men. Michael said, "It could be dangerous. How do you expect him to react? I doubt he'd be happy to see you."

"I have no idea how he'll react and I don't care if he wants to see me," said Deb. "I want to see him. I need to see him."

"Michael's right. This could be the worst idea you've ever had, but if it's what you want, we'll go with you. If you're sure.

"I'm not sure. But it seems as though everything is moving in this direction whether I want it to or not. There must be a reason."

Tyler said, "I've got your back, Mrs. C. Just tell me what you want me to do."

"I don't want you or anyone to do anything. Just come with me."

The four of them stood outside Maggie's Bar. Although it was a warm night, Deb shivered. Michael put his jacket around her shoulders and said, "You really up for this?"

She peered through the darkened bar windows, unsure what to say. She straightened her back, shook her head violently and without a word, walked through the door.

It was your basic college bar, dimly lit, scuffed wooden tables and well-worn chairs. The scent of stale beer filled the air. Country music played in the background, twangy songs with their love 'em and leave 'em lyrics. It was packed. The crowd, mostly students, were gathered in clumps, joking, singing, swaying to the music.

Deb spotted an open two-spot near the bathroom. She said to Tyler and Michael, "Susie and I are going to sit over there. You guys go to the bar."

Tyler said, "No, we'll squeeze in at the table with you."

"No," said Deb sternly. "You'll go to the bar. You can keep an eye on us from there."

Looking completely out of place, the two well dressed middle-aged women made their way to the empty table and sat down. A girl in cowboy boots and Daisy Dukes came to take their order.

"Purple Jesus," said Deb. To Susie, she said, "When in Rome..."

A surprised Susie laughed and ordered, "Whiskey with a beer back."

The waitress gave them a look, then headed to the bar. Deb's eyes followed her. She saw her talking to a young man who went off to make the drinks. *Phew*, Deb thought, *not him. Maybe he isn't working tonight.*

Meanwhile, Tyler and Michael stood near the end of the bar where they could keep an eye on Deb and Susie. They took a few minutes checking out the guys behind the bar, wondering which one was Johnny.

It wasn't hard to tell. Michael spotted him first. He nudged Tyler and jerked his head in the direction of a man at the other end of the bar. "That's gotta be him," Michael whispered.

The man, the only other guy in the place over 30, was leaning on the bar talking with a young, good-looking girl coquettishly giggling and hanging on his every word. He was good looking, tall, slim, with graying hair at the temples. He reached out his hand to push the girl's hair from her face, and leaned over and kissed her. She pulled her head away, said something, seemed to force a smile, then picked up her purse and walked toward the restroom. The man pulled something out of his pocket. What was it? Looked like a small vial. He opened the vial and poured its contents into the girl's drink, glanced over at the bartender and winked.

Michael and Tyler stared at each other, both wondering if they should do or say anything. Before they had a chance to act, the girl came out of the restroom. She started walking toward a group of kids but stopped when the man called out to her and motioned for her to come over. She stopped, thought a moment, then shrugged and went back to the man. He grinned, lifted her glass and handed it to her. He then picked up his bottle of beer and clicked it against her drink.

Just then, the waitress approached the man and after a short conversation, pointed at Deb and Susie's table. The man took the tray of drinks from the waitress and walked away.

Michael and Tyler were so immersed in watching the action at the end of the bar that they didn't notice Susie had gone to the bathroom until their eyes followed the man's journey to Deb's table. Tyler made a move, as if to go over, but Michael stopped him. "Give it a minute," he said.

Tyler nodded, then walked over to the girl Johnny had been talking to. He whispered something to her, picked up her drink and poured it on the floor.

By this time, Johnny was at the table. "Here are your drinks." Announcing each one as he placed them on the table, "One whiskey back. One Purple Jesus."

When he spoke, Deb's breath caught in her throat. She turned and took in the once familiar face, now lined with crow's feet, the lips a bit thinner. His face held the same mocking expression she once adored, and now despised. She looked straight into Johnny's dark brown eyes and said, "Thank you."

"Any time, little lady." He stopped mid sentence, almost dropping the glass as he set it down.

"Deb?" Recognition, then incredulity, replaced the usual self-satisfied smugness.

"Hi Johnny." Composure relayed but not felt.

Johnny grabbed hold of the end of the table.

He paused a minute, then regrouped and said, "Well I'll be damned. Look at you. I almost didn't recognize you. You look good, Deb. Really."

"Thanks. I'd know you anywhere," replied Deb still eyeing him up.

"Yeah, I keep myself in shape," he said patting his flat stomach.

Deb picked up her drink and swallowed. She nodded toward the drink, "Hasn't changed. Tastes pretty much the same."

"I use real vodka now. No more moonshine." He was pulling out his good old boy charm for her.

"Why don't you have a seat?"

"I'm kinda busy." *What the hell does she want*, he wondered. "Don't you see the crowd here?"

"I don't care. Sit," Deb said emphatically.

A bit surprised, Johnny hesitated, then sat down in Susie's vacant chair. "Ok. I'm sitting." Nervous laugh. "Now what? Want to talk over old times?"

"Not really. Though I thought it was important to see you."

"Couldn't keep away from me, huh?"

Deb was amazed. It was as if Johnny had no recollection of their last encounter. *Is this really happening? Does he not remember?* She spotted Susie coming from the bathroom and, with her eyes, motioned Susie to join the guys at the bar.

"I gotta say, it's been pretty easy to stay away from you."

"C'mon girl, don't be like that. We had some good times, you and me, didn't we?"

"Is that what you call it? How you remember it?"

"Sure. Remember that cabin in the woods where we'd put on some music, have a couple of beers, get stoned? Then we'd, like they say today, get busy. Good times." He looked at her wistfully.

"Sure. I remember. You were always so charming, the real Southern gentleman, or so I thought."

"I was, wasn't I?" He laughed. "Still am, darlin."

"I don't think so, Johnny. I don't think you were ever that. It was just a mask."

"A mask? What the hell you talking about?"

She stopped and took another long drink from her glass. "The mask that came off the last time I saw you. Tell me, Johnny. You ever think about that night?"

"Not sure I do. We had a lot of nights." Did she detect a smirk?

"The last night I saw you. The night you and your buddies forced yourselves on me." As her voice rose, she too stood up, catching the attention of others in the bar.

Johnny looked around nervously. "Hush now. Everybody'll hear you." He smiled and waved at the table next to him, shaking his head with a grimace to indicate she was crazy. To her he said, "Oooh. You mean the night you tried to kill me."

"Yeah. Exactly. That night."

"Look Deb. It was just one of those things. We were drunk. High. Things just got out of hand. You're not still pissing about that, are you?

After all these years? Get over it, girl."

"You bastard."

"You bitch."

They glared at each other.

Deb sank back in her chair. "You know, Johnny. I don't know what I was thinking coming here. Maybe I was hoping you had changed. But for the good; not like you changed me. I was never the same after that. I never will be. That night haunts my every moment. It doesn't matter what I do, that will not change. You stole my, my, I don't know, my soul. Maybe I was hoping that the part of me you took somehow worked its way into you, made you a better person. But I guess not. You're still the same old narcissistic cowardly asshole you always were."

Deb picked up her pocketbook and started toward the door. Johnny grabbed her arm and yanked her toward him, hissing in her face, "You deserved it. And you're still the same bitch you always were."

"Maybe so, Johnny. Difference is, I care about the damage I've done. Do you?" She raised her knee and shoved it forcibly into his groin. "Maybe you'll remember this. I know I will," she smiled.

As she strode out the door, she fished her cell phone from her purse and called Joe.

Deb woke to the feel of a wet tongue licking her hand. She wiped it on the sheet and got out of bed, greeting the dog as she dressed and made her way to the kitchen. She put the kettle on, made the coffee, fed the dog, picked up the paper and pulled out the cereal boxes from the cupboard. Joe came into the kitchen, poured himself a cup of coffee, grabbed the sports section and sat at the kitchen table.

"Morning, hon."

"Morning. Grape Nuts or Corn Flakes?"

ABOUT THE AUTHOR

Jane Waters Bugg is a freelance copywriter and editor. Forced by today's technology, she is somewhat active on Facebook, Pinterest, Twitter and Instagram and has launched a website, thewritingbugg.com. She is a member of the National Association of Professional Women. Jane was born and raised in the Philadelphia area. This is her first novel.

Made in the USA
Middletown, DE
06 May 2018